Love So Sweet

Marie Clare Friar

Published 2007 by arima publishing

www.arimapublishing.com

ISBN 978 1 84549 235 9

© Marie Clare Friar 2007
www.marieclarefriar.co.uk

Cover designed by In Position Media Ltd © Marie Clare Friar 2007

Printed and bound in the United Kingdom

Typeset in Garamond 11/14

Swirl is an imprint of arima publishing.

arima publishing
ASK House, Northgate Avenue
Bury St Edmunds, Suffolk IP32 6BB
t: (+44) 01284 700321

www.arimapublishing.com

Dedicated to the memory of my Gran and Grandpa.

Prologue

So sweet... The phrase is a familiar one to us all. We often use it in our daily lives to sum up the feelings conjured up by such things as the sight of children playing together, a kind thought or action or the amusement created by small furry animals at play. Possibly, though, we most often use the phrase when we try to describe the utter devotion between a couple and the love they display towards one another.

"Isn't love so sweet?" and "They look so sweet together..." These are things we often say about people who are so obviously totally in love with one another.

Love has many shapes and forms. Most of us want to share our love with someone, although for some of us, this may be impossible and we put all our love into our work, our hobby or even our pet. Love has a habit of appearing without warning or explanation, usually when we least expect it. Then it's up to you - you either to embrace it with open arms or kill the emotion altogether out of fear.

For some people, bizarrely, Scotland still conjures up images of tartan, kilts, haggis, whisky, William Wallace and whole host of other stereotypical, stagnant clichés involving shortbread tins and porridge oats ads. They don't see a bustling, modern country with warm, friendly people, keen to develop their culture and improve their lifestyles. They certainly wouldn't think of it as the love capital of the world, but love can be found in the unlikeliest of places. It can start with a bang anywhere, anytime.

When it strikes, it is up to us to grab it with both hands. Family and friends may caution us that it takes hard work and effort to make a relationship last and that we should be aware of how lucky we are to have one another, as many never have the chance to experience this joy...

Chapter One – Bitter Sweet

Travelling through Glasgow and arriving at its West End, you come across many quaint little shops, like newsagents, bakeries and greengrocers. The shops are adequate if you are on a tight budget and are unable to travel elsewhere. And for students, it's ideal – charity shops, bookshops and music shops…

However, if you travel a very short way, the scene changes dramatically. All of a sudden, you come to high street stores as well as five star hotels. This area is also home to many well-known landmarks such as the Kelvingrove Art Gallery and Museum; it's a large, old building housing many of the finest pieces of art and history in the world. There's the world-renowned University of Glasgow, part of which is immediately behind the art gallery and, of course, the equally well-known Western Infirmary to the side of the art gallery.

The West End, round the corner from the Kelvin Hall that connects with the main road, which the museum presides over from above, is where a lot of the tightly-packed shops jostle for position and shoppers' attention. In particular, there's a beautiful, traditional confectionary shop that sits between an old-fashioned bakery and a tiny newsagent.

The baker displays his wares in glass-fronted cabinets; bread is kneaded on traditional wooden benches with marble tops; the antique stoves squat cosily along the white-washed brick walls surrounded by long-handed ladles; all this adds to its atmosphere and charm.

The owner is a short, round man who has a perpetual smile on his face; a look you would swear had been kneaded into place and baked like dough. His expression never changed, unless you made him laugh really hard, then his smile would pull so far back into his head, his molars became clearly visible. Although he always seemed happy, the baker hated seeing children coming out of the sweet shop with a bag full of sweets and crisps; it wasn't a healthy option compared with his bread. But really, with the size of him, everyone knew he wasn't exactly nibbling daintily on pan loafs!

And on the other side of the sweet shop nestled a tiny newsagent that could really only allow four people in at a time, including the shop assistant!

The petite shop, more often than not, had a large queue outside its double-glazed door which was crammed with private adverts and mini home-made posters stuck all over it. The owner was generally regarded as a recluse – he was rarely seen. Those who had seen him thought him to be freakishly thin. He had, apparently, been ill after his mother passed away and he had never fully recovered physically or mentally from her death.

Children nicknamed him 'creepy thin man'. He never seemed to smile and moaned at everything and anything. This trait would sometimes be very amusing, even though he was being serious. At other times, he was truly scary. Some adults were sure he ducked under the counter when they turned their backs, so that he could have a quick drink of something, something far stronger than cola. Then he would jump back to his feet, staring at them, his glassy eyes bulging out of his head, and he would reek of booze.

*

Everyone loved the confectionary shop. Its previous owner had been an Irish woman called Marian. She had been a kind, caring and quiet young woman who adored people - especially children, having two of her own.

Bright and chirpy, she was always there for you no matter who you were. The locals came to trust her so much, they would call on her at the shop for a chat or a free and comforting counselling session. They paid nothing for her services but still got a lovely hot cuppa and cake in the café area while they spilled their hearts out to Marian.

People of all ages - from small children to those much, much older - completely adored her. She was one of those women you just naturally felt at ease with and comfortable around. With Marian, you didn't have to pretend to be something or someone you weren't. She had eyes that welcomed you without words.

Tragically, though, Marian had only been in the new shop for three years before she died, suddenly and totally unexpectedly, of a heart attack, just like her father before her, aged only thirty-eight.

Marian left behind her two children, alone without any other immediate family, except some distant cousins from Ireland. They only made contact when they needed something. And when it came to the reading of the will, five of them managed to come to the lawyer's office for that meeting. None of them had managed to make it to the funeral.

When they found out that they were receiving nothing from their cousin, they disappeared again, without so much as a goodbye.

Carla, the elder of Marian's two children, was eighteen at the time and Paul fifteen. Carla, a beautiful and grieving young woman, faced many uphill struggles on her own. Carla was working to make sure her brother's school work didn't suffer and that, with support from social workers, he was able to continue his education as planned. Carla also wanted to keep the shop going, as this was the only immediate and easy way for her to earn any income. She had been shown how to do everything by her mum - everything except how to manage the books. Now that *was* a struggle.

There was also the added burden of maintaining their beautiful home while she also tried to cope with grieving for her mother. Housework had never been her strong point.

Proving that she was capable of being Paul's legal guardian was more difficult than she thought and her mother's lawyer had to intervene twice in order for Carla to keep Paul with her at the house. She had to prove to the social workers that she could handle the conditions set before her, such as the ability to provide for both of them by keeping the business going, being able to pay the bills and so on. It seemed as though the whole world was against her and Carla spent every waking moment thinking of ways to show just how capable she was of looking after her younger brother. Carla also realised how much she needed her brother to distract her from thinking about her mother, having not let herself properly grieve at the time. . The new routine was totally alien to the familiarity of going to school and studying, coming home, having dinner and crashing on her bed for the night. Now, all of a sudden, she was flung into running a business and managing a home, making sure that Paul was okay and doing well at school, with social workers breathing down her neck making unexpected visits to keep her on her toes.

On one occasion, Carla was cleaning a stain on the kitchen floor beneath the window and as she stood up to rinse the cloth she noticed a grumpy old woman standing at the window, breathing white clouds of steam on her nice clean windows, grinning insanely at her. Carla jumped with fright, knocking a fruit bowl to the ground. It was the shock of the woman's appearance that caused Carla to gasp in horror, rather than someone looking through the window, after all she had been used to her best friend appearing at the window most days doing the same thing, except *she* only pulled silly faces! All this to ensure that Paul was treated well and safe with his own sister! 'How moronic' she always felt as though she was being accused of beating him or something. The social workers even went as far as to wait outside the school every morning and evening for the first few weeks to make sure that she was there, which to say the least, was ridiculous, but that was their job one supposed. Carla was just so numb from everything that she had to deal with simultaneously that she became almost zombie like in her daily routine, but she never confronted the social workers.

Carla had given up her dream of going to university and becoming a photographer in order to pay the bills. Keeping a house and grieving for your mother is a lot for an eighteen-year-old to manage. Giving up high school two months before final exams, beginning from scratch to learn how to take on and manage a business. How to balance books and take care, not only of herself, but more importantly, her younger, distraught brother at a very difficult age. That's a lot for anyone to deal with, let alone an eighteen-year-old schoolgirl with ambition.

The harsh reality was just too real at times. Carla's saving grace at the time was her best friend, Rachel Shaw, with whom she went to school.

After seeing what happened to Carla's mother, despite Carla's protestations, Rachel touchingly decided not to go to university herself. Instead, she went to work in her mother's bookshop a few doors down from Carla's sweet shop, to learn how to run that business. Rachel was able to take Paul home at night and look after him till Carla returned from work.

Much of the time Rachel even stayed over, because it was often very late when Carla got home. Sometimes, Rachel's mum, Linda Shaw, would pick Carla up and take her home and cook dinner for them all.

Whilst dinner was cooking, Carla would go straight to the study to start the mind-numbing task of keeping the shop's books up-to-date. Linda, having tried and failed to bring Carla down to join the others for dinner, would then take Carla's food into the study for her to eat, but she would always be too busy to even look at it.

Inevitably, Carla lost a lot of weight, worrying about what would happen if she didn't keep on top of things. At times, she would be found sleeping with her head resting on small mountains of books, stacked on the desk around her. Sometimes, she was still holding a fork full of food, her arm propped up by books, suggesting she'd fallen asleep just before she'd eaten. This was the only time she got rest before starting all over again the next morning.

Carla felt bad that people outside of family were having to come in and help her. Some of the customers who had been very fond of Marian and her children, popped in to offer hot meals, and help with cleaning and washing. Carla felt they didn't expect her to cope or manage on her own, which made her more determined to do it all herself. Just like her mother before her, she was a very proud, determined young woman. She wanted to prove to everyone she could cope, because accepting help always sounded like failure on her part and that was one thing she could not handle.

Having given up the chance to live her dream of being a photographer, which she was so passionate about, was a major blow for Carla. She knew her grades from the previous year's exams were good enough to get onto the course she had set her heart on and, for most people that would have been the last straw. But she kept plugging away regardless, to keep her tiny family together.

Though she never showed her true emotions to her customers, they always seemed to know when she was having one of her 'I've been better' days. Her eyes, like her mother's, were warm, but could be sad and they gave the game away much too quickly.

She became fed up with people telling her that 'it would be alright'; 'it will work out'; 'have faith'…

The advice just wouldn't stop coming! God help her, she once even got a group of them dishing it out together! She would be stuck there for hours, listening to endless drivel about their experiences. They never had anything in common with her predicament, or helped her in any way. They just held her up and made her head spin!

*

The worst customer for this was old Mrs Betty, who never seemed to shut up and was obviously barking mad. She would always be seen walking down the street talking to herself or, worse, having conversations in bus shelters with the late Mr. Betty. God help anyone who sat in the empty space where Mr Betty 'sat'. Mrs Betty would squeal and shriek at the top of her lungs that they had killed Mr Betty!

Carla didn't mind Mrs Betty that much really - she felt sorry for her actually, which Rachel just couldn't understand.

Rachel found it difficult when Mrs Betty came into the bookshop just to pester her. Mrs Betty lived alone in the large house she owned and was largely ignored by her own children.

Carla knew all this because Mrs Betty's family would often come in the shop and they would tell her what their mother had been up to recently. To be fair, though, they did ask if Carla thought their mother was OK, from time to time. But Carla always felt that they should do more for Mrs Betty, so she always sent a birthday and Christmas card to her.

What bothered Carla most about Mrs Betty, however, was that she would pop up out of nowhere full of gossip and if she found a group of like-minded 'old nosy crows' Carla wouldn't be able to move them from the shop all day.

Mrs Betty would also insist, of course, that a space be left at her table with a chair, muffin and cup of tea for her dear Mr Betty, which meant some customers had to take their cakes and drinks away with them to sit elsewhere. Sales would definitely be much better without all those 'nosy crows' around!

Eventually, after several long months of hard work, long hours, and sleepless nights, Carla managed to get Paul through his exams. She even managed to re-vamp the shop to attract more customers and beat off the trendy American coffee chains, expanding her range of homemade cakes and introducing specialist teas and coffees, smoothies and wholefoods.

She bought several more tables and chairs for people to come in, sit down, relax and enjoy their drink and cake. A new chocolate fountain sat in the shop window to attract attention. Her secret weapon was the scent of home-baking, which could be picked up halfway down the street.

Mrs Betty, inevitably, was always shocked and disgusted with the changes that Carla had made to the shop. She believed it was going to attract unwanted outsiders into the area. Carla could only guess that 'outsiders' meant everyone that she didn't know or like; Mrs Betty was very particular with whom she graced with her and her husband's 'presence'.

Every time Carla added something new - like the music system, for example - she would have to spend a good while considering whether it was worth the aggravation from Mrs Betty, who was described by Paul as 'the old fart that lingers'.

His rude nickname for the old bat always made Carla laugh, often when looking into Mrs Betty's face. Carla's suppressed laughter normally resulted in contorted facial expressions that had to be explained somehow!

*

Paul struggled with the fact of his mother being dead. Away from Carla's watchful eye, be it at school, in the back room of the shop or in his bedroom, he had been hiding away so he could have a quiet cry to himself. It wasn't as though he was ashamed of crying: he was just scared that if someone saw him he wouldn't be able to stop. Paul may have been a tall, strong boy, but inside he was frightened of being alone.

The only one who knew about this was Rachel. She would find him doubled over in a corner, sometimes, in his room. He grew very fond of Rachel, for all that she was doing for him. When Paul eventually went back to school, the only people who would approach him were his teachers. His best friends couldn't even look him in the eye. The truth was they didn't know what to say – or they were scared to say the wrong thing and make him cry or run off upset. Paul, though, didn't see it that way.

He believed his friends were uncaring and thoughtless. Not even a card or a simple 'I'm sorry' came from any of them. He would always receive the same pathetic look of sympathy from anyone who knew him and of his mother's death. This look would make his blood run cold in his veins and make him feel small and insignificant. This infuriated him. On top of everything he was going through, he had not only lost his mother, but now he was losing his friends too.

Paul couldn't understand why his so-called friends acted like this, avoiding him as though he had some sort of disease. All the time, he was comparing his friends to those of Rachel and how supportive and loving she was to him and Carla. All Paul wanted was company that could help him cope and move on. Instead he was stuck with the same thoughts and dreams of his mother. Carla did her best to find time to be with Paul. She helped him with homework. When she had time, Carla would sometimes bring the ironing into the front room to watch TV with him. The effort she put into thinking of ways to be with him really made the pair stronger.

This, however, did not stop him from getting into trouble in school. Paul frequently ended up in fights with boys who picked on him. So when his class had blocks of gym, Paul would physically take it out on them, pretending it was just rough and tumble. Knocking them into walls, tripping them up, causing fights to break out. Carla once was called to the head of the year's' office, to be warned about his behaviour. Paul eventually managed to suppress his anger, though he did still blow his stack verbally on a regular basis.

Paul began to take an interest in photography after watching Carla with her camera. She had always loved having her camera handy - just in case. It was up at a loch Ard one morning when they went for a drive, though, that really fuelled his interest.

Carla drove into the car park near this beautiful open loch. The surface of the water was completely undisturbed, like a mirror reflecting the image of the vast green hills and trees alongside it.

Carla took out her camera bag and began to set up her camera. As she did this, Paul watched his sister's meticulous care and attention she paid to both the camera and the contents of the bag. He sat up and leaned forward without realising he had done so to get a closer look at what she was doing.

When she was finally ready to begin taking pictures, Paul watched in wonder as Carla surveyed her canvas. Then, with sudden intrigue, Paul got out of the car and walked alongside her, keeping a respectful distance to allow her room to move. He watched her with every shot as she changed features on the camera. Carla caught him looking and told him to pick up her other camera. Paul and Carla spent hours out there, even when boats and kayaks eventually disturbed the serenity of the water. They found plenty to snap. They re-established their once strong bond and made it even stronger. Paul realised then that, as long as he had his sister, he would never be alone - and no one was going to change that...

At last, through the darkness of everything that had happened, Paul had found something that really interested him. Picking up a camera allowed him to take himself to other places – losing himself in the joy of capturing beauty in his lens. Carla would often find him with a camera, either taking pictures or fiddling with it. This would always make her laugh, as he began to remind her a lot of herself. She, too, would spontaneously want to take pictures.

Chapter Two – And life goes on.

Three years on, Carla was still working hard running the shop, supporting her brother Paul who was now going to university to study photography – the course she herself had dreamed of taking. And yes, Mrs Betty was still watching over Carla's shoulder faithfully and doggedly, as if it was her full-time job!

Carla felt it was hard enough having to give up photography as a career, which she had desperately wanted to do, but to pay for her brother's own photography course was almost more than she could bear. In lesser people, this may have resulted in resentment. Yet for Carla, the only thing she really wanted was to see her brother do well in life and be happy - she had no thought for herself.

She knew that she would probably be working in the shop for the rest of her days and she felt that it probably was to be her career. In any case, neither the money nor the energy were there to start again – at least, not yet.

But she did daydream sometimes, gazing out of the large window in her bedroom, but not about how life could have been. She dreamed about what it could still be. She always tried to be optimistic about her future, because she believed that everything would work out in the end.

Carla really believed this - it was precisely this thought that helped her through the ordeal of her mother's death and the struggle to look after Paul and the business over the last three years.

Carla had become well-known and admired locally for her brave and mature behaviour following her mother's death. People often acknowledged her efforts to raise Paul. More than that, she was also renowned for her beauty - her dark hair and dark mystical brown eyes were stunning.

Carla's beauty had attracted many admirers and a range of interesting offers, up to and including marriage, usually from several besotted students each year. Carla never complained, as it was good for her morale and also good for the business!

Then a funny thing happened one Valentine's Day, while she was making up special hampers for love-struck couples. The hampers were packed full of delicious cakes, sweets and bubbly, intended for sharing. Much to her surprise, she received one of her own baskets with an anonymous card in it! She didn't mind really - it was a lovely thought and that's what counts, isn't it? It was another sale and it gave something for Paul to relish!

*

It was a surprisingly warm day for Glasgow in September. It was the first day of the new academic year at the university, Paul's' first day. Carla, for the first time, had kept the shop closed that morning to take him to matriculate and to gather all the information they needed for the year ahead. She pulled her small and elderly car into the car park and turned off the engine.

"Before you go in..." she said to Paul, stopping him from leaving the car, holding his arm and making him fall back into his seat.

"Aww, you're not gonna cry on me now, are you?" He winced at her, smarting at the pressure on his arm.

"No, I'm not. I just want to give you this." Carla reached into a large brown box hidden behind her car seat.

"It's just something to give you a start, so you don't have to borrow one, and..."

Before she could finish, Paul almost grabbed the box from her hands and ripped the wrapping to pieces, like a child on Christmas morning, which made her smile.

Opening it frantically, Paul stopped suddenly, holding the flaps of the box open as he stared at the contents. Then he looked back at Carla, who was watching him intently, waiting for a reaction.

"What the... when did you... how did you?" Paul stuttered, trying to take it all in.

"I bought it a couple of weeks ago, do you like it?"

"Like it? I love it! This is the best camera available! Wait, that's not a..?" His mouth gaped open, as he lifted one box to reveal another.

"It's a laptop. You're going to need that, too, I'm guessing." Carla watched him, wondering what he was thinking, yet knowing what he must be feeling. "Carla..." he began, too full of emotion to finish. He reached over to give her a big hug. He kept hold of her when he looked into her eyes. "You're an idiot, you know that? Can you afford this?"

"Yes, I can, I made sure of it. Look, hurry up and get your stuff, because the longer you're in here, the longer the shop stays shut and we need to pay our bills. We still have to pick your books up from Rachel's."

Not knowing what to say, Paul got out, smiled at her through the window and ran off, knocking innocent students out of his way as he headed rapidly for class. Carla simply smiled with pride and joy as she watched him disappear...

*

People come from far and wide to study at Glasgow University and this year was no exception. The airport was full of new arrivals and through the crowded arrivals lounge walked a young man, tall, dark and truly handsome. Just arrived from London, he was nervous yet excited... a new city, a new challenge waiting for him at university...

He walked slowly through the arrivals area, weaving in and out of a sea of bodies, all talking. After collecting his bags, the handsome young man found himself climbing onto a crowded bus and finding a seat. When he was finally able to relax, he began reading over his instructions for accommodation and registration in the university information pack.

He watched the sights pass by as his bus sped along the motorway. The airport gradually disappeared, then he saw industrial units and shopping malls and several tower blocks of flats. Then he began drifting away, thinking about his mum and sister back home. Both had cried at the airport and, when he left, his dad was trying to console them, even though he was sure his dad had tears in his eyes as well. It brought a lump to his throat.

In no time at all, it seemed, the bus came to a standstill, bringing him back to reality with a gravity-defying thud. Clambering off with his two cases and two rucksacks, he began looking round to get his bearings. Looking across the street he saw two people standing at the other side. He realised he knew them!

"Marti! Sarah! Wait up!" he yelled at the top of his voice.

"Hey, Drew!" The tall, pale, young man with long, dark hair shouted back immediately. The two newcomers crossed the road to meet up with Drew, smiling widely and extending hands.

"Thank goodness for meeting you guys! I've no idea where I'm meant to go from here," he said, exasperated and bewildered.

"Well, come on, we're on our way to the campus now," said Marti. "Here, give me one of your bags... Bloody Hell, what have you got with you? Your mother?"

"Don't start," Drew said, waving his hand dismissively while rolling his eyes, struggling with the bags he'd slung over his shoulders.

As Drew, Marti and Sarah made their way round to the university's main entrance, Carla and Paul who were just leaving the university passed by them in their car. Paul had just enough time to collect his text books before his first seminar.

"There's that girl I was telling you about, Sarah," Marti said, nudging Sarah and turning to watch Carla's car pass onto the main road.

"Oh, so that's who you were talking about? Now I'm with you!"

"Yeah," Marti replied in a choked sort of voice, his face contorting as he struggled to lift Drew's heavy case once more.

Drew looked up from his chunky university pack, which he'd been trying to read intensely for the last ten minutes.

"What and who are you two talking about?" he said, looking around quizzically. His two friends rolled their eyes heavenward.

"Never mind, I'll tell you later," Marti said, patting him on the shoulder. Marti increased his pace to get to the university quicker to relieve his aching arms from Drew's deadweight suitcase.

Chapter Three – A fresh start

Back at Rachel's mum's bookshop, Rachel was ringing up Paul's stack of university books, with their usual extra discount, of course, while Paul stared at her over the counter.

Carla watched the pair of them closely, knowing full well that Rachel was blissfully unaware of Paul's feelings for her. He looked like a puppy as he stared at Rachel, with absolute adoration in his eyes.

Carla's day-dreaming came to an abrupt halt when she glanced up at the wall clock.

"Oh no, Paul - what time was Steven delivering cakes today?" she asked, wiping a stray strand of hair from her face.

" No idea," Paul replied vaguely, from his private world.

"Paul, pick your jaw up off the floor and tell me when Steven said he'd be round or I'll tell Rachel you fancy her!"

"Thanks for nothing, Carla!" Paul retorted, his face turning beetroot red.

Rachel smiled and looked out of the shop window.

"Too late Carla," Rachel said, nodding towards the sweet shop. "That's Steven driving away now!"

"What?" Carla exclaimed, running quickly to the window, skidding into a pile of books. "Damn, damn, damn!" She glanced from the kids gathering outside her sweet shop to the rather sheepish look on Paul's face.

"Sorry," Paul mumbled, his face an even brighter crimson colour now. "I seem to have a habit of distracting you from your work."

"I'll get you for this, you little bugger!" Carla smiled thinly. "You're going to have to start playing your part in our business, Paul...you'll need to remind me when deliveries are coming. Just help me out a little, will you?"

Paul felt bad - he knew how much Carla did for him; sometimes, he felt like a passenger, a piece of baggage in their business. A brief and awkward silence filled the bookshop.

"We'd better open the shop," Carla said with a sigh. Paul gave one more look of adoration at Rachel before quickly turning to leave the building.

After walking along the street to their sweet shop in silence for a few minutes, Carla jabbed her elbow into Paul's ribs. They burst out laughing in the middle of the street, attracting the attention of passers-by and customers queuing outside their shop.

"Sorry we're late, guys," she told them. "My brother has other things on his mind today!" Carla opened the door to let the kids in, hugging Paul as he handed her the rest of the books he didn't need for the day.

"Good luck, and enjoy yourself," she told him with a smile.

"Thanks, Carla – see you later."

Carla watched Paul as he left for his first seminar. She realised just how grown up he had become and her eyes welled up slightly. She tilted her head back to force the tears back and, as she looked up, a large cloud parted and the sun beamed down on the entire street, warming her face and drying her tears.

"Hi, Mum," she whispered, smiling into the sunlight. "Things are okay, they really are." She closed her eyes and basked in the joy of the moment before going inside the shop to serve her impatient customers…

*

The bell sounded at the end of the hour-long seminar. Paul's fellow students dispersed quickly, disappearing down the long, sunny corridors. Many of the students still looked dismayed and nervous, overwhelmed by their new environment.

A group of four boys left the room ahead, whispering quietly among themselves. They turned left along the corridor and disappeared down the stairs, while Paul waited for the lift.

Once outside, near the traffic lights, Paul bent down to tie his shoe laces. Whilst bending down, he heard the voices of the same four boys from his class, whose conversation had, apparently, consisted solely of sport and then, as they crossed the street, it seemed that one of them spotted Carla's sweet shop.

"Let's go to Carla's, I'm starving," one of them said. "I fancy a mint marble." He nudged one of his friends knowingly.

A mint marble was one of Carla's many specialities; it was chocolate at the top of the rectangular block and mint at the bottom, mixed and swirled in the centre, combining both flavours with the creamy centre. This was one of her best-selling confectioneries. As the boys approached the shop, another member of the group pointed Carla out to the others.

"Well, boys, there she is!" the young man said as he pointed towards her. Carla was reaching into the window to use the chocolate fountain while a couple of young kids licked their lips outside.

"Now, that is one fine piece of candy, eh, boys?"

"Aye," they all replied with thick Scottish accents, peering into the shop.

Paul found himself immediately resenting them lusting after his sister. He felt blood rush to his face. He suddenly felt very protective towards her and decided to put an end to it.

"Hey, sis!" He banged loudly on the window and waved. The four guys jumped back, startled.

Carla waved and smiled sweetly. Paul, however, delighted in the boys' embarrassment. He smiled smugly at them from the middle of the shop door, blocking the exit of several other young customers.

"Paul, I don't know what's going on with you," Carla said, "but those kids need to get back to school and if you want your lunch, it's already on the table. Paul, would you move?"

"Huh? What? Oh, right, sorry kids." The kids gave him sour looks while they walked under his arm as he held the door open for them. One even stopped to stick out his tongue at him.

"Lovely!" Paul responded sarcastically but grinning.

"What did you expect? And what's with the grand entrance?"

Paul tilted his head not very discreetly towards the shop window, rolling his eyes in the direction of the four guys, who were still gawking at his sister. Carla smiled at them, and then she waved to them. The boy's eyes opened with shock. They all turned bright red and, after a moment's confusion, they took off like a pack of hounds. Two even collided with each other while trying to make their escape, much to the amusement of Paul and Carla who just burst out laughing.

"Aww, great, salad again," Paul said sarcastically, looking at his lunch.

"Shut up and put the kettle on, would you?" Carla replied before she went back to serve some children. "Yes, sweetheart, what can I get you?" she asked a young and very rotund boy, who was obviously a regular to the shop.

"I'll have a mint swirl," the tubby boy said in adoration as he looked up into Carla's eyes. Carla smiled at him across the counter. As she turned, she caught sight of the same four boys who had returned to stare at her through the window.

"Hey, Paul - your friends are back," she said, without drawing attention to the fact she had seen them.

"Tell them to get lost, it puts your customers off," Paul shouted back, his answer muffled by food stuffed into his mouth.

Carla glanced at them again while she served the tubby boy and another group of sugar addicted kids that had just arrived.

Suddenly, like a ghost appearing in the night, Mrs Betty popped up out of nowhere!

"Oh Norma!" Carla shrieked, slapping her hands to her face. "You must stop doing that to me - I just about go through the roof every time!"

"Can you see God too, dear?" Mrs Betty asked. She stood holding two empty cups; her head tilted awaiting Carla's response. An almost toothless grin split her face.

"No, Norma, I don't…I'm sorry."

"My dear, please call me Mrs Betty, you know how upset my Daniel gets."

"OK, Mrs Betty – now, do you want another cuppa?" Carla changed the subject and avoided Mrs Betty's nosy stare by nodding towards the two empty cups in the old woman's hands.

"Yes, please, dear," Mrs Betty replied before glancing sideways at her invisible-to-everyone-but-her husband. "No, Daniel, you're on a diet!" She swiped at an invisible arm reaching for a slice of chocolate cake on the counter. One of the children waiting to be served opened his eyes in alarm, silently mouthing the words "fruit cake" when his eyes made contact with Carla's.

"It's OK, Sean, she's not talking to you!" Carla giggled. "Mrs Betty's disciplining her husband for being naughty. Go on, help yourself to a muffin, Sean, it's on the house today."

Mrs Betty merely smiled sweetly and took her two cups of tea to a nearby table.

"But her husband's not there, Carla!" Sean whispered hoarsely, stating the blindingly obvious.

"Sshh, don't tell her that, she's lonely! Believing that he's there keeps her happy, you see." Carla circled her index finger round her temple in the universally time-honoured way to emphasise the point.

"You should sell her as part of your stock, being a fruit cake, an' all," Sean stated with wide-eyed wonderment.

"Sshh… she's not that bad, honestly. Why don't you take her cakes over to her?"

"No way, she's mental," Sean said, turning up his bottom lip. "I'm outta here!"

Sean grabbed his muffin and a packet of sweets and ran out the shop, half expecting Mrs Betty to turn into a bat or something.

Carla giggled again, revealing even, white teeth in her pretty face. She selected a nice piece of cake and took it over to Mrs Betty.

"Thank you, dear," Mrs Betty said.

"No cake for Daniel, then?" Carla teased, playing along with Mrs Betty.

"Not today, dear, he's putting on a bit of weight, don't you think?"

"Yes, Mrs Betty," Carla grimaced, rolling her eyes, "He certainly is a bit chubbier these days!"

Carla rubbed her open palms on her apron and walked quickly back to where Paul was finishing of his lunch.

"That woman will scare off all my customers - the way she sneaks up on people!" Carla sighed.

"I told you to call the nut house, but you choose to allow her to terrorise everyone, so on your head be it" Paul retorted.

Meanwhile, outside, another discussion was taking place as to who should go in and ask Carla out on a date. As the four youths discussed it, Marti, Drew and Sarah strolled towards them.

The three of them were lost in their own animated conversation when they noticed the four guys talking among themselves outside the sweet shop.

"Hey guys," said Marti. "What's happening? This is Drew, he's just arrived from London."

"So what brings you here then?" one of them asked.

"English Lit.," Drew replied.

"Tough subject," one replied. Drew wasn't sure if he was being sarcastic.

"I guess…but I have a passion for writing," he replied, giving the guy the benefit of the doubt.

"Wait, you're telling me that you've come from London to Glasgow to study English - there's something Irish about that, if you ask me!"

"Look guys, what's going on?" Marti said, confused by the change of subject. "Why are we out here when we could be inside?"

"We're trying to pluck up courage for one of us to ask Carla out," explained one of the group.

"Ask who?" Drew asked, an eyebrow raised.

"What, you mean Marti didn't tell you? Come on, Marti, is this a wind up?" One of the guys, Pete, grabbed hold of Drew and pulled him in front of the window.

"That there is Carla Devine, the sweet shop owner," Pete remarked, nodding his head in Carla's direction. Drew leaned slightly to one side to see her face better, but she was surrounded by a group of schoolchildren at the counter.

"I think *you* should do it, Marti - I pissed myself laughing the last time you tried," Pete mocked.

"What happened last time?" asked Drew, unable to take his eyes off the window.

"Marti only got as far as putting his hand on the shop door when he saw Carla's wee brother come in the back door so the big moron legged it!" The group slapped Marti on his back. "Chicken!"

"Shut it, you lot - at least I had the guts to try! It's time for the newbie to give it a go I think."

All eyes turned to Drew, putting him on the spot.

"Come on guys, you know that's not fair!" Drew stood rooted to the spot, looking at Carla properly for the first time. She *was* stunning. His heartbeat accelerated quickly.

He wondered why the guys kept bottling out trying to date her - it wasn't as if she was ugly. And her smile switched the sun on...

All of a sudden, Drew felt several hands pin his arms to his side, forcing him towards the door. He barely got out "Hey, guys!" before he was shoved forward, landing spread-eagled on the shop floor. The door swung shut, drowning out peels of laughter from his mates who made a very rapid exit. Several customers, and Mrs Betty in particular, scowled down at Drew, muttering a pejorative 'Kids!' under their breath.

Mrs Betty nudged her imaginary husband's arm and pointed a skinny finger at Drew, cackling wildly as she did so. Drew sat bolt upright, went bright red in the face and wished a massive deep abyss would open up in the floor to swallow him.

"Well, you're not the first big entrance today but certainly the most entertaining," said a voice from above Drew. He looked up to see Carla, her hand held out to help him up. Her head was framed by a halo of light from the display lamps above her, giving her the appearance of an angel. His heart raced when he slipped his hand into hers, pulling himself up.

"Are you OK?" she asked quietly, her voice full of concern.

Drew couldn't speak at first. He was entranced by her beauty and still felt a little embarrassed by his unplanned grand entrance. And those eyes of hers...they were just so warm and inviting.

"Are you OK?" Carla repeated.

"I am now," he said. Carla smiled and pulled her hand gently away from his.

"I'm Carla."

"I'm Drew."

"Drew - that's a nice name. Pleased to meet you, Drew."

Drew felt himself going red again and a brief silence fell between them. Carla reached up to Drew's hair, pulling a bit of fluff out of it.

Her touch was electrifying, but all he could do was smile like an idiot. Her eyes seemed to bore into him. What was in that look?

The four guys watching from outside were completely blown away as they watched Drew strike up a conversation so easily with Carla. How come he could do it and they couldn't?

"What are they saying to each other?" Pete grumbled, frowning through the shop window.

"Who knows?" Marti shrugged, feeling jealousy well up in him as well. He didn't like the way Carla kept smiling at Drew. His idea seemed to have back-fired.

When Drew finally emerged from the shop, five or six minutes later, he continued to walk forward as if in a trance, then stopped at the kerb to stare blankly across the street.

"Well, what were you guys talking about?" Phil, another one of the group, said to Drew, as he stood there, zombie-like.

"What did she say?" asked another, Kevin.

"Huh?" Drew muttered, his face glazed with a far-away look.

Marti waved his hand in front of Drew's face, to try and get some sort of reaction.

"Earth to Drew – come in, Drew..!"

But Drew remained unmoved.

"OK, boys," Marti said at last. "Give Carla a round of applause for bewitching yet another victim!" The others slowly clapped as they watched Drew.

"Come on, mate, what did she say?" Pete cut in. "You didn't ask her out? Did you?"

"Well?" the group chorused as one. Pete punched Drew playfully in the chest to bring him down to earth.

"No," Drew said, eventually, drifting back into focus. Recognition seemed to flood back into his eyes then, smiling, he said: "No" a second time.

"So what's up then?" asked Marti.

"She asked where I get my hair done and told me not to go back there unless I liked the windswept look."

The group looked knowingly at his bedraggled hair, laughing at him.

"Mate, I think I know why," Eddie said, pointing out Drew's new style in the reflection on the shop window. Drew went red – again - from embarrassment.

Without completely being aware she was doing it, Carla watched Drew from inside her shop. Paul stood alongside his sister, leaning on her shoulder and following her gaze.

"Hot totty?" he whispered in her ear.

"Shut up and eat your lunch," Carla said, spinning on him, punching him a bit too hard on the shoulder. "Where's that tea I asked you for?"

"Your Highness!" Paul mocked, bowing low. "Coming right up."

*

Later that night, while Carla sat reading a book while she waited for Paul to get in from university, there was a knock on the door. Carla got up to answer, expecting that Paul must have left his keys.

It was Paul, but he was not alone.

"What are you lot doing here?" Carla asked, puzzled. She looked enquiringly at Paul and the 'Gang of Four' from earlier on in the day, plus Marti. "What's going on now?"

"These guys saw me in the shop and wondered if I would bring them round for an introduction," Paul explained, grinning like the Cheshire Cat. What he didn't tell Carla was that this was payback time for embarrassing him in front of Rachel earlier!

"Paul, I want a word with you...inside now," Carla said sternly, her lips pursed into a thin line across her face. "But..."

"No 'buts' - *now*, mister!"

Paul gulped hard. He could see he had no chance to argue or defend himself so he went inside, slamming the door loudly behind him.

"How dare you use me to become popular!" Carla exclaimed once she turned around towards him.

"Chill, woman! First off, this is revenge for the bookshop incident with Rachel and second, being with *them* is never gonna make me popular. I reckon that's how you would say touché, sister!"

"Is that so? Well, two can play at that game," she said, yanking open the front door. Pete saw her coming and stepped back.

"Sorry boys, Paul's not coming out to play tonight – he's grounded, so you'll have to come back in a month... Night, night. And you, Paulie!" She mocked her brother. "Go and put on your jimjams so I can come up and tuck you in!" Carla grinned wickedly before slamming the door in the boys' faces. Paul looked like he was about to explode. Veins stood out in his neck and he flushed a rather dramatic shade of vermillion red. Again.

"That will be the door shut then?" Eddie remarked, somewhat sarcastically. The boys stared open-mouthed at the tongue-lashing going back and forth between Carla and Paul, but the glass was too thick to make out what they were saying to each other.

"That's that, then," Pete said to no-one in particular. "We didn't even get our feet over the threshold..."

"She wouldn't ground Paul at his age, would she?" Eddie asked as they sauntered back to their car.

"Buggered if I know," Marti said, "we should call her the 'Ice Queen'."

"And don't come back again - ever!" Carla shouted over the intercom when they neared the gate.

Carla meant every word she had said and followed through by grounding Paul. Over and above that, he had to go to the shop and do her routine chores every morning - mopping the floor, wiping the counters, cleaning the machines and dispensers and refilling the sweet jars.

Then he would go to university and, between lectures and seminars and tutorials, he would have to come back to the shop and serve customers to allow Carla a break. And that wasn't the end of it.

After university, he would have to do all their collective chores at home before sitting down to study. This was very hard in the extreme, he felt, but Carla wasn't prepared to be pushed around by an adolescent for the sake of a practical joke and she stood her ground.

"Now do you understand what I go through every day to keep us going?" Carla said to Paul on the last day of his 'sentence'.

"I guess," Paul said sullenly. "But all I did was get you back - it was a joke."

"I don't have time for all that, Paul," she said wearily. "It's just something extra for me to worry about." Then she softened her tone as she handed him a packed lunch. "This is for your lunch at Uni. Just be home in time for dinner, will you?"

Paul sulked a while longer and then, smiling, he pecked his sister on the cheek.

"Yeah, OK. Fair dos - I'll lay off the practical jokes for a while."

"I'll believe it when I see it," she said, slapping him on the shoulder. "Anyway, I think you've got the message now."

Carla watched her brother walk off down the driveway. Her heart was full of love and compassion for him - after all, he was the only family she had left now that mum had died. And she knew in her heart that their circumstances would mature him quicker than most.

Chapter Four – Closer

A few days later, Paul learned of his first assignment for grading and had two weeks to complete it. While he sat in the library, trying to come up with ideas for his project, Carla closed the shop in preparation for her visit to her mother's grave.

It was the third anniversary of their mum's death and she promised herself she would never forget to visit the grave on the anniversary as well as on her mum's birthday.

Driving slowly into the grounds of the cemetery, through the tall black gates and up along the winding road, she parked as close to the grave as possible. Then she walked up the cobbled path to her mum's headstone, which lay close to the top of a small slope.

The wind started swirling around her, tugging at the green plastic bags in her hand. Her hair fluttered across her face.

Carla stood solemnly at the foot of the grave for a long time until she seemed to shake herself back to the present. She noticed litter lying around and set about tidying the place up, a bit like her mum would have done to her room when she was a little girl. She stuffed the rubbish into an empty supermarket bag, plucking up a few weeds in the process. She seemed to work in a daze, silent and lost in her own thoughts.

"That's better, Mum," she whispered, before lifting a beautiful plant out of one of the green bag she'd been carrying. "I know it's your favourite, Mum." She dug a small hole near the head of the grave, planted the tulip and then sprinkled on some water that had collected in a nearby glass jar.

Carla knelt there for a long time, talking out loud about how everything was going; how Paul was and how she'd been teaching him lessons in respect. She told her mum how the shop was running and that she didn't have to worry about them and that funny old Mrs Betty was still calling in with her dead husband. Carla chuckled, knowing her mum would be laughing too.

A quick glance at her watch made Carla realise that she'd lost all track of time. She quickly got to her feet, brushed her jeans down and buttoned up her long black coat.

"Mum, I miss you so much. I wish you were still here. I'm lost without you." She blew a kiss before turning away, her gloved hand wiping away the tears that had formed in her eyes. A sigh of wind that blew through the trees seemed to answer her. She was almost sure it whispered 'I'm here'.

*

Driving back home, Carla decided to stop at the supermarket to get some shopping for dinner. She was far away, thinking of her mum, when she walked into the supermarket and headlong into Drew in one of the aisles. Her basket crashed to the floor.

"You sure know how to sweep a girl off her feet," Carla said, trying not to grin at Drew's awkwardness.

They banged their heads as they simultaneously bent down to pick up the contents of her basket.

"Damn! I can't do anything right!" Drew muttered, rubbing his forehead. "Are you OK?"

"Apart from a lump the size of Texas threatening to come up on my forehead, life's great!" Carla pushed the spilled items back into her basket, concealing a smile behind her long hair.

"I'm sorry, Carla." Drew extended his hand to help her up, gripping her hand in his. They stood facing each other, eye to eye. There was definitely something there - they both felt it. Carla felt light-headed, almost giddy.

A brief silence hung in the air, making them shift the weight on their feet awkwardly.

"You can let my hand go if you want," Carla said at last.

"I just can't get it right with you." Drew seemed dejected.

"I didn't know you were trying." Carla smiled, tilting her head forward to hide the reddening of her cheeks behind a whisp of hair.

"I'm new in town...I don't know many people - but I'm glad I keep bumping into you, at least it's a friendly face."

"Literally!" Carla smiled.

They turned to walk down the aisle towards the tills.

"So you run that sweet shop all on your own then?"

"Yes - well, mostly. Paul helps when he can. We've been doing it for three years now."

"And how's it going?"

"Pretty good really. What about you?"

"I'm at Uni, doing English Lit."

"Really?" Carla surprised, spinning to face him. "Photography was what I wanted to do."

"Well, why didn't you?"

"Because Mum died three years ago and I needed to leave school to keep the shop going and Paul needed a 'responsible' guardian."

Carla half-turned to Drew and smiled at him. Drew felt his heart trip in his chest, its beat accelerating rapidly. How gorgeous she looked, he thought. Those brown eyes catching the last glint of daylight. He wanted to crush her into his arms.

"It must have been so hard…"

"What?"

"Giving up your dream to look after Paul and the shop."

"It's just a season in my life, Drew…I'm young and it'll pass. I've got plenty of time to play catch-up. That's how I look at it, anyway."

"I really admire that in you, Carla."

"Can I help?" the till operator enquired, breaking the spell. Carla started unpacking her shopping basket onto the counter. Drew used the opportunity to say goodbye.

"I enjoyed bumping into you," he said.

"In more ways than one!" Carla smiled as she watched him move away.

After putting the shopping away, Carla and Paul were sitting watching the news on TV when the doorbell rang.

"I'll get it, your Highness."

"Why, thank you, jester."

Carla assumed it was Rachel, so she sat back and waited for her to enter the room.

"You have a visitor," said Paul, rolling his eyes up into his head, nodding behind him.

"Drew?" Carla stammered, standing rapidly. "What are you doing here?"

"I was passing by and decided to see how you are…"

"How I am?"

"Your head…" Drew smiled, tapping his forehead. "You said you expected a lump the size of Texas to spring up?"

Carla laughed, and it reached her eyes. Her face flushed. Then she became aware of Paul, standing scowling behind Drew.

"Paul, fancy making us all a coffee?"

Paul gave Carla and Drew a sour look before turning towards the kitchen. Drew wiped the palms of his hands nervously on his jeans.

"Please sit," Carla said, beckoning to a chair.

"I'm sorry, can we start again?"

"Sure..."

"How *are* you?"

"Well I've been better, but I thought that men are meant to make girls go weak at the knees, not knock them senseless."

Drew laughed. "I'm glad to see it hasn't affected your humour."

Carla looked at Drew as if for the first time. He appears to be a bit of a rough diamond, Carla thought, while staring at him, but he had lovely eyes and a disarming smile.

"Is there anything I can do to make it up to you?" He seemed almost desperate to make things up to her. It was quite sweet, she thought.

"Mmm..." mused Carla, pursing her lips. "That's dangerous, suggesting something like that."

"The offer's there...."

"You're willing for me to choose your fate for my revenge?"

"Well...if you put it like that..." Drew began tentatively before being cut off by Carla.

"You're not going to chicken out?"

"I don't think you'd let me!"

"OK...how about working for two weeks in my shop when you have no lectures on?"

"You drive a hard bargain!" Drew groaned, but inwardly his spirits soared at the thought of being close to her without having to make excuses to see her all the time.

"Deal," said Carla, holding out her hand.

Drew had never felt a hand like that before...so soft and smooth. She had never felt a hand like his either for that matter – it was firm but gentle. She sensed the strength in him. A delicious silence, full of tension, fell between them.

They were staring at each other without realising it, only breaking away in embarrassment when Paul entered with the coffee.

"Look, I've got an essay to do for Thursday so I'm off to my room..." Paul told them, but he didn't move, willing Drew to pick up the hint and leave.

But Drew and Carla sat down on opposite sofas, completely ignoring Paul, so he turned and headed off up the stairs, stomping just a little.

"Allow me," Carla said pouring the coffee from the cafetière. "One lump or two? Sugar, that is…not another lump on the head!"

Drew grinned at her, looking intently into her eyes.

"Quite the comedian, hey?"

"Paul!" Carla called after her brother suddenly. "Drew's going to help out in the shop for two weeks."

"What?" he yelled from his room. "What for?"

"Compensation for crunching my head." Carla looked at Drew and smiled mischievously. "That'll wind him up!" she whispered conspiratorially.

Paul re-appeared as if by magic in the doorway, frowning at Drew.

"I could do that for you…help you out, I mean."

"Well, then, you can both work in the shop. I could use the extra pairs of hands."

"But…"

"No buts, young man - do you want me to make it three weeks?" Paul scowled before slumping into an armchair. The thought of working alongside Drew annoyed him for some reason. He didn't want anyone moving in on his territory at a time when Carla was clearly vulnerable. It wasn't the first time he had had to be protective towards his sister.

Carla, however, ignored the blatantly sexist and paternalistic attitude of her younger brother and turned to talk to Drew.

"You're going to have to tell me when you can work, so I can work out some kind of rota for the both of you." Carla wanted to make sure that the pair were not left alone together, hence the need for a rota. Carla would be there at all times and Drew and Paul would take it in turn to help out.

"Well, I can start tomorrow morning as I don't have my lecture till one, then after that I'm free," Drew told her willingly.

"Is that the same most days?"

"Yes."

"Well, then it's sorted, you can do the morning and Paul can do the lunchtime shift, after that we can all try and deal with the evening rush…Deal?"

"Deal!" Drew smiled.

"I don't want him left alone with you while I am at uni," Paul said suddenly.

"Don't you trust me then?" Drew asked quizzically. Carla was surprised by Paul's deepening attitude towards Drew; after all, he was only trying to help her.

"Paul, calm down! What do you think is going to happen?"

"Well, I don't know," Paul said quietly into his sister's ear, flushing red in the face, "I mean, we hardly know the guy, Carla... And all this for some corny payback for a bump on the head."

"Give us a break...What's wrong with him? He's just a student like you...not some criminal!" Carla quietly replied back to him before turning to Drew. "Are you OK to do the work, Drew?"

"Yeah, sure."

A silence fell between them again, broken only by the sound of coffee being sipped and slurped.

Drew drained his cup. "I'd better be getting off now and I'll see you in the morning," Drew said as he stood to leave.

The three of them walked out towards the front door, which Carla opened to find Rachel standing there gawking at them from the doorstep, her focus zeroing in on Drew. A secret smile curled the corners of her mouth.

"And what are you doing here?" Rachel said, to Drew, folding her arms across her chest.

Was that jealousy that Carla detected? It made her feel good somehow. She had something that Rachel didn't!

"I just popped in to see the walking wounded," Drew quipped. Paul stood behind Carla in a huffy silence, hands on his hips.

"Well, I'm off – g'night, Carla..."

Drew's smile was electrifying and Carla felt her heart flutter like a trapped rabbit's.

"Well, goodnight...and thanks for popping in...and don't forget tomorrow!" she called after him.

"Not likely!" he called back as he walked rapidly towards the gate. The street light glowed behind Drew's body and then he was gone into the night.

No one said anything for quite a few moments...

"So what's going on here then?" Rachel said finally, moving up to stand close to Carla on the top step.

"As if it isn't obvious!" Paul snorted before spinning on his feet. "He's 'In Love' with her and she... well, for some strange reason, she seems to like him, too!"

Rachel's eyes went wide, looking at Carla for confirmation.

"Get inside, you Muppet," she hissed, taking hold of Rachel's elbow.

Chapter Five. Give me a reason.

Bright and early the next morning, Drew was waiting patiently outside the sweet shop for Carla to arrive. It was a cold and very wet morning. In other words, very typical Scottish weather, in his limited and southern experience! Standing with his back to the shop door, he looked up and down the street for a sign of her arrival.

Unbeknown to him, Carla had actually been there for a while, silently watching him from the dark interior of the shop. She turned the lights on at last and stepped outside.

"You trying to hold the building up, Drew? You look mighty suspicious!"

He swivelled towards her, smiling.

" Well, I used to have fingers and toes, but I'm not sure now… it's freezing out here! Let me in, woman!"

"Go through to the back room, it's nice and warm. Want some tea?"

"You bet," Drew said, rubbing his hands as he came through the now opened door. "Man, it's cold out there!"

He followed her inside the unusually silent but delicious-smelling shop. It had her stamp all over the place. The beautifully-laid out shelves, a vase full of flowers by the window… quaint pictures hanging on the wall by the tables in the café area. He felt alive being alone with her here… that amazing aroma of something baking… the perfumed smells, the feminine atmosphere that she had made her own. It was like being at home again…like putting on a favourite pair of slippers. But more exciting.

Drew didn't realise it but Carla was watching him through the serving hatch, smiling silently to herself.

"How do you take your tea?"

"Milk and one sugar, thanks." Drew took a seat.

"So, what's your favourite flavour?" Carla asked handing him a cup of tea.

"Mmm?"

"Favourite flavour…of sweets…I could see you sniffing away there."

"Oh…let me see… mint and strawberries were always my favourites"

"An interesting choice. Which smell is the strongest to you in here?"

"Coconut, I think."

"So your favourites are mint and strawberry but you smell the coconut...that's curious." She sat down next to him and warmed her hands round her cup of tea.

"Does that mean something? Does it say who I am?"

"No, it's just a curiosity of mine...linking people to flavours. Finish your tea and then I'll show you the stockroom. It's the least interesting part of the whole place but it's the first step."

"You're enjoying this, aren't you?" Drew asked, looking at Carla over the rim of his cup.

"What?"

"Having me at your beck and call..."

Carla had the grace to blush, hanging her head forward to hide her embarrassment. Drew loved the way her full, silky hair fell forward, hiding her face and he smiled.

"Come on...let's show you the shop before the kids get here..."

Drew took the last swig of his tea and stood up to follow her. A short while later, Carla had shown him everything of importance in the stock room, including the circuit box and fire exit.

"Any questions?"

"Yeah, how do you remember what everything costs with out looking at the board?"

"Well, I've been doing this for a long time, remember, so it's all up here," she said, tapping her head, "but here's how I learned to remember it." She bent down and pulled a worn piece of paper out from under the counter. "This is the cheat sheet - I place it next to the till and check it every now and again. Here, have a read."

Drew took the sheet from her, frowning.

"I'll switch on the machines and open the door while you absorb that," she suggested. "Oh - and by the way, get ready for a rabid mob of kids - it gets kinda mental in here very early and very quickly."

Drew rubbed his hair and wondered what on earth he had gotten himself into. This was going to be harder than he thought.

"Don't look so worried!" Carla said, from somewhere near his elbow. "It'll be old hat in a few hours..."

As the first swarm of school-age customers arrived, the look of concern on Drew's face deepened to fear. The kids stampeded through the door as if it was feeding time at the zoo. Carla watched Drew's body language and facial expression change to panic, with amusement.

"They don't bite...I promise," she whispered in his ear. "OK guys, calm down and we'll get everyone seen quicker, alright? This is Drew, everyone - he'll be here on a temp basis for about a fortnight." The kids settled quickly at the sound of Carla's voice and turned to swivel their heads to look at Drew like a family of meerkats.

That broke the ice. Drew seemed to become more confident with every customer he served but it wasn't long before a bell sounded loudly and the shop almost emptied, much to Drew's bewilderment. Carla had had the bell installed to warn the schoolchildren that school was about to begin.

"C'mon, mister!" demanded the remaining child - a fat red-headed kid with black teeth. "Move it, will ya?" Drew pursed his lips trying desperately not to respond. Carla and Drew's eyes met for a brief second and they both smiled at each other. He loved it the way she swept up loose strands of hair behind her ear.

No sooner had the rush of kids begun than it ended. Carla held the door open for the last of them to leave, a rather attractive girl from a senior school down the road.

"That Drew's really cute...but a bit of an idiot, he gave me sherbet lemons."

"And what did you ask for?"

"Sherbet dip dabs," the girl replied as she left the shop.

Carla turned to look at Drew and smiled when their eyes made contact. Was she falling for him?

"Never mind, Rebecca - I'll give you a freebie when you come around this afternoon!" Carla shouted after the girl now running towards school. Rebecca turned and waved once before carrying on.

"And you do this everyday?" Drew said, from behind the counter.

"For the past three years."

Drew let out an impressed sigh and followed Carla into the cool of the back shop. He got the feeling that this was going to be one of the hardest and longest months of his life, but the sheer joy of being near Carla made him feel better...much, much better!

*

As the day wore on, with the flow of customers fluctuating predictably, Carla and Drew took it in turns to take a short break, while the other served. Lunchtime duly arrived and Drew asked to be shown how to work the smoothie machine, but Carla gave him one instruction too many.

As he turned the machine on, Carla moved away to refill an old man's cup of coffee. While she talked to the old man, Drew stood watching her and pondered the relationship that she had clearly developed with her customers. Whether frequent visitors or first timers, they were all met with the same warmth and kindness.

Suddenly, Drew felt a severe chill and dampness encroaching on his right foot and looked down at a huge puddle of smoothie juice all over his shoe.

"Aww, what the heck?" he yelped.

Hearing his cry, Carla came back to see him almost paddling in the slippery fruity stuff.

"You're meant to eat your fruit portions every day, not swim in it!" She laughed. Go on…get yourself sorted out. I'll mop this up…"

"Sorry…I thought the machine turned itself off automatically once the glass was full!"

"No harm done…Go on…get yourself cleaned up. I'll deal with it!"

"Typical!" Paul appeared out of nowhere and spoke with contempt. He'd entered the shop a second or two after Drew had gone to the toilet to clean himself up. "Just typical, I knew we couldn't trust that clown! Look at you doing all the work on your own…wait until I lay my hands on him!" Paul yanked the mop angrily out of Carla's hands.

"It was an accident!" Carla exclaimed, stepping back to watch Paul's frantic effort to clean the floor. "He's been here all morning, you know!"

"Yeah, he seems to have a lot of accidents, you better dock his wages."

"It was an accident – his only one so far, I'll have you know - and he isn't getting paid, he's only doing this to make it up to me."

This was something the hot-headed Paul either didn't realise, or chose to ignore - that Drew was, in fact, a volunteer. He had clearly made his mind up that Drew was out to sabotage his sister or con her…or both.

Paul was about to apologise to Carla when he saw Drew returning from the washroom. Paul opened his mouth once to say something then seemed to think the better of it. He carried on mopping with vigour.

Inwardly, however, Paul felt bad for jumping to conclusions about Drew. He moved quickly into the back room to wash his hands before coming back to serve customers. Then the phone rang.

"It's for you Carla," Paul said, holding the phone out to her.

"Who is it?" she mouthed silently.

"Rachel," Paul replied, covering the mouthpiece with his hand.

"Hey Rach what's up?"

"Hiya, Carla…Did he pitch up for work?"

"Who? Drew…yes he did…"

"Amazing! He's quite a hotty, actually…"

Carla felt a twinge of jealousy for the first time.

"What's up, Rach?"

"I've got four box seats for the next footie match - you interested?"

"Like hello!…Who did you get them from?"

"A friend…Someone who wouldn't take 'no' for an answer."

"Great…who are you inviting?"

"Well, I really don't want this guy to think he can make a move on me, so I was going to ask Paul to come and act as a bodyguard."

Carla burst out laughing, causing Paul to frown at her. She turned away from him to discourage him from listening..

"You'd better watch you don't lead him to believe that he's got some kind of chance with you - it would crush him!"

"He doesn't like me like that, does he?" Rachel sounded genuinely surprised.

"Let's put it this way, if this guy whose given you the tickets even smiles at you, I'll be visiting my brother in a prison! For some reason, he's quite hot-headed these days and prone to wild attacks of jealousy!"

"Do you think I should take him then?"

"Well, knowing you, you ain't got any other guy friends that could do it for you and we're not pretending to be an item just to save your neck."

"No, but it would be funny to see his reaction when he gets the invite…"

"No, it wouldn't - it's not fair on him to wind him up…"

"Well, ask him anyway. Who will you bring, I wonder?"

"Shut up Rach, I'll have to think about that one…"

"Yeah, sure…as if we can't guess anyway!"

"Rach! Anyway…I'll call you back later, OK?"

Carla put the phone down and looked thoughtfully at Drew. Of course he would be her choice. She smiled, watching him serve the last bunch of lunch-time kids before going to classes at uni. He had such a cute, innocent way around the children. They seemed to love him.

"Everything OK, Drew?" she asked moving closer to him.

"Oh, yeah, fine…"

"You sure?"

"Yep."

"Who were those guys you were talking to?"

"Just some mates from uni...you remember Marti?"

"Oh, yes...how could I forget? Could you come and see me when you've finished serving? Thanks."

Marti wandered back to the counter.

"What's all that about?" he asked pointedly. "Wants to see you privately, hey?"

"Give it a break, man, there's nothing going on between us..."

"Not that you wouldn't mind, hey?"

"Give it a break, Marti!"

"You do realise you're the source of a bet?"

"Let me guess," Drew said sarcastically. "I can't last the whole two weeks in here with Paul?"

A couple of other guys drifted over to listen to the conversation.

"On the contrary," Pete butted in. "The bet's that you *can't* get her to go out with you...we lose if you do," Pete said, throwing an arm around an uncomfortable Marti, who shrugged it off just as quickly.

"So you see," Marti added. "We have a vested interest in your success!"

"Let the fun begin!" Pete laughed, punching Drew none too gently on the shoulder.

Paul watched all this from a distance. It didn't take a rocket scientist to figure that something was up...and that it involved Carla. The sideways glances towards her from the group of guys made sure of that! Paul just didn't trust Drew or his mates and studied them through narrowed eyes...he would pull Drew's head off if he did anything to hurt his sister. He wasn't the first to want to date her but, so far, he was the most successful. He could tell by his sister's body language and frequent glances in Drew's direction that she felt something for him too.

Drew wasn't insensitive – he quickly became aware of Paul's poorly hidden hostility and frosty manner whenever he was close to Carla. He knew Paul was protective of her and decided to walk carefully around him rather than upset him. But for now, he revelled in Carla's presence as she went through the intricacies of the cappuccino machine with him...

"You'd better start heading up to the uni so that you're not late," Paul told Drew, glancing significantly at the clock. Both Drew and Carla stared at him blankly.

"Actually, he's right, Drew…better not be late," Carla remarked.

"Yeah, on you go mate," Paul said gleefully.

"Chill out, Paul, you'd better get going too, you know!"

"Not until he goes," he said, nodding at Drew.

"Oh, good grief - have you listened to yourself lately? You sound like a two-year-old! In fact, most two-year-olds I know behave better!"

Drew shifted his feet with embarrassment. A stony silence, charged with tension, filled the air.

"Right I'm off, Carla - I'll see you later."

With that, Drew walked out and headed off to his lecture. Paul, who now saw the opportunity to get him on his own and grill him, grabbed his bag and ran around the counter.

But Carla caught his jacket from the other side and pulled him back, causing him to fall backwards down on top of the counter facing the ceiling. Carla's face then appeared above him and, as he stared at her, she said quietly: "Leave him be, you've scared him enough, alright?"

"Fine, Carla – just let go, OK? I'm late."

"I mean it, Paul."

"I heard you - let go." Paul had not realised that Carla had already let go, so he pulled hard and flew to the floor in front of an old man who had his granddaughter with him. The little girl deliberately dropped her ice cream cone on his head as he started getting to his feet. In that situation what could anyone do but laugh?

Which is exactly what everyone in the shop now did - including Carla. Embarrassed, humiliated and angry, Paul stormed out of the shop, throwing the cone to the ground. But he turned and smiled wickedly at Carla as he left - and she knew what that look meant.

Trying to get to him before he ran off, she headed for the door. By the time she got there, however, he was gone and already catching up with Drew.

Carla was now furious with him, so she walked back in and made the little girl a new cone and gave her a bag of sweets to congratulate her on having such a good aim. Then she started to clean the empty tables as she muttered under her breath: "Oh boy, you're so dead…"

*

Drew, meanwhile, was standing at the traffic lights waiting for them to change to the green man, when he heard someone running behind him. He turned to have a look, saw that it was Paul and suddenly felt a twinge of alarm coarse through his body.

"Wait up, mate!" Paul yelled. Drew, trying to cross the busy road without waiting for the lights to change, knew that it would be safer for him to make his own way across.

At the other side, having managed to avoid causing an accident, Drew looked back to find Paul had gone. Assuming that he had moved further down the street to cross the road, Drew turned around to walk on only to find Paul standing right in front of him.

To his astonishment and fright, Drew jumped back and began falling back onto the road into oncoming traffic, when he was suddenly pulled forward.

"No, no, pal, you don't get away that easily. If you end up dead, Carla would only blame me and I am not losing my sister because of some guy. You OK?" Drew, who was still in shock, nodded, stunned into silence. Staring at him, Paul then pulled Drew's head under his arm to lock him in a headlock, but made it look playful so that no one thought that he was attacking him.

"Now we're going to have a little chat."

Drew had been frantically trying to pull free of the headlock. He stopped suddenly, exhausted.

"How the Hell did you get across the road so fast?" he demanded.

"Never mind that - what's with the guys and all the whispering in the shop and that guy... what's his name...Marti? He's always whispering to you and then he shuts up when Carla and I get near him. You planning on robbing the place or something?"

"Give it a rest!"

"What's it all about, Drew? And your plans with my sister?"

"Look, Paul, there's nothing going on with Carla and me and, as for planning a robbery...Well, all I can say is stop watching those action movies, they're messing with your head!"

"You've got something up your sleeve...I'm watching you, OK?"

Paul's voice was low and threatening. "And I'm telling you one more time -keep your eyes off Carla and your mates out the shop!"

Drew made an attempt to pass Paul but Paul grabbed at his collar. Drew responded by latching onto Paul's shoulders, pulling him in close.

They eyed each other without flinching, knowing that the first guy to let go or back away would lose the stand-off.

Down the road, Marti, Sarah and Pete caught sight of the struggle.

"What's that all about, do you think?" Pete asked.

"Oh, no!" Marti sighed in exasperation. "If Paul finds out we've made a bet involving his sister, he'll kill Drew...and us!"

"Bet? What bet?" Sarah interrupted, confused.

"We'll fill you in later," Pete said as they hurriedly crossed the road to pull Paul and Drew apart.

"Easy guys, what's going on?" Pete said putting his hands on both their shoulders, "easy now...come on, break it up!"

"It's fine - just a friendly chat, that's all... right Drew?" Paul said slowly, before pulling away from Drew.

"You bet!" Drew replied to Paul as he walked off.

"What's this I hear about a bet?" Sarah said, catching them up.

"Drop it!" the three of them told her simultaneously.

"I'm telling you guys - if you don't let me in on your secret you'll never see me again!"

"So be it," Pete said without looking back.

"Come on!" Sarah yelled, stamping her feet. "Be fair!"

"OK, I'll tell you," Drew said, spinning to face her. "These clowns here have made a bet that I can't get a date with Carla!"

"What? You're not going to try it are you? Do you realise what Paul would do to you if he found out? He'd go bananas! That guy's got real anger issues – I've seen him really lose it at school."

"He seems OK around Carla."

"She's the one who keeps him calm!"

"Does she know how Paul behaves?"

"I doubt it..."

"Well, the best thing we can all do is avoid him from now on, eh?" Pete suggested

"So what do I do about all this?" Drew asked.

"Just be cool around Paul...Don't do anything that makes him get suspicious."

"Sounds like that's easier said than done..."

"We'd better get to class." Marti butted in anxiously. "Five minutes to go..."

As they headed into the lecture halls, Sarah's mobile phone rang. She answered the call, which was from a friend she used to go to school with, who was now at another uni.

"Hi, Jane, how are you? No, it's cool – just on my way to a class…"

Marti tried not to listen to the conversation but Sarah's words drifted over to him as she meandered away form the group. He heard: 'I love him' and 'No, I haven't plucked up the courage yet.' Naturally, he became curious about the call and the topic of the conversation. He was just about to ask Sarah what the conversation was all about but when he turned to look at her she was halfway down another passage already, heading for her lecture hall.

*

Half past three came and Carla wondered where Drew was, when the shop door opened with a tinkle of its bell. Carla looked up to see Rachel standing there.

"Well, don't look so pleased to see me… Ooh wait, don't tell me - Drew's a no-show! I should have guessed."

"Trust you to think that way…But I must admit, he *is* late…I've a sneaky suspicion Paul has something to do with this."

"Let's hope Drew's not swimming in the Clyde with the rats."

"That's a bit extreme…Paul wouldn't do anything to hurt Drew."

"Really?" Rachel retorted, with more than a hint of sarcasm.

Carla pondered Rachel's comments. Could Paul really be that angry? To do something as drastic as that? No, he's not like that - Rachel's just trying to wind her up.

"Good grief, Carla - that's the biggest batch of mint marble I've ever seen you make," Rachel said, breaking into Carla's thoughts.

"Mmm? Oh, yes… I heard there's a coach trip stopping off near here and I wanted to be ready, just in case."

"You're sure it's not to impress someone?"

"Oh, Rachel…not you, too? Put a cork in it, OK?"

Rachel giggled mischievously, helping herself to some of the delicious marbled confection.

At that moment, Drew walked in. Rachel hugged her shoulders and blew Carla a lover's kiss, glancing sideways at Drew.

"Give it a rest!" Carla hissed under her breath.

"Morning, Drew," Rachel said, emphasising the sway of her hips as she headed for the door.

"Push off back to your bookshop!" Carla shouted after her.

"What's that all about?" Drew asked, putting his bag in the corner.

"That's just Rachel for you...high on helium, I think..."

"Helium, eh?" Drew replied, chuckling. "Maybe I should try some of that..."

Drew and Carla were still smiling into each other's faces when Paul walked in. With his arrival came tension and an awkward silence crackled between him and Drew.

"What are you doing back so early?" Carla asked, folding her arms defensively.

"Forgot this." He grunted, picking up a heavy book. He threw a long, almost threatening look at Drew before heading for the door.

"Bye, then," Carla shouted after him, but he didn't respond.

"What's eating him?" Carla said.

"I think he has a problem with me being here..."

"Really? Why?"

"Just a hunch..."

A silence fell between them, which grew into an awkward silence. Both started fidgeting with confectionary displays. The awkwardness grew. Thankfully, the phone rang, spurring them both into action.

Carla picked up the receiver while Drew turned to serve an older couple who had just walked into the shop.

"Yes, sir?" Drew enquired of the old man.

"You're new here, aren't you? Are you Carla's boyfriend?" the old man asked bluntly.

"No, it's nothing like that," Drew assured him, looking sideways at Carla, who was still talking on the phone.

"It's about time," the old man continued, ignoring Drew's protestations. "She's been lonely for so long and..."

"She's *not* my girlfriend!" Drew said politely as he put his left hand straight into a cake by accident.

"I know that her baking is to die for, son, but if you really wanted cake, I'm sure she'd give you some," the old man said with a twinkle in his eye.

As Drew began wiping the cake off on a cloth he asked: "What can I get you sir?"

"I'll have a cup of tea and a mint marble…the same for my wife over there, please."

"I'll bring it over in a minute, sir…"

"Right-oh, sonny," the gentleman said, tapping the side of his nose. "You'd better get that cleaned up!"

*

"Have you asked him out yet?" Rachel asked Carla over the phone.

Carla cupped the phone in her hands and turned to make sure Drew wasn't within earshot, but he was busy doing teas for the old couple.

"Not yet…I'm as nervous as Hell…It's not like I ask guys out every day…"

"Well, hurry up, woman -   ask him to the match and do it quickly…There's only a couple of hours left and you don't want to end up without a date."

"OK, I'll do it now…Bye!"

Carla put the phone down and looked over thoughtfully to Drew. Her heart fluttered away in her chest. What if he turned her down? It would ruin their relationship and that would be the end of him coming to the shop. But she so desperately wanted to go out on a date with him…There was a feeling growing in her that she'd never felt before.

He wasn't half that bad-looking either. As if seeing him for the first time, she realised just how handsome he was, in a plain, rugged sort of way. And he had a child-like innocence with a maturity beyond his years, all wrapped in one. Carla suddenly found this very appealing.

Nothing further was said until about half an hour later, when the old couple stood up and headed for the door.

"Your secret's safe with me!" The old man tapped the side of his nose again, giving Drew a wink and smile, revealing gaps in his teeth. Drew smiled weakly at him.

"What was that all about?" Carla said as she locked the door behind them, flicking the sign on the glass door to 'closed'.

"Just a nice old guy who thinks he knows something," was all Drew would say.

Carla cleared her throat, swiping back a loose strand of hair behind her ear. Her heart fluttered. Well, here goes nothing!

"Drew…I was just wondering…" she said fidgeting nervously with her hair. "How would you like to…" Her voice trailed away weakly.

"How would I like to what?" The sun caught Drew's eyes, turning them a dark hazel green. Carla looked deeply into them, feeling her face flush.

"Well, Rachel was given four tickets to go to the football match tonight and I wondered if you'd be interested in coming with me?"

"Yes," Drew said, perhaps a shade too quickly. "That would be great..."

"Great!" Carla said, a bit too enthusiastically to be cool. "Come round to the house at six...You can leave here early."

"Why do I need to go home early to get ready for a football match?"

"We've got an executive box...So it's a suit and tie for you."

"A suit and tie..." Drew looked thoughtful.

The two of them worked silently together, cleaning the shop and preparing shelves of confectionery for the next day. Drew caught Carla glancing at him occasionally. They smiled spontaneously at each other when their eyes met. Carla was becoming increasingly aware how special it was to be alone with him...

"Right Drew, you'd better head off," she announced just before half past four. "I'll see you at six. Remember, smart dress."

"OK... pink and fluffy?"

"What?"

"You said I must wear a dress..."

"Ha ha! You'd better leave now, smart Alec..."

Paul walked through the front door just as Drew exited it. They made no eye contact with each other.

"Rachel phoned to ask if you'd act as her bodyguard tonight at the football match," Carla told him, without looking up.

"Why?" Paul said excitedly, dropping his bag behind the counter. "You're kidding me, aren't you?"

"I'm not...She was given the tickets by a guy that may be trying to make a move on her so she needs you to protect her honour. Or something."

"I wouldn't miss it for anything! Are you coming?"

"Yes I am."

Carla walked through to the back room to start locking up, avoiding Paul's eyes.

"You're acting all shifty suddenly...What's up, Carla?"

"I'm not shifty. You have an over-active imagination, Paul."

"There's something else you haven't told me, isn't there?"

"Look, we haven't got long to get home and get changed. By the way, your suit is in my wardrobe."

"Why do I need the suit?"

"We've got an executive box tonight."

"Cool!"

"Yeah, so give me a hand to secure everything and we can go."

Paul ran round and bolted shutters down, unplugged machines and turned chairs up on to the tables. His mind was spinning. A date with Rachel! He couldn't believe his luck! The thought of her drove any suspicions about Carla's secretiveness far from his mind.

Chapter Six. Just good friends

Paul looked at his watch. It was half past five. He ran up to Carla's bedroom and knocked on the door.

"Carla, I need my bow tie done."

She came to the door, tying the bow expertly for him. As she did so, she realised how tall he was becoming – quite the young man. Paul studied her face.

"Why have you got so much make-up on and why are you wearing your good earrings?"

"I haven't been out in a while so I want to make the most of the occasion... Is there a problem?"

"No...I just wondered."

Paul's sixth sense kicked in again. His earlier suspicions returned. Why was she looking so good? Carla finished fixing his tie.

"Well...Don't you look handsome, " she said, stepping back to focus on him. "For a clot that is..."

Paul faked hurt feelings, turning down the sides of his mouth. The doorbell rang.

"That'll be Rachel...Go let her in will you? Oh - and try not to look like a lovesick puppy."

Paul raced noisily downstairs to open the door, panting like an idiot. A beautiful vision greeted him as he hurled the door wide open. He had never seen Rachel look so amazing. He just stood there with his mouth open...His heart was racing.

"My coat," she said, turning for him to remove it from her shoulders. Paul eased the expensive-looking coat off her shoulders, noticing how soft and pure her skin looked. A gentle waft of her perfume reached his nostrils. He thought he had died and gone to Heaven!

"What...what would you like to drink?" he stammered nervously.

"Do you have sparkling water?" Rachel asked in a level voice, trying to hide her own excitement at seeing Paul. He looked so different all dressed up... He looked like a man now...not a boy.

"I think we do...I'll go get you a glass. Take a seat."

"Where's Carla?"

"Still getting ready."

"OK."

A taxi pulled up outside as Paul moved through to the kitchen. Rachel pulled the lounge curtain to one side, revealing Drew walking up the driveway. She caught her breath. She thought Paul looked great in a suit but Drew was drop-dead gorgeous! She opened the front door before he had a chance to knock, nervously patting down the front of her skirt.

"Rachel..." Drew said, as he looked up at Rachel. "You look lovely..."

"As do you ...very handsome, I mean..." she said stepping to one side.

"Where's Carla?"

"Getting ready...Up there," Rachel thumbed towards Carla's room. "Go into the sitting room and I'll see how she's getting on," Rachel said, feeling all excited for Carla.

She blushed red and ran up the staircase, just as Paul returned with the drinks for Rachel and himself. He stopped in mid-stride, staring at Drew with his mouth wide open.

"The penny has just dropped..."he said, glaring at Drew.

"What do you mean?" Drew asked casually, not rising to the bait. Paul put the tray down and walked closer to Drew, looking him straight in the eye.

"I got suspicious when I saw Carla getting all dressed up tonight...I should have guessed..."

"What's the problem, mate?"

"You're making a move on my sister, aren't you?" Paul said, raising his voice, "I don't trust some loser from outta town who'll break her heart as soon as uni's over!"

"Look, she asked me to come to this, so wind your neck in, I'm sure I'm only here to stop some other guy hitting on her!" Drew said louder than he had intended to.

"Shut up you two," Rachel said from nowhere, "Carla's about to come down and if you two ruin her first night out in a long time she will never forgive you - and neither will I."

As Rachel finished speaking, Carla entered the doorway. She wore a beautiful three-quarter length dress, her hair down and in slightly loose curls. Everyone looked at her in amazement.

"Wow, Carla - you know it's a football match were going to, not some kind of ball?" In reply, Carla tapped Paul playfully on the face, almost hard enough to be considered a slap.

"I'll second that," Rachel agreed.

"But what's he doing here?" Paul jerked his thumb in Drew's direction.

"Please, not now, Paul...let's call a truce for tonight."

Rachel cast a fierce glance in Paul's direction, as did Drew. Paul nodded and shrugged, accepting her plea.

"Well, what do you think?" Carla asked Drew.

"You - well, umm...you look great..."

"OK, great," Carla said, slightly disappointed. She was kind of hoping that Drew would fall at her feet. What she didn't realise though, was that Drew was completely gob-smacked by the transformation in her. She had taken his breath away.

Carla turned to put her coat on.

Rachel was also flabbergasted by Drew's response and glared at him. A sour silence fell over the room. Then a loud blast of a car horn sounded as their taxi pulled up.

"Look, if we are actually going to go to this match, we'd better go now," Paul said, looking at his watch. Rachel grabbed Paul's arm and dragged him out of the door to the car, much to his surprise. But he had time to realise that it felt like heaven walking arm-in-arm with her.

"We'd better go then," Carla said, avoiding Drew's gaze.

"Yeah," was all he could say at first. Then he held her by the elbow as they reached the top of the steps at the front door. "Look, I couldn't say how beautiful you are while Paul was staring at me, Carla. I just want you to know that I think you look stunning...just totally gorgeous. I can't believe you're my date...You look so different without your apron on..."

Carla put her index finger to touch Drew's lips, smiling broadly.

"Thank you Drew, I hoped you couldn't be so indifferent to me..."

They stood staring at each other in the soft moonlight. It felt as if a magnet was pulling them together, inevitably, irresistibly...

"My Lady," Drew murmured, bowing slightly, offering her his hand to guide her down the short flight of steps.

"Quite the gentleman!" She giggled before heading off towards the waiting taxi.

*

The traffic heading into Hampden Park was severely backed up. By the time they finally exited the lift, the executive lounge to the side of the private boxes was full. Several men straightened and smartened themselves up when they saw Carla and Rachel but immediately lost interest when they realised that Paul and Drew were with them.

Once they'd ordered their drinks, they made their way over to the large window to have a look out onto the stadium. Rachel spotted her 'friend' on his way over to see her but she made an effort to avoid making eye contact. Carla diplomatically ambled away with Drew to tell him about the stadium.

While Carla was explaining various details and history of the ground to Drew, Rachel received a tap on the shoulder. She turned round to look into the eyes of the man who'd given her the tickets for the game. She knew from the outset that it was a mistake to talk to him.

"So how do you like the evening so far?" the man said, cockily preening himself. He smelled like he'd bathed in a vat of aftershave.

"It's great, thanks, John, I was just saying so to my boyfriend, Paul…"

"Boyfriend, hey?" John leaned forward to shake his hand, but Paul was determined not to return the gesture.

"Paul!" Rachel hissed quietly under her breath. The two shook hands. Paul squeezed extra hard to make a statement.

"How do you do?" Paul said firmly.

"Pleased to meet you, I'm sure," John replied, but looking at Rachel. "Come with me, dear, I have something to show you…"

Carla had been watching this out of the corner of her eye and moved quickly over to Paul.

"Bodyguard - time for some action," she whispered urgently in Paul's ear. Paul seemed to snap out of a his trance and took four large steps before catching up with Rachel.

"Excuse me, but I think you'll find Rachel's with me," he said, tapping the man on the shoulder.

Paul took a hold of Rachel's free hand and pulled her towards him - much to her delight!

"Erm…" John stammered as he looked at them, slightly miffed.

"Nice to meet you…eh – John, was it?" Paul replied sarcastically as he walked Rachel away.

John stood, his face flushing with frustration. He lifted his glass of whisky to his mouth and threw it back, swallowing the contents before storming back to his table.

A while later a group of girls came round from a betting agency to take bets on the game, obviously most of the men bet and when they came to Drew and Carla he ask her predictions and put the money on for her as he didn't know what the players were like.

"Right Carla, I think I'll leave the predictions up to you!" Drew remarked quietly, as he passed the betting slip to her.

"Sure…now let's see…" Carla began to tap the pen on her chin as she pondered over the possible team line up. As Drew stood up, to retrieve his wallet from the suit pocket, he caught a sneaky look at Carla. A quiet smile crept onto his face just as the young girl interrupted him.

"Emm, can I ask how much you are wanting to put on the bet, sir?" the brassy girl asked, her tone hinting at the need to hurry the bet along.

Drew looked down at Carla, who suggested: "Put ten…no make it fifteen!" she exclaimed having looked back at her slip and confidently smiled at him.

"You sound very sure…are you? He smirked.

"Actually I am - here you go, girls!" As Carla handed the slip to the girls, Paul scribbled frantically on the sheet. Rachel was too busy looking around, in case someone famous was in the room.

Ten minutes later, the headwaiter announced that the match was about to begin and that everybody should take their seats.

Drew led Carla out to the seats, which were on an outside balcony, then Paul guided Rachel through the doors behind them. Paul made sure that he sat right behind Carla and Drew so he could hear everything that was being said between them. For the rest of the match, though, everybody seemed to be having a good time - except the man who had invited Rachel and her friends. Paul even forgot about watching Carla and Drew and started watching the football, becoming more involved and animated as the pace of the game intensified.

At half-time, everyone had come back into the warmth of the executive lounge for cups of tea and coffee to heat them up. So far, Carla's bet was going really well and she and Drew seemed quite upbeat about their predictions.

However, Paul's hopes had already been dashed, as he had predicted a one-nil win and as it stood, it was already two-one.

Which put Paul in a slightly sombre mood. As for Rachel, she was too busy keeping an eye on John, who seemed to be stalking her, worrying what he was doing, in case she had to utilise Paul's role as bodyguard again.

The atmosphere became electric again as the teams walked onto the pitch for the second half. As the night wore on, the stadium became a wind tunnel, but the fans didn't seem to care. Their chants grew in volume, urging their teams on. Carla started to feel the bitter cold more and more. Drew saw her shivering and took of his large outer coat, wrapping it round her.

By this time, Paul was too engrossed in the game to have noticed the exchange of looks between the two of them.

Ten minutes before full-time, the score still stood at two-one and a free kick had just been awarded about a yard outside the eighteen yard box. The stadium was on its feet in anticipation; Carla gripped the railing in front of her as fans below their balcony were cheering on the player who had stepped up to take it.

The bet was that it would be a three-one win and Carla had actually named the first goal scorer and had guessed the man of the match. Now they had one out of the three predictions right. If they got all three correct, then a lot of money would be heading their way.

Which was why Carla was gripping the railing so tightly. Their predicted man of the match stepped up to take the free kick, then smacked it right in the top corner of the net.

The raptures of celebration consumed the stadium - everybody at the home end was jumping and hugging everyone beside them. Paul had grabbed Rachel, threw her up in his arms and twirled her round; everyone was celebrating - except Carla. She couldn't believe what she was seeing unfold in front of her, as she looked at he piece of paper. Drew tapped her on the shoulder and pointed to Paul and Rachel's reaction.

"They don't even know about our bet yet and look at them."

"I know - but I just hope that Rachel realises just how much he really likes her and doesn't break his heart."

"Really, he's in love with your best friend?"

"Has been for a long time. I only found out when he was lying sleeping on the sofa one day and mumbled about his undying love for her."

"Oh - when did he find out you knew?"

"When I mentioned it at dinner that night. He was mortified!" They both laughed, before Carla then said: "But Rachel only thinks it's lately that he started having feelings for her, so until he tells her otherwise, please don't say anything."

"I promise." They looked back at the stadium which was still rejoicing at the goal as the final whistle sounded. Had there been a roof on the stadium, the crowd would have lifted it clean off with the sheer volume of their screams. Getting back inside, they collected their winnings quietly, then suggested to Rachel and Paul that they should start heading home before the roads got too busy. So they headed for the exit…

*

John, the man who had provided the tickets for the group, was clearly very frustrated at Rachel. He was drunk and suddenly started hurling abuse at her.

"Well, aren't we a smooth little operator…" he hissed viciously at her, narrowing his eyes and pointing.

"Excuse me!" Rachel replied, displaying a horrified expression. Carla then quickly stepped in.

"Never mind him, he's drunk…Paul, take her over there" Carla whispered urgently in her brother's ear, desperate to keep both of them away from John. But John had already worked out that it was Carla who had made Paul take Rachel over to the other side of the room.

"So who are you then? Some bloody guardian angel or something?" He was becoming so loud that everyone in the room had stopped to watch.

"He's only embarrassing himself. Don't you join him," Carla said to both Paul and Drew. Paul nodded and continued walking, as Drew stayed fixed to her side.

John, filled with anger at her remarks, grabbed her arm and flung her to the floor. The other men in the box had to help restrain him as Paul and Drew made a dive for him, Rachel ran to Carla's side as the three men were restrained.

"What the Hell do you think you're doing, mate?" said one of the men who was holding Drew, as he tried to wriggle free of the man's grip on him. John didn't answer as he was wrestled to the ground. It seemed the police were there almost instantaneously - at first, they didn't see Carla sitting on the floor. The man who had assaulted Carla was quickly escorted out of the stadium, straight into a police car then taken away to be charged. Another policeman went over to Carla as other officers took statements and asked: "Are you OK, miss?"

"Yes, but I think I've hurt my ankle."

"Wait here and I'll bring the paramedics up to have a look at you."

"No, I'll be fine," she insisted,

"Well, we're going to charge this guy, so we need to know everything that he did, especially the injuries that you have sustained, so you'll need to wait there in any case."

Carla realised that she had no option and sat back with a sigh.

As Carla was finishing her statement, the paramedics arrived.

"OK, let me have a look," the first one said. "Oh dear, looks like you're taking a trip to the Western, lass! You're going to need an X-ray for this – there could be a fracture"

"Oh no!" Carla tried to rise in protest but fell back in pain as her ankle gave way.

"Do you have a car with you?" said the blond and very handsome paramedic to Paul and Drew. But they were so shocked by her need to visit the hospital that their only response was to shake their heads helplessly.

"Right, Steven, help me get her up. Looks like we'll have to take her in…" The two paramedics picked Carla up and strapped her into a wheelchair then headed for the lifts, followed closely by Rachel. At the exit they moved outside and wheeled her along, through the crowd with people staring at her.

Carla even heard someone saying: "Bettcha she's drunk!" By this time, Carla was mortified. When they reached the ambulance, Rachel climbed in with her and Paul and Drew both also tried to follow.

"Sorry guys, only one person can come in the back."

"But I'm her brother." Paul protested.

"Paul, you and Drew go and get a taxi and pick the car up from the house, you and I are the only ones who haven't had a drink and Carla wants me with her," Rachel said, as Carla looked at her confused, trying to work out when she may have implied that.

"But…" Paul interrupted a bit put out.

"So we'll meet you at A and E. Well - go on." Rachel waved them off as the medic closed the doors.

"Right - OK." So Drew and Paul backed off and ran off to get a taxi home. Carla now found herself in an ambulance with Rachel for company.

*

Finally, when they got to the A&E, Carla didn't even react to the commotion happening around her as she knew it would be pointless.

Then, out of nowhere, she heard: "Hello pet, have you hurt yer leg?" An old drunken man was swaying beside her as she lay on the trolley.

"Oh blimey, not tonight!"

"What's your name, hen?"

Carla tried to grab a passing nurse. "Nurse, I'm in a lot of pain - please, is there anyone that will see me?"

"Sorry, love – we're busy tonight. It's Saturday – I'm afraid we've got a few in who are worse off than you. We'll get to you as soon as we can, I promise."

"Hello, is it really sore, pet? I'm a doctor - dae ye want me to have a look at it for ya?" The drunk moved forward staggering with his hands outstretched.

"No, I'm fine thanks." Carla ruffled the blanket back over her ankle and pulled back from his touch.

"No – it's nae problem, come here..." He swayed towards her unsteadily.

Then Rachel suddenly spotted him as she was waiting for Paul and Drew to arrive. She ran over to move Carla, but as she did so, a young boy sent a wind-up toy skittering across the A&E floor, which Rachel managed to step onto.

Just then Rachel flew right into the drunk and knocked him to the floor beside her. As he sat up, she did too then the drunk turned round to face her and sprayed vomit on her.

Carla started laughing uncontrollably, as the young boy whose toy Rachel stood on started to cry, as the toy lay smashed to pieces on the floor. Rachel was gagging and trying to scrape off some of the vomit that had been shared with her, as a nurse and a janitor pulled the drunk to his feet.

Just then, Paul and Drew walk in and, seeing the A&E in the mess it was in, with the high-pitched whining of the child, Carla laughing hysterically and Rachel on the floor green in colour from the smell of the vomit, they stopped dead in their tracks. Carla saw them and her laughter became even more uncontrollable, which caused the nurse to stare at Carla and move towards her.

"Oh, now she's become hysterical with the pain - get her in there now." Carla just kept laughing, so much so that she could be heard down the corridor for a few more minutes. Then nothing - the waiting area fell silent.

Paul walked over to help Rachel up and take her to the toilets, he then gave her his jacket to put on so that she could take off the now-ruined corset top that she had on. A while later, Carla emerged, having to be wheeled out to the waiting area by the nurse, this time bearing a stupid grin on her face, looking spaced.

"What's wrong with her?" Paul asked, tilting his head slightly, to see her face better.

"We just gave her some strong painkillers and strapped her leg up. Here are a few more painkillers for when this lot wears off, but she can't have these till at least five hours from now. It's best to put her to bed when you get her home."

"Ok thanks, nurse. Come on, let's get you home."

Getting Carla out of the car, once they got home, required both Paul and Drew. Paul then carried her the rest of the way to the house, as Rachel ran to the door to open it and get her bed ready. Up the stairs in her room, Paul laid Carla down and Rachel sent him downstairs while she changed Carla into her pyjamas.

A while later, Paul was pacing up and down the front room waiting to find out how Carla was doing, with Drew sitting watching him. Rachel came down and closed the door quietly behind her.

"Is she ok?" Paul asked urgently.

"She's sleeping, thank goodness," Rachel replied as she glanced at Drew, who looked drawn and pale.

"Right, let's go, Drew," Rachel said briskly. "We've all got an early start tomorrow. She won't surface till the morning, so there's no need to wait around. Paul, if either of you need me for anything just phone me, ok? Night, then."

Giving Paul a kiss on the cheek and dragging Drew behind her, Rachel left to go home.

In her car, Rachel and Drew sat quietly as Rachel drove. Then Rachel remembered that Drew and Paul had been alone in the car on the way to the hospital.

"So, Drew, how was Paul with you?"

"Fine. Well, I mean, we didn't talk, he was worrying about Carla too much to bother about me," Drew responded sounding tired.

"Yeah, so you and Carla - what's happening there then?"

"I don't understand…"

"Well, do you fancy her?"

"I think she's a lovely person."

"Don't avoid the question Drew."

"I'm not, I didn't realise that accepting this ride home meant we were playing Twenty Questions."

"Look, all I wanted to know is, do you fancy her? That's all."

Drew turned to look at her, smiled and went back to looking out of the window. Rachel got the distinct impression that Drew *did* like Carla, but that something was holding him back from acting on his feelings.

She dropped him off and went home. However, as she got in, Rachel realised that she had left her purse in Carla's room. She would have to go back for it - she needed to go to the suppliers the next morning to hand in a new order.

*

Reaching Carla and Paul's house, Rachel saw that the front room's light was on so she went to the front window. Paul was sitting there with a bottle of lager and seemed to be very upset. Rachel walked up to the door and knocked on it, as she felt using the doorbell might startle them. Paul came to the door and was surprised to find Rachel standing before him.

"Are you OK?" she asked, walking forward and taking a hold of his arms.

"Yeah, I'm fine - what's wrong? She hasn't moved." Paul replied, thinking Rachel had been worrying about Carla.

"I forgot my purse - it's in her room, I'll just go get it."

"OK."

Rachel quickly ran up to Carla's room to find her lying in exactly the same way she had left her in. With a sigh of relief, she spotted her purse sitting on Carla's bedside cabinet. Bending down to pick up the purse, Rachel glanced at Carla, gently smoothed her hair away from her face, smiled and headed back down the stairs to find Paul again sitting on the couch moping. She walked over and sat down beside him.

"Hey, what's up? And don't fob me off again 'cause I've never seen you like this before."

"I know that it wasn't serious, but seeing her in there tonight got me thinking. I never realised how much I need her and depend on her, she's all I've got, Rach. What would I do if anything happened to her? She's always been there for me, you know. Even when Mum died, she was - she was always there for me." He burst into tears and Rachel pulled him into a hug, as she too shed a few tears as she remembered how much she had also leaned on Carla.

Carla hadn't just helped him, She had also been there for Rachel when she was having problems too, especially with her own mother. She wondered what she would do without her best friend to look after her.

It took them a few minutes to calm down, just sitting there together, then, as they moved away, their eyes met.

Then they were kissing, although neither knew who started it. The kiss lasted for a long minute before they gently pulled away.

"You know, don't you?" Paul said while brushing her hair behind her ears.

"Yeah, Carla told me how you feel."

"I know it feels weird, but I've tried to shake it, believing it was some stupid crush, but I can't and I thought I would never be able to tell you."

"Well I know now, but what do we do?"

"I don't know, what do you think we should do about it?"

"Do you think we should ask Carla how she feels about it first? After all, it could be weird for her."

"Yeah, you're right." They sat in silence for a few moments, Pauls' arm around Rachel's shoulder, both thinking about the situation.

"Look, let's leave it till tomorrow, when Carla's awake and feeling better, to talk to her about it," Rachel suggested eventually. "I'll just head off just now, I need to be up early to get to the suppliers." They both stood up to walk to the front door.

"G'night, then."

"Goodnight, Paul." They gave each other a final peck on the cheek, and Rachel walked off to her car and headed home. In the car, Rachel found herself smiling. She had looked in her rear view mirror and caught a glance at herself, which meant only one thing - she was falling for Paul.

Chapter Seven – The great pretender

The next day, Rachel arrived at the suppliers and handed over the order for the stationery. Opening up her purse to take out the company bank card, a piece of paper fell to the ground. Rachel handed the card over, then bent down to pick up the piece of paper thinking to herself, I didn't leave a bit of paper in there, she opened it and began to read, 'Rachel and Paul up a tree k.i.s.s.i.n.g'.

"Oh, my God – did she see us?" Rachel exclaimed out aloud. Clearly, the man who had taken the order from her was becoming rather worried about her, by the look on his face.

As soon as Rachel had picked up all the supplies and put them into the car she phoned Paul on his mobile.

"Paul, it's Rachel - is Carla up yet?"

"Hey, no - but hang on and I'll just check." In the background, Rachel could hear Paul running up the stairs, opening a door and calling out:

"Carla - you awake? No, Rach, she's not moving."

"Go tickle her!"

"What? Why?"

"Paul, just do it!"

"There's still no reaction - oh, my God, is she alright?"

"Yes, Paul, she's alright."

"Well, why are you getting me to check her?"

"Just curious as to when she's going to wake up. I need to talk to her - look, I'll phone you later."

"Rach, can we talk about last night?"

"Later, Paul, OK? I need to get back to the shop. Remember, Drew is working today so you have to let him in and help him unless Carla gets up and is feeling better. OK, bye…"

"Bye, then," Paul said, as she hung up. Standing over Carla, looking down at her, Paul wondered why Rachel had so urgently wanted him to check whether she was awake or not. After a few minutes deliberating, he went downstairs and left to go to the shop, leaving a note on the fridge door in case Carla should wake up and wonder where he was.

As the door closed and the car could be heard driving away from the house and out of range, Carla sat up and laughed, then lay in her bed for a while thinking of how to wind them up further.

The night before, when Carla had been taken into the examination room in the hospital, she had had to explain why she was laughing so hysterically. The doctor examined her ankle and diagnosed the condition to be only a bad sprain. The nurse then handed Carla two painkillers and left the room to fetch the doctor's prescription of painkillers for her from the trolley.

Carla knew that she was not very good with strong painkillers - in the past, they had caused her severe headaches. So Carla only took one of the tablets, and placed the other in a paper towel and then in her coat pocket.

Carla had, in fact, fallen asleep in the car, meaning that there was no chance of her bursting out laughing. At the house, when Rachel was changing her into her pyjamas and turned away, Carla dropped her hand down and tipped Rachel's bag to the side, causing the purse to slip out. When Rachel went home, Carla was surprised that Rachel couldn't tell the difference in weight of her bag without the purse and decided that she would wind her up. She put the note in as she had seen them through the banister kissing. She saw and heard everything that went on and how upset they were about the thought of losing her if they fell out or if something ever happened to her, before she hobbled off to bed.

Shortly, Carla got up to have something to eat so that she could take some more painkillers – her ankle was throbbing. She decided to phone Drew, as she knew that Paul wouldn't be at the shop for another few minutes.

Carla told Drew what she had done, and was immediately told not to mention the conversation at all, so that she could phone Paul later, as he would be upset that she didn't phone him first.

"Listen, would you like to help me stir it up further?" she asked him. "You would only be feeding me more information about them - I can't keep tabs on them when I'm meant to be out of it."

"Sure, what do you want me to do?" Drew was getting excited about the whole undercover operation to which he was being assigned.

Carla gave him some ideas about what to ask Paul. She knew that, if Drew could get him to talk about something so personal, Paul would confide in him, which would help the two to get along.

She did not reveal that part to Drew, though. She felt it best that it seemed as though he was able to break the deadlock between them on his own.

"Great, OK - I'll phone you later, then."

"No, just text me then delete the message and any replies. If Paul got hold of your phone, he would go ballistic."

"Sure, no problem."

"But remember - be subtle about it. He would suss that something was up if you came out and blatantly asked him."

"OK, right - that's him coming, I'll speak to you later. Bye."

"Bye…" Carla sat on the kitchen counter eating an apple. She started laughing again then proceeded upstairs to shower and get ready to make her grand entrance later.

Once Drew and Paul opened the shop and settled in after turning all the machines on, waiting for their first customers of the day, Drew decided to ask his first question.

"So, Paul, great game last night, eh?"

"Suppose so, yeah." Undeterred by his lack of enthusiasm, Drew pushed on.

"Hey, listen - I must say that, last night, you and Rachel really looked like a lovely couple." Paul wheeled round and Drew thought for a split second that he had blown it.

"You think so?" Paul asked, blushing slightly.

"Yeah - I mean, I even said it to Carla."

"What did she say to that?"

"Oh, just something about how weird it would be, her brother and best friend together. And how awful it would be if you two got together and then split up – she'd be torn between you."

"Oh…" Paul said, disappointed because Carla was right - it would leave her in an awful predicament.

"So how do you feel about Rachel?" Drew enquired further.

"Yeah, she's nice."

"Oh, come on! It's just us two guys, you can tell me! I can see by the look on your face every time her name is mentioned. When she was on your arm last night, you both seemed to be rather enjoying the situation."

"Really? You could tell?"

"Well, I know I haven't known you for long, but it was as though you'd had a personality change." When Paul heard Drew say that, he realised that he had only ever seen one side of him and was always on the receiving end of his 'Mr Hyde' side.

"Look, mate, I'm really sorry about the way I've been treating you, it's just I don't want to see my sister get hurt and I also don't want to lose her."

"I assure you, mate, I'm not someone who will hurt her, or take her away from the only family she has left."

"But you do like her though, don't you?"

"I do, I like her a lot."

"You know what? You're alright, pal, and I'd be happy if you asked Carla out. But you ever do hurt her and…"

"Yeah - you'll beat me to a pulp." They both laughed.

"Well, that's me sorted," Drew said – then: "Why don't we help you with *your* girl problems?" They sat down together and talked until customers came, then after serving they would go back to talking and doing some male bonding.

*

While all this bonding was going on, Carla was frantically getting ready and decided to text Drew to see how everything was going.

'How r u gettin on, has he said anything?'

For a good few minutes, there was no reply, which panicked Carla a bit. What if she had texted during a conversation and Paul had asked what it was? She left it a bit longer, just in case that 'no reply' meant he was close to Paul, or they were still talking. Hoping for one rather than the other, she went into her bedroom to dry her wet hair, but she kept glancing back through the door at her mobile phone to check.

She couldn't stand it anymore! She picked her phone up and called Drew's, but she got his answering machine. Thinking that maybe he was now trying to phone her, she hung up and waited and waited and waited some more – but nothing.

The house phone rang and, just as she was about to answer it, she remembered that no one but Drew knew that she was up.

It could be Rachel, trying her luck testing her, so she let it ring out and immediately rang 1471, to find out the number of the last caller. It was Drew, so she phoned him back on her mobile.

"What took you so long?"

"Paul and I have been talking - now would be a good time for you to get down here, he's gone to get Rachel, so that the three of us can talk about the situation."

"What situation?"

"The Paul/Rachel situation. By the way, do you want them together or not?"

"Wow, you seem to be really good at the whole 'stirring them up' malarkey."

"Well, I am and I'm not, 'cause they really seem to be besotted with each other and 'in love'."

"In love? You heard my brother say the word 'love'?"

"Not in so many words," Drew admitted, "but he definitely implied it."

"Right, OK - I'll leave now. Keep it going and remember - you have to be just as surprised as they are when I walk in."

"Right - see you later then."

"Oh, how's the shop? No problems, I hope."

"It's fine - don't worry, we're taking care of it. See ya later."

"Bye." Carla grabbed the house keys and went to the door as the taxi had arrived just at the right time.

Back at the shop, Paul walked in with Rachel just as the phone rang.

"I'll get it - could be Carla." Paul said quickly. Drew made his way over to Rachel.

"So you and Paul then..." He said with a twinkle in his eye.

"What?"

"Paul told me he has feelings for you."

"He did?"

"Look, your secret's safe with me. Don't worry, but I think that, if the two of you are getting together, then telling Carla sooner rather than later would be a better idea." Rachel didn't say anything, she just nodded as she watched Paul put the phone down.

"Was it Carla?" Rachel asked.

"No, the police."

"Why didn't they phone the house?" Drew asked

"We didn't give them the number." Rachel said, looking slightly worried. "Well, how did they find out about the shop?"

"Apparently, someone at the match told them where she worked," said Paul.

"OK, so what did they say?" Drew asked.

"They said the guy is being charged and they just want us to know that the other men that were there are ready to testify in Carla's favour."

"Well, that's great," said Drew.

"Yeah, she'll be so pleased, maybe they won't have to call her!" Rachel said. Shortly after that they were all sitting round one of the tables talking, when a taxi pulled up outside. Seeing it, Drew picked up the cups

"Refill?" he asked.

"Yeah, thanks pal." As Drew reached the counter, Carla stepped out of the taxi and began walking to the shop door. Paul and Rachel couldn't see her because they had their backs to the door, Drew looked up and his eyes lit up upon seeing her.

Paul, noticing that Drew had become distracted by something, spun his head round and jumped to his feet to welcome Carla with a big hug. Rachel also got to her feet and grabbed her after Paul had finished his hug.

"How are you?" asked Rachel.

"Why didn't you call me? Did you not see my note?" Paul asked, smiling.

"Yes, I'm fine, and yes, I saw your note - I just wanted to come down to see if you were looking after the shop. So what's going on, any news?" Carla sat down and looked over to Drew, smiling sweetly.

"Hey, you OK, Drew?"

"Yeah, I'm fine, how are you? Would you like a drink?"

"Great, yes please."

"Wait - when did you wake up?" asked Rachel, suspiciously.

"About an hour and a half ago, it was the best night's sleep I've ever had!" They all burst out laughing,

"But how did I get into my pyjamas?"

"That was me," Rachel answered, as she sipped her tea.

"Thank God for that - I thought I did it myself and didn't remember doing it. Or worse!" For a good ten minutes, the four sat talking about the night before but tending to talk about the more enjoyable parts.

Drew and Paul took it in turns to tend to customers as they came in, allowing Carla and Rachel to chat.

"Carla, by the way the police called and said that they have a number of witness to the assault last night and the guy is being charged." Rachel looked over to her friend to gauge her reaction.

"Fantastic, I hope I don't get called, but I probably will, since I was the one he did it to. Listen, I was thinking - why don't we all have a quiet night in? We haven't had a meal together in ages - I'll cook. And that means you too, Drew," Carla insisted before the comment was implied only for Paul and Rachel.

"That sounds great, but you ain't cooking," Rachel insisted.

"Yes, I am and if you're that worried, Rach, why don't you help?"

"Sure, but don't you do too much!"

"OK, that's settled - let's say half-past six for seven, is that ok?"

"Yep, fine by me," said Rach and Drew in unison.

"Right, I'm off to the shops now - Drew, do you have any food allergies or preferences, before I buy the ingredients?"

"None that I know of, " Drew assured her.

"So what you thinking of making?" Paul asked.

"Well, I thought I'd start with - umm, let's see - mini salmon toasts with chilli snaps, then pasta with mussels in white wine cream sauce."

"Stop it, you're killing me here!"

"To finish?" asked Drew, wearing a face like a starved puppy as was Rachel.

"And to finish..." she added hobbled over to the door. "...A soft centred chocolate pudding and vacherins of strawberries with a passion fruit cream."

"Right you - get out, it's too much for me!" Paul started to jokingly push her out of the door.

"Wait, do you want a hand?" Drew shouted after her.

"We can't leave Paul here on his own," Carla said, looking at him, disappointed.

"Well, I could stay here and help Paul out, till Drew comes back!" Rachel suggested innocently. Drew and Carla both look at her smiling with a look of, 'Oh really!' on their faces.

"Don't give me that look, I'm helping you out here."

"Well if you're sure," Carla said, very sarcastically.

"Come on, Carla, before they change their minds." Drew took Carla by the arm, smirking.

"Oh, someone's eager," said Paul, with an equally sarcastic tone.

"Shut up, Paul let's go, Drew." And off they went down the street to the supermarket. On their way, they enjoyed a laugh at the conversation they had had with Paul and Rachel, back at the sweet shop.

*

After being at the shops the pair headed back to Carla's house. The taxi pulled up outside the gates of Carla's home. Drew jumped out and typed in the security number, then the gates opened slowly. He hopped back into the taxi, before it drove up the long driveway to the house.

Once they had put away the shopping, Drew and Carla sat down to have a cup of tea before he headed back to the shop.

"Thanks very much for helping me with this, Drew - would you like another cup of tea?" Carla asked, pointing to the kettle.

"No, I really should get back, before Paul kicks my ass for being gone so long." Drew stood up and walked over to the sink and placed his mug in the basin.

"Well, Paul can get mad all he wants - you were helping me."

"Well, all the same, I'd better go!" Drew made his way out of the kitchen to the front door.

"Now remember - you're my mole, I need regular updates!"

"Which must make you 'Secret Squirrel' then!" Both laughed as Drew opened the door.

"Are you sure I can't call you a taxi back?" Carla asked, leaning against the door for support.

"No, really, I'm fine - there's a bus stop a couple of yards from the gates. You take care and rest that ankle."

"Thanks again, Drew."

"You're welcome - and I'll speak to you later, OK?" Drew leaned in to give her a kiss on the cheek and she also leaned in for the kiss. But both had their eyes closed, their heads tilted in the same direction, so when their lips touched, they were so overcome with shock, they didn't pull back.

Their heads didn't move as they opened their eyes and stared at each other for a moment, then they separated. Without a word, Drew ran off down the driveway, leaving Carla standing there, pouting slightly, her eyes wide open from the surprise. , She could only watch him disappear.

Getting through the gates and hiding behind the wall, crouched down with his head in his hands for a couple of minutes, Drew sat there, mentally kicking himself. With his head between his legs, he stared at the ground - then a pair of feet appeared.

"I'm sorry about that kiss, I didn't mean to, " Drew said, shaking his head, looking up.

"You've kissed her already!" Drew, startled by the male voice, looked up to find Marti, Pete and Sarah standing over him, all three looking shocked and amazed.

"Emm, I mean..." Drew stuttered, trying to find a good explanation, but he struggled to think quickly on the spot, as he didn't want Carla to be the subject of a bit of amusement for them in the style of a bet.

"Well, come on, Romeo - do tell! Are you two dating?" Pete asked excitedly as he knelt down beside Drew, thinking only of their bet.

"How did you do it?" Pete said pushing for an answer.

"Were not dating." Drew held his head, leaning against the brick wall.

"You could have fooled me!" said Sarah, playfully smiling down at him.

"Right - let's get you home," Marti said, reaching down to help pick Drew up.

"No, I have got to get back to the shop, my shift doesn't end till six."

"Fine then - we'll drop you off." Pete retorted as he ran round the side of the car.

"Can we go, though, because I'd quite like to get back?" Drew asked, in a sullen tone, as he made his way slowly over to the car.

"Well, get in then!" They all got in quickly and headed off.

When they reached the shop, it seemed to be on the brink of bursting at the seams. The four in the car stared at the mass of bodies, squeezed like sardines into the sweet shop.

"Right - I need to get in and help. Thanks for the lift, guys."

"Wait a sec!" Pete said, pulling Drew's jacket and making him fall back into the car.

"You've got to talk to us about what's going on with you two."

"Later OK? They need me, so let go." With one almighty pull, he freed himself from the intense grip of Pete, then ran into the shop, making his way through the crowd.

"What do you reckon that was all about?" asked Sarah, looking quizzically at Marti and Pete, whose heads were looking in the opposite direction,

"Don't know, but I intend to find out." Marti said, as Sarah started the engine and moved off...

Five minutes later, Drew finally made it to the counter where Paul and Rachel were swamped by the screams and demands of the children. Drew decided it was time to put Carla's crowd control method to use.

"OK everyone - calm down and you will get seen quicker, I promise," he shouted. "Now quieten down and line up - well, come on – who's first?" Initially, they just looked at him blankly, then they realised that they did want to be seen more quickly, so they did as they where told and order was quickly restored.

Drew turned to see Paul and Rachel standing there in disbelief at his ability to take control. How had he succeeded where they had failed? Drew just smiled serenely and began to serve. Slowly but surely the crowd started to dwindle. Finally, they were able to sit down to relax and have a cup of tea. Then the clock rang, which caused three of them to jump. Paul fell off to the side of his chair and landed face down on the floor.

Rachel and Drew looked down at him, to check he was alright before they all began to laugh, at the irony of forgetting about the bell. They had been so overwhelmed by the stampede, they were certain that it was well past the time the children needed to be back at school. It hadn't even dawned on them that the bell hadn't yet gone off.

The phone rang as Paul struggled gamely to his feet.

"Drew, would you get that, please? he asked. Drew walked over and picked up the phone,

"Hello - 'So Sweet' - can I help you?"

"Well, I think you have helped me enough today already, don't you?"

Drew's faced flushed as he realised that it was Carla. He moved further into the back room, to be out of ear shot of Paul and Rachel. But they were still distracted at Paul falling off his chair.

"Hi Carla, how are you? How's your ankle?"

"It's fine, I just phoned to check how you were. You kind of ran off and didn't wait to talk about…"

"Yeah, I'm fine now, thanks, feeling a lot better. Er, do you want to speak to Paul? He's got a funny story to tell you - hold on…" Carla was baffled by Drew's awkwardness, and could do nothing but wait for her brother to come on.

"Paul, Carla wants a word."

"Thanks, Drew. Hey Carla - listen the funniest thing just happened…" Paul filled Carla in on the morning's events and described the surge of customers they had received in the few hours, since he'd been in charge of the shop. Not that he was, in any way at all suggesting that he was possibly better at running the shop or anything.

Meanwhile, Drew sat down in a kind of a daze. Rachel started dropping tiny marshmallows into her tea. She had been watching him.

"Are you OK, Drew?" At first he didn't respond, until she placed her hand on his arm to bring him out of the trance.

"Yeah, I'm fine."

Unbeknown to them, Paul had seen this touch and, unable to hear what was going on, had zoned out from listening to his sister. "Hold on, Carla - Rachel wants you." He beckoned Rachel over. As she began to talk to Carla, Paul made his way slowly over to the table, watching to see if Drew would look up, expecting Rachel, but he never did. Paul sat down, still watching him.

"You OK?" Paul asked.

"Yes, fine," Drew answered, sounding strangely fed-up.

"Nice girl, Rachel, isn't she?" Paul asked, deliberately watching and waiting for his answer.

"Yeah, nice girl, you shouldn't wait, just ask her out, in case someone beats you to it." Drew said quietly, without looking Paul's direction.

"Why, do you want to ask her?" Paul asked, watching him intently.

"No way - I think she's a great friend, plus I would never go after a girl that a mate of mine likes." Paul suddenly sank back into his seat, having misjudged Drew's intentions towards Rachel.

"I do like her - I mean we are and we aren't going out, because I haven't actually asked her out yet."

"Well, I would talk to Rachel, when she comes off the phone, about telling Carla tonight at dinner." Drew was looking out the large windows onto the street with a blank expression on his face.

"I don't think we should tell her something like that, when she will be stressed out of her mind with the catering arrangements."

"What - it's only dinner," Drew said dismissively, as Paul nearly fell off his seat again.

"Only dinner? She lives for her idea of being the perfect hostess! I mean, you must have seen how fussy she is with food."

"Well, now that you mention it..."

"You know I'm right. And for your own sake, never - ever - say or suggest that it's not that important to be a good hostess, or about having great table arrangements, or the right seating arrangements or, to say the least pal, you would soon see a very dark and ugly side to Carla."

Drew pondered the idea of Carla having an ugly side – and over such silly things as eating arrangements. Paul moved over to wipe down the counters, as Rachel put the phone down.

"Well, how's she getting on?" asked Paul,

"Fine – but she asked me to remind everyone not to bring any gifts or anything and not to be late!" Rachel raised an eyebrow and looked from Drew to Paul in a threatening manner.

"Yeah, yeah!" Paul remarked, waving his free hand dismissively.

"Oh, no - it's not that time already?" Paul yelped, as he caught sight of the clock reflected in one of the tall sweet containers beside the coffee machine. Paul quickly finished filling the water container in the machine, as Rachel picked up her bag.

"Well, I'm going to have to love you and leave you," she announced. "If I don't at least make an appearance at the bookshop before I go out tonight, Mum and I won't speak for the next fortnight and I don't think I could handle the tantrums." Rachel opened the door and was about to walk out when Paul stopped her.

"Wait, you aren't leaving me - I mean - us, it's rush hour! C'mon!" Paul rushed round to the door.

"No, Paul, I have to go. Anyway, you've got Drew here, look how well he handled the last rush of kids... You'll be fine." She leaned in and gave him a peck on the cheek. "See you later, guys..."

Paul started to go through to the back room to pick up some more packets to refill some containers. Rachel took the opportunity to go back to Drew.

"Keep an eye on him, he doesn't deal well with too much pressure, Drew," she whispered. " If you need to talk, you know where I am." She winked at him and walked off. Drew stood gazing out the window in a trance.

"Boo!" Paul jumped from behind Drew to startle him back to reality.

"What was that for?" Drew had jumped to his feet after the fright.

"I've been calling you for a hand, then I come out here find you're staring at that crazy old woman, who's talking to a lamp post."

Drew frowned in confusion, then looked back out the window to see an old woman, who was, indeed, now arguing with the lamp post. She had clearly caught her bag on the loose metal door of the lamp post, while trying to pass it.

Drew laughed as he put his head in his hands and shook it in disbelief. Then, when he looked back up, the windows were full of little faces staring back at him, which made him jump again, much to the children's delight, before they began to flood through the door for Round 2.

Chapter Eight – Mixed emotions

Three hours later, Paul and Drew closed the shop and made their separate ways home to get ready. As Drew turned the corner, he found Marti waiting for him in his car.

"Want a lift?" Marti called to him out of the car window.

"No, thanks, I'm fine."

" C'mon now, I'm not gonna bite - get in, mate." The car door flew open and Drew, against his better judgement, got in. After a good few minutes of painful silence, Marti spoke.

"So how are you?"

"C'mon, why don't you just say what you're really wanting to?" Drew snapped back, knowing Marti only wanted information about Carla.

"Wow, man, OK, I'm not digging. I'm just wanting to know how my pal's doing, since all I get to see of you these days is the back of your head when you're at uni or in the flat, that's all."

It was true - Drew had been neglecting the friends he had made before he had even heard of Carla or the sweet shop. Drew started to apologise, but before he could Marti held up his hand to stop him.

"So how about coming to a barbecue on Saturday night at the fair? You can bring as many people as you want - it'll be great fun, Sarah really wants you to come."

"Oh…" Drew realised he had jumped to conclusions without hearing Marti out.

"I'm sorry, Marti - I'd love to go."

"I'll pick you guys up, then. I mean, you will be bringing her with you, right?"

"She has a name. Also her brother and best friend would have to come too." Marti pulled the car over to the side of the road, then put the hand brake on.

"Are you absolutely mental?" he demanded.

"What?"

"The loopy brother and the best friend!" Marti said, as his eyebrows disappeared into his scalp.

"There's nothing crazy about Paul - and Rachel is a great laugh."

"Well, just don't tell him about what we're doing," Marti was obviously starting to panic.

"What we're doing?" Drew asked, confused.

"Yeah, I could see how much you really liked her, so I convinced the others to drop the stupid bet."

"Really?"

"Really." Marti was now getting honked at by other cars to move, as he hadn't parked properly so he drove on.

"Thanks, mate," Drew said, feeling slightly better now that they had cleared the tension between them.

"No problem. Listen, fancy nipping to the pub to catch up some more?"

"Well - I can't, I promised that I would go to dinner at Carla's and…"

"Right…" Marti sounded disappointed.

"No, look, we can do it tomorrow, OK? Sounds like a great idea."

"Yeah, sure, better make my reservation with you now, before Carla beckons you again." The snide comment from Marti undid all the apologising they both had done.

"Hey, what's that meant to mean?" Drew responded quickly, sounding furious.

"Well, if she said jump, you'd say how high, wouldn't you?"

"This isn't just about me not being able to come to the pub, is it? What's wrong with you, why do you have a problem with Carla?" Drew demanded.

"Nothing, forget it." Marti shrugged and turned away.

"Fine - I haven't got time for this anyway." None spoke for the rest of the journey, and both remained silent even once they reached the flat. Then, as Drew left to go to dinner, he shouted towards Marti's room: "That's me away then - don't wait up."

Marti turned his music up louder as Drew walked out then slammed the door shut.

Drew got into the first taxi that he found, and sat back thinking about the way he'd left things with Marti and how he really felt about Carla. His thoughts swung between Marti and Carla for a while, trying to come to some kind of decision as to what to do, without jeopardising either relationship. Soon after, the taxi pulled up to the electric gates outside Carla and Paul's home.

Drew got out and paid the taxi driver, turned to the electronic keypad and tapped in the code.

"Hi pal, tell the driver just to come all the way to the door."

"Aww God, I sent him away, I'll just walk it."

"Right, well - it looks like a brisk walk in the moonlight for you then...."

"Oh and I thought that you were going to come and pick me up!" Drew responded sarcastically as he hunched his shoulder to keep the heat in.

"You'd better hurry 'cause Carla's starting to get worried."

"Right I'll be there in a minute, just have the door open for me it freezing out here!"

"Will do, mate..."

Drew had already begun to run up the drive, when he heard a series of clicking sounds. Drew hadn't a clue what the sound was, but thought it best to move quicker, so he began to run. Then like a movie scene, where the main character is running and the water (bullets in the films) is turned on behind him, chasing Drew up the driveway (looking like gun fire hitting the ground as the water bounced). The moonlight was gleaming down on him as a brisk cold wind blew against him. About a foot or two from the first step of the stairs up to the front door Drew took a large leap into the air landing just in front of the step, clear from the sprays of the sprinklers. He sat for a minute or two, trying to compose himself before he realised that Paul was standing over him.

"Hey - Tom Cruise, you'd better get in fast! You're two minutes late and Carla has already started panicking that you aren't coming, even though I told her five minutes ago that you were sitting in the lounge waiting just to shut her up. So while you've been playing with the water, I've had my own 'Mission Impossible' in here, trying to keep her away from that lounge to say hello to you."

Paul took Drew's arm and pulled him to his feet. Getting indoors, Paul sat Drew down on the beautiful light grey couch.

Rachel and Carla kept coming in to talk and check on them, bringing in nibbles, until the meal was ready.

In the kitchen, Carla was moving about adding so many ingredients to so many pots, pans and dishes that Rachel couldn't keep track of what it was she was meant to be doing.

"Erm - Carla, could you maybe slow down, 'cause I don't know what the heck you're making!"

Carla stood holding a hot pot in one hand and, in the other, a saltshaker, with a spatula in her mouth. Rachel began to laugh at how ridiculous she looked. Carla then saw her reflection in the mirror behind Rachel and began laughing too.

Paul came in to check on them then, without having said a word, he walked out back to the front room.

Rachel and Carla exchanged puzzled looks, before getting back to work. Rachel began to quiz Carla about Drew, while Carla put the finishing touches to the starters.

"Alright - so what is with you and Drew, then?"

"Oh, come on - don't start that again!" Carla pleaded - but it fell on deaf ears.

"Well, you have got to admit - he does like you and I know that you like him, so do you think anything will be happening between the two of you?"

"I don't know."

"Well, would you *like* something to happen?"

"Why, do you know something?"

"I'm just asking, so would you?" Rachel said evasively, as she moved over to the cooker, where Carla was adding ingredients to more pots simmering on the hob.

"Well?"

"Well - what?"

"Well, come on talk to me."

"I like him, but I don't know... There's something about the way he is around me - I mean, he always seems a little distracted... But I think he's a good friend."

But while Carla said this, she didn't realise that Drew had been standing out in the hall, listening to them talking. Hearing the last comment made him see that the closeness he shared with her could be no deeper than a friendship. In that moment, he realised he should concentrate more on his friendship with Marti than waste his time on a relationship that would never happen with Carla.

Though if he'd waited a minute longer, he would have heard Carla say:

"But I do really like him, OK? I like him a lot and would go out with him if he asked me to." Carla and Rachel finished preparing the starters.

"Right, could you tell the boys to go sit at the table, please?" Carla said, as she added a final flourish.

Rachel made her way through to the lounge. As she got closer, she heard Drew talking about having over heard the girls' conversation.

"She said she just wanted to be friends - she feels that it would spoil the relationship."

"That is what she said?" Rachel heard Paul ask.

"Well, not word for word, but it was implied." Drew sounded completely depressed now.

"Oh, mate, look - give it a while. She's just very cagey about guys in general. She believes that most only see the pretty face in the sweet shop and can't see anything else past that. She'll come around you just got to show her that you're not like that." Paul tried to sound optimistic for Drew's sake.

"I don't think that her feelings will change any time soon," Drew muttered. "Anyway, how do I show her without telling her that I am crazy about her?" Paul looked at Drew in astonishment, Paul had had a fair idea how he felt, but Drew had never actually been explicit about how he felt to any of them. Rachel sat down on the stairs, trying to take in everything that was going on, trying to work out how the wires got crossed, then realised that Drew hadn't heard Carla finish her train of thought.

"Look I'd better go," Drew said from inside the front room. "It would only get more uncomfortable than it already is and I really need to talk to my room- mate."

"If you leave before she serves dinner, how difficult will it be when you appear at the shop tomorrow?" Paul was the voice of reason.

"You're right." Drew sat back down. Rachel stayed out of sight for a minute longer, then casually walked in so Drew didn't come up with another reason to leave.

"Right, boys - the starters will be out in a minute, so if you want to go and sit at the table..." Paul and Drew just looked at her blankly; then they obediently stood up and walked slowly to the table not saying a word.

Rachel went back into the kitchen where Carla stood holding two plates, tapping her foot in frustration at the length of time it took Rachel to come back and help.

"Where have you been?"

"Oh – right, sorry," She took the plates from Carla and walked towards the dining room - in the hall, however, she almost bumped into Paul.

"Rach, do you think we should tell Carla about us tonight?"

"Well, I don't think so, 'cause I kind of overheard Drew and you talking - I don't think that he's in the mood to calm her if she takes it badly!"

"He overheard you and Carla saying something about her only wanting to just be his friend."

"Yes, but had he waited, he would have heard her say that she really likes him a lot. He didn't have his ears flapping at the door long enough to hear the rest!"

"She said she really likes him?"

"Yes - so what are we going to do?" The two looked at each other, waiting for the other to think of something. Then Carla called from the kitchen:

"Rachel, I have more plates for you to take in!"

"Look - take these, put them on the table and stay with Drew in case he runs away or something."

"Right - what are you going to do?"

"Help Carla, before she has a wobbly." They ran off in opposite directions. Finally, at last - they were all sitting at the table getting ready to start eating. Carla looked around at each of them and noticed that they were all wearing very depressed expressions.

"Is everyone OK?"

"Yeah." When all three of them suddenly perked up as if by magic, Carla knew something was wrong.

"What's going on?"

"What?" They chirruped in unison.

"The three of you answering at the same time is really freaking me out now. There's is something wrong, now tell me." Carla looked genuinely agitated.

"No."

"OK - what?" Carla clattered down her knife and fork, sat back in her seat, folded her arms and looked at each of them in turn, waiting for an explanation.

"OK, right - well, it's just…" Drew began to try to explain, but Paul jumped in.

"Drew, I'll tell her." Drew was stunned, as he stared at Paul.

"Look, Carla - Rachel and I have something we need to tell you."

"Wait - if you are about to tell me that you and Rachel are wanting to date and are actually asking my permission, I have already decided on this." Carla paused, wanting to wind them up. She got up form the table and walked over to the window to stare out to the large garden. She was really milking the suspense! Rachel and Paul gingerly rose to their feet.

"Well, what do you think?" Rachel asked quietly.

"If you two think - for one minute - that I am going to allow you two to be together, when you know what damage it could do to my relationship with the pair of you!" Carla was stood facing the window, terrified to turn round, knowing that she would only burst out laughing if she saw their faces.

Paul, Rachel and Drew sat with their mouths gaping.

Carla then slowly turned around.

"I'm kidding! I'm really happy for you both." She ran over to them to give them a hug. Poor Drew just sunk even lower into his chair and into his gloom.

"Right - well then, let's eat…"

But shortly after they'd finished their starters, Carla realised that Drew hadn't said a word to her since they sat down to eat. In her own domain of the kitchen once more, Carla turned to Paul, who had helped her to carry in the dirty plates.

"What's wrong with Drew?"

"Why would you ask that?" Paul panicked.

"He hasn't said a word to me since we sat down - it's not like him at all. Did I do something?"

"No - course not, he's just tired, it's been a long day."

"I think we asked him to do too much, with helping me with the shopping, then going back to work in the shop."

"That must be it. Is that to go on the table? Right, then, I'll take that in." Paul grabbed two hot plates and ran.

"But they're really hot!" she said vainly after he had left the room. Running through the hall and into the dining room, Paul said:

"Coming through - *really* hot plates." He practically threw the plates down and began waving his hands around to cool them whilst jumping up and down. Rachel took an extra napkin from the cabinet behind her, dipped it into the jug of water then wrapped it round his hands.

"Rach, can I see you a second?" The pair walked out to the patio and closed the door behind them, abandoning Drew to his own devices.

"What's wrong?"

"Carla started asking me questions about what's wrong with Drew."

"What did you say?"

"Well, I just said that he was tired and had a really long day."

"Right - so you didn't mention anything about the…"

"God no! If she found out that he had heard you two, she would go mental! Trust me, I know about that, she hates people eavesdropping on her conversations."

"I know – I remember one night she caught you listening in to our phone call, I had to come round to calm her down, though you didn't exactly help matters by teasing her mercilessly about it afterwards."

"Anyway, what are we going to do with Drew? He's becoming more distant as the night wears on."

"I know - look at him, he's so depressed, poor thing. You have to talk to him - I'll distract Carla." Rachel pushed Paul back in to the house and nodded encouragingly at Drew as she passed.

"So…" Paul tried to think about how to approach talking to Drew, but was stuck for words, for a change.

"So - er, listen, mate, I was just talking to Rachel - and she asked me what was wrong with you, 'cause you didn't seem yourself." Drew jolted upright, immediately worried.

"And what did you tell her?"

"Well, I had to tell her the truth, because…"

"You did what? Why? Now she's gone to tell Carla, they're going to have a right good laugh at me."

"No, no! She's trying to help you, trust me, if she didn't think that you were right for Carla, you would never have got this close."

Drew sat there confused.

"But I thought that…"

"You thought, that I was the one that let no one near her? Well, that's partly true, though I am not as bad as Rachel, she has more say than anyone over what happens with Carla." Drew sat there in disbelief.

"Rachel doesn't show how she feels, but she definitely has more say with Carla than you think. Rachel gets close to the person in question, then feeds back what she finds out - that's how Carla decides."

"So, it's Rachel I should have been sucking up to this whole time and not you? Well, that was a waste of time!" Paul's shocked look made Drew smile.

"Mate, I'm kidding!"

Paul exhaled then looked again at Drew again to make sure.

"Really, I'm joking." The pair laughed, as Paul realised Drew was starting to loosen up.

Meanwhile, in the kitchen, Rachel took the dishes containing the vegetables out of the oven. Carla added the white wine sauce to the mussels and stirred, leaving it for a few minutes to simmer and infuse with flavour.

Then Carla turned to watch Rachel, as she placed the vegetables delicately on the dishes. Carla walked up behind her and hugged her.

"Hey - what's that for?"

"I'm so happy for you and Paul!"

Rachel smiled.

"We were worried that you were going to go mental at us."

"What, over the three years'-"

"Two years!"

"...age difference."

"Are you going to rub this in till the cows come home?"

"Certainly not, cradle-snatcher." Carla grinned as she took the mussels off the cooker.

"Right - I'll go and put these out on the table, then come back for the rest."

"Right." Rachel walked through to the dining room, where the boys were laughing, which was a good sign.

"Well..." Rachel said, putting the plates down, looking from Paul to Drew.

"It's OK - I told him."

"Thanks for helping," Drew said.

"You're welcome, but it's up to you now - I can only put in the good word, the rest is up to you!" Rachel lowered her voice, having heard Carla clattering pots in the kitchen.

"Well, what do you think I should do?"

"Just take her somewhere where both of you can relax and enjoy being together."

"Hold on – there's a fair on at the weekend, I completely forgot to ask the three of you if you wanted to come and meet the rest of my friends."

"Perfect!" Rachel said, as Paul nodded in agreement.

"What's perfect?" Carla stood at the doorway, holding a large colander in her hands, smiling.

"The food!" Drew exclaimed, jumping to his feet to help Carla with the dishes.

"Thank you, Rachel there are a few more dishes left, if you could help me."

"I'll help." Drew answered.

"No - you guys are doing the washing-up."

"You what?" Paul exclaimed.

"Don't even start." Carla glared at him, then smiled.

"Fine, it's only fair."

"Good." The girls walked back into the kitchen, then reappeared a few minutes later, carrying the other dishes. As they settled down to eat, Drew raised his glass to make a toast.

"Well, thank you Carla, for this lovely meal and well done to the new happy couple."

"We're not married, mate." Paul joked.

"Shut up and let him finish," Rachel said, elbowing Paul in the ribs.

"To friendship!"

"To friendship" they choresed, and then they tucked into their main course, as some gentle music played in the background. The conversation was relaxed and light-hearted.

A while later, everyone had finished except Drew, so the others sat watching him polishing off his plate.

"Does anyone else want the rest of that?" He asked, pointing to the bowl of mussels.

"No, on you go, pal." Paul patted Drew on the back, pushing the plate toward him.

"You don't have to finish it all, Drew - you won't hurt my feelings, if you can't finish."

"No - this is fantastic, I have never tasted anything as delicious as this."

"But do take your time."

"I love this salad you made."

"I can wrap the rest so you can take it home."

"Really? I don't want to seem…"

"What? Like a greedy git?"

"Paul!"

"What? I've never seen anyone eat so much, except when you and Rachel are watching a soppy movie!"

Rachel kicked Paul under the table. "Shut up." She hissed, scowling at him.

"Here, I'll go wrap it for you, it'll stay fresh for about two days and then if you haven't eaten it, you've got to throw it out," Carla said, picking up the bowl.

"Thanks," replied Drew.

"Here, Paul – you do it."

"What do I wrap it in?" Paul stared vacantly at the bowl, as Rachel got to her feet.

"Here – I'll help you. C'mon."

"If you're not back in five minutes, I'm coming in to get you!" Carla joked as they were leaving the room.

"Oh ha, ha," they retorted, disappearing into the kitchen.

Carla and Drew were left alone. To avoid an awkward silence, Drew went back to eating the rest of the food on his plate. Carla sat watching, not knowing whether to laugh or not.

Paul came back into the room a few minutes later and sat down in his seat.

"What?" Carla looked at him.

"She hit me." Paul rubbed the side of his head.

"Well, you obviously deserved it," Carla said, needing no further information. Rachel then arrived at the doorway.

"Well, did you tell Carla what you just did?" Rachel stood there, with her arms crossed.

"What did you do?" Paul could see that Carla was anxious to know.

"Well, I..." Paul was reluctant to divulge the reason.

"What?" Carla said, calmly wanting to see if her brother was brave enough to tell her himself.

"I..." he continued to stutter, trying to articulate his explanation.

"What? Just tell me - you haven't touched my desserts, have you?" Carla panicked slightly.

"Oh, would you tell her already, Paul?" Rachel said forcefully.

"I dropped the bowl of salad." He couldn't look at anyone.

"Is that all?" Carla laughed, relieved.

"You did what?" Drew said, disappointed.

"Mate, I think that you must have some sort of addiction to her salad."

"It's OK, really, Drew – I've got plenty of ingredients, I'll make you more." Carla insisted.

"No, I don't want to cause any trouble."

"It's no trouble – in fact, why don't you come through to the kitchen and I will show you how to make it." Carla and Drew got up from the table and walked into the kitchen. Paul and Rachel went through to the lounge, for a break before dessert.

"Well – do you think he's going to ask her in there?" Asked Paul.

"No, he will do it with us around, so that Carla doesn't think that it's just her who's invited."

"So it wouldn't be like a date? Right – no of course not." There was a long thoughtful silence between them.

"So listen, when are we going to go out for *our* first date? Now that we have been given the green light." asked Paul, as he looked longingly at Rachel.

"Paul, please don't take this the wrong way, but we're OK just now as we are. I want to look after Carla just now, OK?" Rachel looked sympathetically at Paul who was obviously disappointed with her answer.

"I didn't say we weren't going to go out, but let's think of Carla first." Rachel kissed him lightly on the cheek. Paul then leaned over and started to nibble her neck.

"Ow! C'mon, that tickles - stop tickling me, Paul." Paul finally stopped tickling her.

In the kitchen, Carla finished the salad and poured it into a plastic container. As she went to hand it to Drew, his phone rang.

"Thanks - sorry, I need to take this." Drew turned his back to Carla as he put the phone to his ear. It was Sarah, calling to ask how he was, what he was up to and to let him know the details about the fair.

As Carla stacked all the dirty dishes into the dishwasher, she tried not to listen to the conversation, but she couldn't help overhearing.

Drew and Sarah obviously got on very well, Carla thought, as he was never able to speak to her like that - so free and relaxed, able to joke and share stories and information about university.

Carla felt a pang of jealousy towards this Sarah, for having a relaxed relationship with Drew. It seemed that Carla herself was unable to have something as natural and comfortable like that with him.

Drew came off the phone and apologised for having to take the call - he explained that he hadn't spoken to Sarah for a while.

"Paul and I will tidy up the dining room," he assured her, noticing that she had cleared away the dishes in the kitchen. "You go sit down or do what you have to do with the puddings - we'll get the rest of the dishes."

"OK, thanks!" Carla smiled brightly as Drew walked out of the kitchen - she couldn't help but notice that he was in a slightly chipper mood than he had been earlier.

"Paul!" Drew called out.

"What?" Paul yelled back from the front room.

"Could you help me clear the table, please?"

"Why?"

"Cause I'm asking nicely."

"Fine!" Paul said, pretending to sulk. As he got up and went through to the dining room, Rachel headed for the kitchen.

"What is going on with him?" Carla asked.

"Well, I'm not sure, Carla, but I think Drew's a bit nervous."

"About what?"

Rachel just stood there looking at her,

"What?" Carla insisted.

"You really haven't got a clue!"

Carla stood there and the pair exchanged looks as Drew and Paul walked in trying to balance too many plates in their hands.

The boys' sudden appearance stopped the conversation dead, until they headed back out of the kitchen, to get the rest of the dishes and cutlery with which to load the dishwasher.

"Well – what do you mean by that?" Carla said in a hushed tone.

"He likes you!" Rachel was smiling, brightly.

"I'm not sure he likes me as much as you think!" Carla turned away.

"No, really - he likes you a lot!"

"Well, I just heard him talking on the phone, to some girl called Sarah."

"Yes – and? They're just friends." Rachel couldn't understand what Carla was getting upset about.

"Well, they seemed to be more than that…" Carla sat down at the kitchen table.

"What do you mean?" Rachel asked, joining her at the table.

"Well, it was just the way he was talking to her - he was smiling, laughing, upbeat." Carla rattled on.

"So what?" Rachel tried to play down the significance of the call,

"Aren't you like that when I call?" Rachel continued.

"Well yes and no - it was just the way he was on the phone."

"Yes and no?" Rachel retorted sarcastically, pretending to be upset by Carla's last comment.

"Calm down, Rach, you know I enjoy our chats, but even when he came off the phone, he was all happy and excited about something."

"Maybe he's had a bit of good news," Rachel suggested, trying to help rule out the only reason for his joy that Carla had come up with.

"Look, it's OK, I know I said I would like to go out with him if he asked, but I'm not going to get cut up about it if he doesn't," Carla insisted as she made her way over to the kitchen counter to prepare the desserts.

Rachel recognised that Carla's rapid move away from the table also meant that she had moved away from the conversation and didn't want to discuss it anymore.

As Rachel made her way over to watch Carla putting the finishing touches to her desserts, Rachel noticed several things: Carla's usual delicate touch with her food had become a little slapdash and erratic; she was frowning slightly, meaning that it did bother her that Drew and Sarah were so close; and she had a tear in the corner of her eye.

Paul and Drew came in with the last few dishes and even loaded the dishwasher.

Exhausted, they then headed for the front room for a rest, while the girls finished preparing the last course.

Rachel happened to look down at the plates and had to double-take, as she realised there were too many plates being prepared.

"Wait – have you lost the ability to count, Carla?"

"Huh?" exclaimed Carla, looking at Rachel, slightly frustrated.

"Oh, this? No, I just want to have it ready in case someone decides they want to try something else." Rachel looked at her, knowing that Carla was actually referring – albeit obliquely – to Drew wanting someone else.

"Right - so what about the rest of us?" Rachel enquired further to find out if Carla would open up and talk about how she felt.

"Well, unless you have lost the ability to count, there's two of everything," snapped Carla, as her frustration grew. Rachel knew she wouldn't be able to get Carla to talk that night.

"Oh, yeah, I was never any good at numbers." Rachel played it down.

"Hmm…" Carla grumbled, looking curiously at her. Picking up a large tray, Carla stacked on the desserts – she managed to find room for all but two dishes.

"Rach, could you carry those two, please?" Carla had started to calm down now.

"Sure." Rachel picked up the last two desserts, then smelled them in turn, trying to guess what was in them.

"Those are yours now." Carla said, laughing at her friend.

"Great – thanks." The tension was broken.

As the girls walked back towards the dining room, Carla noticed that Drew was standing in the hall talking on his mobile again. She couldn't take her eyes off him, wondering if it was Sarah on the phone again. In the dining room, Rachel leaned close to Paul.

"Who's he talking to?" she whispered as she put a dish in front of him.

"Some pal of his," Paul said, picking up his spoon to start eating. Rachel placed her hand over his to stop him from taking a bite.

"Who?"

"Sarah from uni, I think." Paul quickly put the spoon into his mouth and took a bite as Rachel turned to look at Drew.

"Sarah…" Carla murmured quietly, not taking her eyes off him, while trying to put the tray down on the table.

"What does she want?" Rachel asked Paul quietly in his ear.

"I don't know." Paul shrugged his shoulders and continued eating.

Carla sat down and turned to Rachel and Paul.

"Let's eat, otherwise there is no point to the hot soft chocolate centre." "There's a hot soft chocolate centre!" Quickly, they started tucking in to the pudding, adding some home-made buttercream icing to it.

As Carla went to take her first bite, she caught a glimpse of Drew, in a pane of glass in the cabinet against the opposite wall; she could do nothing but stare at him.

Rachel saw Carla staring at the cabinet, smiled and reached over. She gently guided the spoon and its contents to Carla's open mouth, as she made an aeroplane noise. Carla quickly snapped out of her trance. Rachel and Paul laughed uncontrollably as Carla's spoon almost fell out of her mouth.

"Did you just do what I think you just did?"

"Yeah, she did and I wished I had my camera - that was priceless." Paul was laughing harder now.

"Carla, laugh a bit, will you?" Rachel pleaded with her. Carla sat there, sad-faced for a moment or two, before finally giving in and she, too, began to laugh. The three of them were soon in convulsions with laughter.

Not noticing that they had been laughing for a couple of minutes, Drew came back in and said:

"That was Sarah - she was telling me to ask if you all are going to the fair this Saturday." Drew had a huge grin on his face as did Paul. Rachel wasn't as upbeat, though, because she was now starting to have her own suspicions about the relationship Drew had with Sarah.

"There's going to be a barbecue there, rides and loads of other stuff."

Carla sat still, looking at her plate.

"Yeah – let's do that," Paul answered enthusiastically.

"Great! Well, if that's OK with everyone, I'll phone Sarah back and tell her the new plan." Drew said, as he turned to head back out the door.

"Listen, just use the house phone, it's in the hall there." Paul pointed through the door.

"Thanks." Drew walked back out to the hall.

"You only did that so you could hear what he was saying," said Rachel.

"Yeah – and your point is?" They all went back to finishing the remains of the first pudding. Five minutes later, Drew returned.

"Right then, that's it sorted." He sat back down at the table, looking very pleased with himself.

"Great – now eat your pudding before it gets cold," Rachel said, hoping to catch the attention of Carla, as Drew was distracted by trying his dessert.

"Which one?" He grinned as he eyed up both plates eagerly.

"Try the chocolate one first, mate - with this." Paul handed him the bowl with the remaining contents of the buttercream icing.

"Thanks, Paul."

Everyone went back to finishing the desserts in absorbed silence. A little while later, the four of them sat back in the tall-backed wooden chairs, relaxing, having eaten their fill.

"Well, it's safe to say I won't need feeding till at least…"

"When? Breakfast?" Carla asked, as they all began laughing again.

*

After a glass or two of wine, Drew suddenly realised how late it was. He was anxious to get back before Marti went to bed so that they could talk and clear things up.

"Look at the time! I'd better go; otherwise I won't get up tomorrow."

"Do you have to? Can't you stay and have another one - at least have a drink while you wait on the taxi," Paul insisted, standing to his feet then heading for the dining room to bring through the bottle of wine.

"Well OK, but I'll go phone the cab now - can I use your phone?"

"Yeah, sure." Carla nodded with a gentle smile.

"Well, this has been a great night, but I am going upstairs to bed now - I have to do the books tomorrow for Mum." Rachel stood up and stretched pointedly.

"Wait till Drew leaves?" Carla implored,, holding on to Rachel's arm.

"Sure - could you pour me a glass of water then, please, Paul?"

"Sure - do you want one, Carla?"

"Yes, please." As Paul poured from a beautifully engraved jug into matching tall glasses, Drew walked back in.

"How long did they say it would be?" Paul asked Drew, while handing the glass to his sister.

"I think we'll have to have that drink later."

"Why?" asked Carla.

"The taxi will be here in five minutes, so I'll wait at the door." Drew made his way back out to the hall, when Paul appeared from the front room door.

"I'll stand with you." He joined Drew out on the steps, at the front of the house.

"No - go back inside, where it's warm," Drew insisted.

"Look, they said they were only going to be five minutes, so five minutes won't kill me." Paul closed the front door behind him as they stared down the driveway awaiting the taxi's arrival. Paul took a quick glance at the front room window to his left, checking the girls weren't watching, then looked back at Drew.

"Listen, I have to hand it to you - for a minute there, I thought you weren't going to ask her, I mean us, about the fair on Saturday."

"For a minute there, I thought that I might not be able to do it either." Drew shivered as he stood waiting. They waited for another few minutes outside in the cold dark night, in silence, the cold air nipping their faces, making their cheeks turn pink. Paul looked at his watch several times, getting agitated at how long it was taking the taxi to get there, after being told it was only five minutes away,

"Thanks for a great night," Drew said to Paul as he continued to stare down the driveway.

"Yeah, it was, must do it again sometime," Paul replied, leaning against the cold doorframe. Standing outside Drew looked around from the driveway, to the beautiful garden then up at the house.

"So listen, I was wondering, how is it that you have this amazing house and grounds, when you own a sweet shop? I mean, if you don't mind me asking?" Paul looked over at him, wondering why he would be asking such a personal question. But he realised that Drew was just making polite conversation to pass the time.

"Well, you see, our mother was born in Ireland, lived and worked on the family farm until she was eighteen. That's when she moved over here, which she did on her own, to work in a hotel, but ended up leaving after two months - she hated it."

"What did she do then?" Drew asked as he sat down on the top step, giving up on the taxi.

"Our mum had a very sweet tooth - she loved sweets, cakes, biscuits, candy - anything that had a high volume of sugar in it. So she asked our grandparents for some money to open a shop." Paul joined him on the top step and sat down.

"But, you see, the shop we have now was not the original my Mum had."

"No?"

"No - she had a very small, box-like shop, which cost her a lot to buy outright, so she couldn't afford a flat at the time. All her money went into the shop."

"So what did she do?" Drew realised he had suddenly become engrossed with the tale.

"She slept in the back room of the shop."

"She never did!" Drew was astonished at hearing that the poor woman had to resort to sleeping on the floor of the shop.

"Had to use four hot water bottles to keep warm, in order to save money on heating. But then as the money started coming in, she opened a bank account of her own, separate from the business account and saved up a good little nest egg."

"So she saved up enough to buy a…"

"No, she managed to start renting the flat above the shop, then a few years after that, my poor grandparents died within months of each other, from the 'flu," Paul said, staring out at the garden. Drew could tell it was still very hard for him to talk about his mother.

"Oh, I am sorry." Drew felt awful for having asked, but Paul patted him on the shoulder to let him know it was alright.

"Thanks - I just wish I had known them. After that, she had to make a difficult decision - whether or not to move back to Ireland or to sell the farm and stay to develop her own little business. Obviously, she decided to stay here, so she sold the farm and land to a development company for houses. They paid well over the odds for the land – it was just at the right time because the Irish property market had started to take off - then she put the money away for the future." Paul stood up and walked down the steps, then began pacing at the foot of them.

"So when did she get this place?" Drew wanted to hurry the story along.

"By the time I was born, Carla was three. Mum told us that our Dad left her for a girl he worked with, and that they headed to England, to get away from having to look after a family."

Drew wanted to kick himself; this was worse than talking about the grandparents and mother.

"So was he married to your mother?" He couldn't believe, of all the questions he could have asked, that was the best one he could come up with.

"Yeah - for five years, before he left." Paul's head drooped down sadly.

"Men," Drew said, under his breath, but Paul heard him nonetheless.

"Well, we didn't miss him, and Mum certainly didn't, 'cause we kept her busy and he never got a penny from her, 'cause she never revealed to him she had all that money. So as soon as he left, she went out looking for a new home to start afresh and found this place." Paul looked around, his home and smiled at what his mother had accomplished on her own.

"Wow! She must have been one Hell of a strong woman, to have looked after you both and the shop as well as keeping this beautiful house going."

"Yep - that was our mum." Paul got up and walked around the front of the steps.

"How did your parents meet?" Drew asked, wishing he could just shut his mouth.

"Oh, nothing interesting really - Dad met Mum at a dance then asked her out. Two years later they were married and a year after that my sister came along then I followed three years later. That's it really." Paul shrugged as he kicked some stones with his hands in his pockets.

"Well, there's nothing wrong with that. If anything, I envy your story." Drew said quietly. Paul looked at him, bewildered that he would have preferred his family story to that of his own.

"Why?"

"At least yours is so short! I mean, my dad met my mum when he was on a date with another woman. The pair dated for about two years then got engaged for the first time." Drew raised his eyebrows as he laughed slightly. Paul looked at him, confused, before Drew continued.

"Look, it's too long to explain, but put it this way, three's a crowd!" He nodded with a grin as Paul stared back at him in shock.

"Well - when you put it like that..!" Paul finally remarked, rubbing his forehead slightly.

They burst out laughing, enjoying the fresh air and bonding - again. Then they looked up as they saw two bright lights from the headlights of a car as it turned into the driveway. The car pulled up, braking quickly, causing the stones on the path to crunch with the weight of it.

"Right, well - I'll see you tomorrow then and thanks again for tonight, I really enjoyed it."

"You're welcome - wait, where's your salad?"

Drew realised he had, in fact, left the house without it, but unbeknown to them, Rachel had been watching and listening through the letterbox. She had opened the door slightly and placed the plastic container out on the top step, without either of them seeing her. As they turned to go back in and get it, Drew noticed the container sitting in front of the door.

"Look, I did bring it out, I must have put it down when I sat down on the steps." Drew picked up the small container and headed down the steps to the waiting taxi,

"Yeah, I'm sure!" Paul said suspiciously, looking towards the door and spotting the letterbox lid flap open. He stepped back into the door, causing the letterbox to slam shut, which made him grin as he worked out who was behind it.

As Drew turned to wave goodbye, Paul was still grinning, which confused him. As Drew got into the taxi, Paul saw the look on his face and he burst out laughing as he realised that Drew hadn't worked out what had happened with his salad.

"Never mind! Listen, text me later ok? See ya." Drew closed the taxi door and gave Paul the thumbs up as the taxi drove off.

As Paul pushed hard to open the door, he heard a thud come from behind it. He stepped inside to find Rachel lying clutching her forehead.

"Well, serves you right," Paul said unsympathetically, but helping Rachel to her feet as Carla came out of the front room.

"Haven't you got that assignment to finish, Paul?" Carla leaned against the door for support, although she hadn't used the crutches for a good part of the day, her ankle was still weak, and she had been on her feet most of the day.

"But…" Paul tried to protest, but Carla was having none of it.

"No buts - just go! You'll thank me later."

"Where have I heard that one before?" Paul looked back to Rachel, gave her a kiss on the cheek and headed for the stairs.

"And where's my kiss, brother dearest?" Carla said, tapping her cheek mischievously.

Paul sighed and came back down the steps he had climbed and walked over to give her a kiss on the cheek, then went to his room.

Rachel was staying the night, to avoid going home too late or too drunk, as her mother would have lost the plot with her. Rachel often stayed over to avoid fights with her mother - she even had her own room, which used to be Carla's before she moved into her mother's master bedroom. And Rachel had accumulated a small collection of clothes for any eventuality waiting for her in the wardrobe, in the event of an unexpected stay.

"Right, Rachel - you'd better get to bed, too, if you've got to play accountant tomorrow."

"But what about the dishes and the mess?" Rachel gave a small yawn.

"I've got it covered - now go, it's just a case of putting the rubbish in a black bag, and putting the rest of the dishes in the dishwasher. No big deal, now move." Rachel reluctantly went to her bed but, before she closed her door she called back down from the landing.

"If you need me, call me, OK?"

"OK," Carla replied quietly, as Rachel shut her door. Carla pottered round, clearing up, loading then turning on the dishwasher and washing machine. She sat down to give her ankle a rest, having poured herself a well-deserved cup of tea.

As she sat there, holding the handle of the mug that Paul had made for her at school years ago which said 'Best big sister in the world', she looked around at the empty kitchen, remembering when she and Drew were in there, making his replacement salad.

She re-played over in her mind Drew's part of the conversation, trying to find a way that she could have been mistaken about his relationship with Sarah. But her mind kept returning to the fact that both times he had come off the phone to her, he was happy, upbeat and talkative, which was very much the opposite to the way he was with her.

Tense, shy, nervous, jumpy sometimes - Carla couldn't help listing what seemed like symptoms of an allergy, with her being the cause. Finally, she finished her tea, made up a hot water bottle, locked up and turned off the lights on her way to bed.

*

Drew sat in his room, in the large chair beside the window, staring out at the black night sky, thinking about how much he had enjoyed the evening he had spent with his new friends. After a while, he heard movement and saw, underneath his door, a shadow passing as the light shone through.

Drew quietly got to his feet and tiptoed to his bedroom door and swung it open so fast that it hit his bedside cabinet with a loud clatter. He went into the kitchen, but Marti wasn't there. He checked the toilet - not there either - and just as he began to think that it must have been his imagination, Drew heard Marti cough and it came from the direction of the large three-seater sofa in the communal sitting room. Gingerly, Drew walked over, as though expecting Marti to jump from the couch to scare him.

"Hi, Marti," Drew said gently, as he approached the back of the sofa.

"Hi!" his friend replied sharply.

"Don't be like that with me!"

"Hmm!" Marti grunted, un-amused.

"Look, I'm sorry - are we going to talk or are you going to sit here like a three-year-old?" Marti turned his head around, very slowly, his face sporting a frown that reminded Drew of 'The Exorcist' or some other scary film.

"I'm not the one who has abandoned his mates for some bird," Marti said, turning his head back round to face TV.

"Some bird? Oh, c'mon - you're not jealous because I've become friends with her, are you?"

Marti didn't move or respond.

"You are, aren't you?" Drew found this incredibly funny.

"Am not!"

"Are so - you're like a child, behaving like this, when you should be happy for me."

"Look - that's not the point, Are you dating this girl?"

"No…" Drew replied defensively, unsure where this was leading.

"Well, why invest so much time in someone you can't and will not have? You're my mate too, I would like to see you more than just when you leave in the morning and when you get home at night" Marti lay there stretched out on the couch as Drew stood gaping at him.

"I promised her that I would help out for a while - after all, her ankle's in that state because of me, remember.'

"Well, I think she's using you."

"Why would you think that?" Drew came round the other side of the couch, to face Marti.

"I've just got a feeling that she is, alright?" Marti waved his hand in the air at Drew to tell him to move aside, as he was blocking his view of the TV.

"What do you suppose I do then?"

"Well, the uni is having trials for the football team and the word is that you're pretty good." Sitting upright.

"Where did you hear that?"

"So it's true then?"

"I wouldn't say that I'm pretty good, or anything like it, but I'm OK, I suppose."

"Well, then, that's how you can do it, when you have finished playing Benson for her you can play footy with the rest of us then come for a drink afterwards…"

"So when are they?" Drew was feeling satisfied that he was finally getting somewhere with Marti.

"Saturday morning," Marti said, his eyes never flickering from the TV.

"What? This Saturday, but that's the day of the fair!" Drew exclaimed, stunned.

"Yeah - and?" Marti shrugged the comment off, wanting to see what he would choose to do.

"Well, that's when we're all meant to meet up, so I can introduce you to her," Drew said, panicking over whether or not he would still be able to meet the others.

"What a surprise! She comes first again." Marti said, as he tried to guilt-trip Drew into calling off the meeting with Carla.

"Hey hold on - you wanted to meet her just as bad as the rest, I didn't say that I wouldn't go to the try-outs."

"Well, are you?" Marti sat back in the couch staring at him.

"Of course, why not? I'll ask her to meet us at the fair afterwards."

"Wow!" Marti applauded him sarcastically.

"A decision made without Her Majesty's royal blessing - very impressive."

"If you want me to do this, then cut it out."

Marti stopped the applauding and held his hands up to show he had stopped, as he tried to hide the deep grin of victory on his face. The two left the conversation and talked about the other guys who would be trying out. By the time they headed to their rooms, both felt relieved to have settled their childish dispute, though Marti believed Carla would have to be expelled from Drew's life altogether if he and the other guys wanted more time with him.

In a way, Marti was very jealous of Drew being able to talk to Carla, never mind spending so much time with her in the shop and going out for meals, football matches and helping her with her shopping. Marti was always used to being the one who attracted the female attention. He was tall, fit, very good looking, with dark silky hair and more than a hint of danger about him.

Also, when chatting up foreign women, he would start talking like Sean Connery and really turn on the charm. Oh, how they fell for that trick! Though of late, due to his jealousy towards Drew, his moods had been making him considerably less attractive.

Even as an adolescent, Marti remembered liking Carla. Back then, he couldn't even look her in the eye without blushing when he was taken into the shop with his mother. He would watch Carla sit behind the counter transferring freshly-baked cakes or cookies into little paper holders then arrange them on a plate to place into the display cabinet. His mind would often have switched off completely while he watched her. The nearest he ever got to her was when Carla went round the shop one sunny day, clearing and wiping the tables down. His mother and her friend were sat chatting away beside him as he stirred his empty cup with a straw. Carla approached him and smiled: at first he just sat there smiling helplessly at her. Then he sprang back in his chair, realising that she was, in fact, right in front of him.

"Are you finished with your cup?" Carla asked him, in a sweet childish voice, as she pointed to the cup.

"Emm…I…Umm…" He was so flustered, his hand moved across the table and knocked the milk jug over his mother's black suede handbag. Carla immediately put her tray down, on the opposite table and helped his mother. Then she turned her attention to the spill, dabbing a towel over it before using a damp cloth to stop more milk being sapped up by the bag.

Marti couldn't move - he was fixed to his chair with his arm floating in mid-air, transfixed by the scurry to save the bag. Marti never forgot the embarrassed look that Carla gave him before moving off back behind the counter. Their paths rarely crossed again as Marti would seldom approach the counter to avoid Carla. Instead, when he and his mother would go into the shop Marti would slink away into the corner table, then sit with his back to the shop looking out the window, hoping Carla wouldn't come near him. Marti, to this day - even though Carla probably wouldn't remember him - still allowed this to hang over him when he had plucked up the courage to try and talk to her. His pals never found out. Really, he was hoping that Drew would have an embarrassing moment with her that would see his 'relationship' on whatever level disappear...

Chapter Nine – Trials of the heart

The next few days passed pretty much as usual - the routine was just the same, the shop was doing well and Rachel and Paul's relationship was also going well.

Drew and Carla were still good friends but, secretly, Drew was gathering the courage to ask her out that Saturday at the fair. Drew forgot that he hadn't informed any of them that he would be trying out for the football team on the Saturday morning and that the plan was now for them to meet up later at the fair.

So on Friday night, as Paul was locking up, he asked Drew about plans for the following day.

"So what time are we meeting you tomorrow then?"

"What?"

"Tomorrow, at the fair." Paul prompted him, wondering if he was feeling OK.

"Sorry, right - well, you see the thing is."

"You're not pulling out of this, are you? Carla and Rachel are getting really excited about this and I really don't want to have to go home and break bad news… This will also be the first time she's shut the shop on a Saturday morning…Carla even got Rachel to put a sign up to say when we would re-open," Paul said defensively, with one hand still on the door handle.

"No, it's OK…What it is - I have try-outs for the football team first thing in the morning, so what I was going to suggest was that you three meet me at the fair later."

"Aye, OK - wait, you play footie?"

"Yeah - why are you so surprised?"

"Just didn't have you down as a footie player that's all…Well, anyway we'll see you at the fair - let's say, for about half-past twelve?"

"OK, the trials will be over then. If I'm going to be a bit late, I'll text you."

"OK, then, mate - night." Paul spotted an empty plastic bottle lying on the pavement and turned round.

"Hey, Drew - heads up!" Drew turned round to see Paul doing a few tricks with the bottle then flipped it across to him. Drew brought the bottle down with his foot, spun around, matching some of Paul's moves, then kicked it high up into the air. He spotted a round black metal bin with an open top, near to where Paul was standing, so as it came back down, he chipped it into the top of the bin.

Paul stood impressed, and then turned, waved and walked off, taking the odd glance back in disbelief at what he had just seen. Drew grinned from ear to ear all the way back to the flat, through the dark, cold streets of Glasgow, glowing in the light of the bright yellow and orange fluorescent colours, feeling optimistic about tomorrow.

*

Saturday morning and Drew was up well before Marti, which was part of his plan, because Marti took ages in the bathroom, gelling his hair and brushing his teeth. So Drew ran in, got showered and shaved, then went back to his room.

"Oh, shit!" he heard a short while later. The expletive came from Marti's room, then Drew heard hurried steps travelling from one end of the flat to the other, banging of doors then water running in the shower. Drew kept laughing at Marti, who kept repeating various other expletives as he rushed to make up for sleeping in.

Eventually, with fifteen minutes to get to the pitch, Drew and Marti were ready and for the entire trip there Drew wound up Marti by mimicking him.

"Oh, shit. Oh, shit!"

"Shut it."

"Oh, shit."

"I am gonna throttle you, if you don't…"

"Oh, shit."

"Right!" Marti began chasing Drew along the road, the pair of them laughing as Drew continued to taunt his flatmate. But Drew was too quick for Marti, he would slow down to let Marti catch up, then speed up again if he got too close. Getting to the pitch side, they quickly took off their tracksuits. Underneath, they were wearing a football top and shorts and they quickly put on their boots and signed in.

There were a lot of spectators watching, including a group of girls, one of whom Drew recognised straight away.

It was the little schoolgirl, Rebecca, who came to the sweet shop everyday. She obviously had a crush on him. Then on the other side of Rebecca's group, Drew spotted Sarah standing on her own waving at him. He waved back realising, that this was not going to be as easy as he thought.

The coach came out and separated everyone into two teams of eleven aside, Drew and Marti were to play against each other, meaning they were competing against each other for that position on the team, which probably wouldn't go down well afterwards regardless of who was picked.

The game started on a high - Marti was passed the ball at one point but took his eyes off it, only for it to be taken by one of the strikers. He watched in horror and disbelief at how easily the guy had taken it from him.

Marti then watched Drew heading up the field, getting a superb pass into the box, which he took with his right foot. He aimed it for the top corner of the net, but the keeper managed to push it behind for a corner, much to the disappointment of Drew's groupies.

The game provided entertainment, with many chances and plenty of fancy footwork, but the first goal came in the second half for Drew's team. After that, Drew himself provided a fantastic free kick only a few yards from the eighteen-yard box, straight to the head of a fellow midfielder.

Later, Drew also managed a goal but, as he came back off the ground from being jumped on in celebration by the team, he looked up to see Carla and the lovebirds standing applauding him, which merely caused Drew to become all the more flustered. He quickly moved off – clearly embarrassed, while trying to re-focus on the game.

The rest of the try-out went as well as it could have, with Drew panicking every time the ball was passed to him, though he eventually lightened up and played like he had done the night before, when he had showed off some of his skills to Paul.

Marti started playing better, too, but a little more viciously. At one point, he tackled a striker and sent him flying into mid-air. When he calmed down, he realised that it was actually one of his own players!

Drew would occasionally hear a few chants from the young schoolgirls, but the most enthusiastic chanting came from Sarah, on the opposite side of the pitch, who had been cheering him on the whole time.

This did not go unnoticed especially by Carla, who watched Sarah waving to both Drew and Marti and receiving cheerful waves back.

Carla did try, on a few occasions, to wave, but she was positioned at the wrong area of the park for Drew to see her.

Finally the trials ended and the boys were told that the list of players picked would be posted on the notice board in uni the following day.

After quick showers for the footballers, they all then head off to the fair with Marti trudging and sulking behind them, Sarah at his side to keep him company. At the entrance of the fair, standing in line to pay for their ticket, Marti's mood didn't seem to be having any affect on the rest of the group - and even Sarah left his side to join in with them.

As soon as they all got through, the group make their way past the amusements over to the barbecue area where Drew spotted his other friends and guided Carla and company through the mass of people who were playing at the amusement stands.

"Hey, Drew! Over here!" Pete shouted over. He grinned when he spotted that Carla and Rachel were with Drew. Pete sat down and whispered to some of the others as they approached the seating that had been saved for them all. It was clear that the tables had been pulled together to make enough room for them all to fit around.

"Thanks, Pete," Drew said, ushering the girls to their seats. "Here have a seat. Carla, Rachel do you want a burger or hot dog?" Drew asked, as they settled themselves in.

"Thanks – emm, can I have a burger please, Drew?"

"Sure - and what do you want, Rach?"

"I'll have the same, thanks."

"Sarah?"

"Can I have a burger too *and* a hotdog? Thanks." Drew and Paul headed off to join the queue. Marti slumped into his chair throwing down his sports bag, causing people around to stare, before turning back to their own groups.

For a few minutes, everybody at the large group of tables sat silently, exchanging uncomfortable looks. Carla couldn't stand it any more.

"So I'm Carla and this is Paul, my brother." Some of the boys round the table sat up straight and listened intently. "And this is my best friend, Rachel."

"Hi!" they all said.

"So are you all at Glasgow uni?"

"Yeah!" Again all together.

"Is it just me or has someone turned on the surround-sound here?" All of them laughed, but as the laughter faded, the awkwardness returned. shortly afterwards. Drew and Paul came over with the girls' orders and sat down to tuck into their own food. having only taken a few bites, Carla stood up.

"Right, what does everyone want to drink?" Drew immediately jumped to his feet. "No - I'll get them."

"Drew, sit and finish your burger, I've got this." Drew did not argue, he smiled and sat back down.

Carla took a napkin and wrote down the group's order and walked off to one of the two drinks tents, which were set up away from the decking area. From where they sat, the group could keep an eye on her as their tables were raised up from ground level, giving an almost balcony overview of the park and its busy goings-on.

Carla stood in the queue for over ten minutes with Paul, Drew and Rachel making regular trips to check that she was alright and asked if they could help.

At first she found it nice to be asked, but then she became irritated because it was as though she was a child who needed supervision. This was quite ironic, because she happened to be standing in line for the drinks tent, where proof of age was required to purchase alcohol.

Eventually, Carla finally got served. It took another five minutes for the barman to gather the complete order for her and place it all on the one tray. Carla paid, picked up the tray and gingerly turned, watching the contents of each of the glasses so that she could pace herself to avoid spilling them.

As she headed for the decking area, a large, solid body walked straight into her at speed and knocked two drinks to the ground. Actually, it was amazing that only two of them fell off, given the impact. The man helped to steady Carla by grabbing the tray and helped her to put it down on the nearest table.

"I'm so sorry," the deep masculine voice said. Carla hadn't taken her eyes off the drinks till they were on the table then she stood up and looked at the man straight in the eye and as their eyes met the two blushed and became flustered,

"I'm so sorry, here - let me get you another two."

"No, it's quite alright, I'll get them…Wait, did I just say 'it's quite alright'? Wow, I sounded like my mother there."

"Well, that doesn't sound like such a bad thing and anyway, I insist," he said, heading back over to the tent, where one line, Carla noted, was full of women. He just walked passed them and went straight to the head of the queue and ordered the drinks. He seemed oblivious to the queue of women, who were positively swooning around him - or so Carla thought.

She stood watching him in delight when she suddenly realised that she was actually staring at his bum.

She turned away grinning, secretly having enjoyed it but slightly embarrassed at having been so blatant. The man returned to see Carla standing with her back to him,

"Are you OK?" She spun around very quickly, startled by his sudden return. She jumped back in alarm and fell into the chair behind her.

"Are you OK?" The kind, polite stranger put down the glasses he had brought from the bar and helped Carla to her feet. As she stood up, Carla began to laugh at her own clumsiness and the man stood watching then began to laugh with her.

"Has anyone told you that you have the most beautiful smile?" he said at last.

Carla stopped laughing and blushed a deep colour of red,

"Wait, we haven't even been properly introduced - I'm Carla." She reached out to shake his hand.

"Pleased to meet you, Carla - I'm Alex." He smiled warmly at her, which made her go all tingly and blush again. They stood shaking hands for a couple of moments without saying anything, just grinning at each other.

Then Alex said: "Right, then - can I help you carry this somewhere?"

"No, thanks, it's ok - I can manage."

"No, really - please allow me?" Alex picked up the tray and looked down at her. Although Carla knew she was tall for a girl, Alex was at least six foot two and was devilishly handsome. She noticed he wore a black t-shirt and black jeans with smart leather shoes - and his dark hair and green eyes had completely entranced her.

"OK - well, we're over there." Carla pointed to the large group. Alex allowed Carla to walk in front to show the way, which gave her time to regain her cool.

While all of this had been happening, Drew had been intently watching. Who was this handsome man standing talking to Carla? Drew had seen the way that this stranger had made Carla act - it made him furious to see her openly flirt with this guy and his mood plummeted to his boots.

Sarah's friend, Jane, arrived on her own and Sarah brought her over to introduce her to the rest of the group. For some reason, Jane was immediately drawn to Drew, although he was barely aware of her as his mind was elsewhere.

Jane said 'hi' to everyone and noticed that there was a free seat beside Drew free (he had been saving it for Carla) so she sat down, breaking Drew's troubled reverie.

"Hi, I'm Jane," she said in a very friendly voice.

"Hi," he replied vaguely, trying to see past her head, trying to keep Carla in his sight.

"So I hear that you did really well at the trials today."

"Oh – yeah," he said, not really listening and not even making an effort to seem as though he was listening.

"Yeah - I just love football, maybe if you make the team I could come and watch you play."

"Yeah, sure," he said again.

"Great! Er…" Jane noticed that Drew's eye line was focused on something behind her. She turned around to see where his attention had been - it certainly wasn't with her. She saw that he was staring at a tall girl and a handsome man.

The new couple started making their way over towards their seating area, continuing to gaze warmly into each other's eyes.

It was a bit drastic, but Jane knew of only one way to get Drew's attention in order to get him all to herself, so she leaned forward quickly and kissed him. Drew froze, utterly so shocked by the kiss. The other boys around the table, sensing some fun, whistled loudly at them, egging them on to keep going. Carla looked up to see Drew kissing with a girl. Who on earth..?

Then she realised it must be either Sarah or her friend. Carla looked away to avoid making eye contact with Drew or the newcomer as she walked up the steps followed by Alex.

Paul and Rachel were outraged by what had just happened and sat fuming at Drew and the new girl. As for Marti - he sat grinning, knowing that Drew had screwed up big time with Carla. He had seen her reaction to the impromptu kiss. This was brilliant – he couldn't have made this up!

Carla and Alex began handing out drinks; Drew managed to push Jane off him, wiped his lips in distaste and sat sullenly looking the other way. As Carla placed his drink in front of him, she didn't look his direction. Drew knew straightaway that Jane had really messed up his chance of asking Carla out. This new guy took a seat beside Carla and the two became engrossed in conversation, without introductions even been made.

Drew's blood boiled with anger and he wanted to shout out 'She's mine!'. But the fact was she wasn't and there was nothing he could do about it... Shortly after that, Alex and Carla headed off to start playing some of the amusements with Rachel and Paul.

Drew stood up and started following them. Close behind him was Sarah, then Jane, Marti and Pete - all wanting to see what would happen, leaving the rest of the group to become increasingly raucous at the table.

*

Two hours later, Alex was carrying a large bag of soft toys, which he and Carla had won between them. Eventually, they came to the coconut shy, where you could win a small teddy for knocking down one coconut. If you knocked down three coconuts, the prize would be a massive and tacky white or brown teddy,

"Wow, look at that big thing!" Carla stopped to point out the large green teddy.

"Do you want it?" Alex asked.

"No – it's OK, we've won enough."

"No – here, you want that, so c'mon." Alex took her hand and walked her over to the stand.

"No, let's go get a drink instead," Carla said, hoping that the suggestion of quenching his thirst would be an adequate distraction.

"Hi, can I have two shots, please?" Alex picked up his six beanbags, looked down at Carla and winked confidently.

He threw his first two beanbags and knocked down two coconuts with ease. When he turned to smile at Carla, she was beaming at him. Alex turned, brought his knee up and swung the beanbag hard and fast at the last coconut standing, like an Australian fast bowler, much to the delight of the onlookers. Paul and Rachel had caught up with them and were joining in the excitement. Carla just stood smiling at Alex.

"What colour?" the man behind the stall asked.

"It's the ladies choice," Alex said, feeling very pleased with himself. Paul patted him on the back, while Rachel and Carla stood looking at the number of teddies from which to choose.

"Well - what colour?" he asked her.

"Could I have the brown one, please?" Everyone watched the very large, round man climb to the back of the tent to haul down the brown teddy, which was in a clear plastic bag to keep it clean. The stall owner decided to make the most of the moment.

"A pound a go," he yelled to the onlookers. "C'mon, win a lovely teddy for your girl, like this gentlemen did! A pound a go, guys - make her smile like this beautiful young lady." As he handed the large bag to Carla, the crowd began to applaud the pair, much to Carla's embarrassment.

Paul decided to have a go and win something for Rachel but only managed to win a small Sponge Bob Square Pants soft squeaky toy. Rachel was touched by the thought, but Paul was clearly embarrassed by the fact that, in light of Carla's booty, all he could manage was a silly children's squeaky toy...

Later, Alex managed to get Carla on his own.

"Carla, I've had a fabulous day and I'd very much like to do this again – would you go out with me?" She hesitated at first, but she could see this was making him very embarrassed at the prospect of being turned down.

"I would love to!" Carla responded with a smile, making his handsome smile return. "Why don't you come round to the shop tomorrow?"

"You own a shop?" Alex sounded surprised his face was still beaming with joy.

"Yeah, a sweet shop."

"What's it called?"

"So Sweet - do you know it?"

"Know it! Are you kidding me? It's only one of the best sweet shops in Glasgow. I thought I recognised you." Alex sounded so excited.

"Yes, I do, so many people come into the shop, its hard to remember everyone that comes in...- so will I see you tomorrow?"

"Yeah, sure - what time?"

"Say about lunchtime?"

"Great! Well, unfortunately, I have to go now. I need to report to my new boss in an hour."

"Oh, you've got a new job?" It was Carla's turn to find out a bit about this exciting new man.

"Yeah, but I'll tell you about it tomorrow - I need to nip home and get my course work, to start moving in to my room." Alex handed Carla the bag of toys he had been carrying for her.

"Well, congratulations on your new job and thank you for my toys." Carla opened the bag of smaller toys, pulled out the first one that came to her and handed it to him. It was a little teddy, dressed as a teacher.

"Here," Carla said, holding it towards him.

"No, I can't accept that." Alex shook his head at her, "You won that!"

"Well, you're going to have to, after all I get to decide what to do with it! And I want you to have it... Carla held the small bear out to him smiling. "You can use it as your little mascot for your new job," she suggested.

"I'll put him on my desk." He accepted the gift and smiled warmly.

"You have a desk? Very impressive." He laughed and bent down to give her a peck on the cheek, which surprised not just Carla, but Alex as well.

"I'm sorry - I don't know what came over me." Alex seemed very embarrassed by what he had done; he took a step back as his face began to flush.

"I have never heard a man apologising for giving a kiss," Carla said, trying to play it down but rather glad he *had* kissed her.

"I didn't mean to."

"You didn't mean to kiss me? Well, you certainly know how to flatter a girl." Carla grinned widely, waiting for Alex to look at her again so that he could see that she was joking.

"No, I meant it! I didn't mean to give you a kiss that surprised you, is what I meant." Alex looked at her but now, he was too flustered himself to see that she was smiling happily.

"Is every kiss not a surprise?" Carla decided to take a different approach by making him think more about his answers.

"Now that I think about it, on some level, I suppose it is..." Alex smiled, feeling a little more relaxed now that Carla hadn't taken offence. Suddenly, he looked down at his watch.

"Is that the time? Listen – here's my number..." He picked up a napkin from one of the nearby tables, wrote his number on it and handed it to her.

"Here's mine." Carla picked up another napkin, Alex then offered his pen, she took it from him and wrote down her own mobile number.

"Call me if you get lost tomorrow."

"I doubt I will get lost, but I will call you." Alex gave her another peck on the cheek and headed for the exit, turning around to wave a few times before disappearing out of sight.

Rachel saw her chance to quiz Carla, so she took hold of her arm.

"Well - you! What was that all about?" Rachel nudged Carla, making her smile widen.

"What do you mean?" Carla played the innocent, but was unable to wipe the smile from her face.

"OK - don't start me, you fancy him, and don't say you don't, 'cause I know what that look means on the face of Carla Devine." Rachel raised one eyebrow, while continuing to nudge Carla for an answer.

"Alright, I do." Rachel watched Carla's face flush with embarrassment and she started to laugh.

"What?" Carla asked, with a quizzical look on her face.

"Nothing. Come on. Let's get Paul and get the shop open, it's been closed long enough." Rachel roughly guided Carla back over to the table where Paul was sitting.

"Oh no- the shop! What time is it, where's that brother of mine?"

Alex had completely distracted Carla into having such a great time at the Fair, she had completely forgotten about the shop, which she should have opened an hour earlier. The shop did great business on a Saturday and this was the first special occasion which had warranted a brief closure.

Carla tapped Paul on the shoulder and, as he stood up to leave, Carla called to Drew: "Bye, Drew!"

Then the three hurried off to open the shop.

Drew was left standing there, not knowing if he was meant to follow later on to help in the shop or if he was needed at all anymore. Marti got up and went over beside Drew, put his arm around his shoulder.

"Well, mate - welcome back to reality, let's get you another drink, I think you're gonna need it, lover boy!"

Marti walked off laughing, not realising that Drew was actually pretty upset, having lost his chance to be with Carla.

Jane made her way back over to where Drew was standing, and put her arms round his neck.

"Well, why don't you come back to the table and we can have another drink?"

"Do you honestly think that, after what you have done today, I want to be anywhere near you?" He shrugged her off angrily.

"She was no good for you," Jane insisted, trying to look and sound sympathetic.

"Yeah, know her that well do you?" Drew snapped, causing Jane to sit back in her seat, shocked and embarrassed. "Now leave me alone!" Drew stormed off, heading back to his flat, unaware that the people around them had stopped to watch the arguing.

Marti watched his friend and realised that he hadn't been very helpful, when Drew needed him the most. So Marti handed his drinks to Pete and ran off after Drew.

Chapter Ten – Falling out of love.

Back at the flat, Drew flung the door open then slammed it shut in a fury. He went to his bedroom, throwing his bag down with such an almighty crash, his aftershave bottle smashed. It leaked out all over the floor, which raised his blood pressure even higher.

The smell of the fluid leaking from the bottom of his bag onto the carpet became almost overpowering but he couldn't be bothered cleaning it up, so he lay down on his bed and covered his face with a pillow, trying to drown out his thoughts.

Fifteen minutes later, Marti came in but, by this time, Drew had fallen asleep under his pillow, a leg and an arm hanging off the edge of the bed. Marti knocked on the door but, hearing no snoring, he opened it and went it.

Finding Drew draped across the bed, he panicked and rushed over to the side of the bed. He tossed the pillow away, pulling Drew's arm and leg onto the bed,

"Drew, come on mate, she's not worth it, Drew!" Marti yelled, grabbing his arms and began violently shaking Drew, when suddenly, Drew woke up.

"What the Hell are you doing? Get off!" Drew shouted. Marti was so relieved that he swung his arms round him, Drew pushed him off and Marti leapt to his feet.

"So you're OK, then?"

"Well, I was sleeping, until I was rudely interrupted. Why did you do that?" Drew's rubbed his tired eyes before he looked over at Marti.

"I couldn't hear you snoring."

"So, you complain when I snore and now you complain when I don't. I think you need help." Drew got to his feet, rubbing his neck and lower back.

"I couldn't hear you, so I came in and found you lying as though you had smothered yourself. I thought you'd done yourself in, mate."

"Well, I haven't, but I think I need to see a chiropractor." Marti looked on, worried now about the pain he had apparently inflicted on Drew.

"Sorry, pal, I didn't realise I shook you that hard."

"I don't think this was all your fault, but you didn't help - I think it must've happened when I was playing today. When I was tackled, I got up and tried to shake of the stiffness in my back, but I reckon you must've made it worse." Drew stretched to see if he could tell how bad it was.

"Hey - Jane is studying to be a physiotherapist, I'll give her a ring." Marti felt as though he had produced a miracle cure.

"No, not Jane. Anyone but Jane, and do you really think I want someone who's still in training to touch me? I'm in agony here." Drew's back was stiffening up but he wasn't too sore to straighten up quickly at the mere mention of Jane.

"Oh, c'mon, she won't try anything - I'll have a word with her."

"No," Drew insisted.

"Hey - do you realise how much it would cost to get a physio at short notice?" Marti exclaimed, already holding the phone.

"Fine, but if she tries anything...and this is only cause I'm desperate."

"OK, I get it you don't like her, right. I'll go give her a call so don't move."

"I don't think I could, even if I wanted to." Drew lay down on the bed, obviously in a lot of pain. He didn't move until Marti came back.

"Right, she's going home to get her stuff and will be round in twenty minutes - she told me you shouldn't move till she gets here."

"I'll try *real* hard," Drew said sarcastically.

Marti could see that Drew was still angry with him for a lot of things; he sat down with his back leaning on the bed.

"Look mate, I'm really sorry 'bout what's been going on...Just don't want to see you getting used, that's all" Marti looked up at Drew from the floor, hoping for a sign from him that he was accepting his apology. Though all he received was a look of grimace, as Drew winced in pain.

"Marti, where is she!" Drew rubbed his lower back, in too much pain to think about what Marti had been doing.

"She's on her way, pal...Do you want me to get you anything?" Marti turned with a genuine look of worry. Drew heaved a heavy sigh.

"Look, Marti whether you were looking out for me or not, it was none of your business... But the damage is done - she's with that other guy now." Marti kept still as Drew looked at him. "You were the complete bloody opposite of helpful, just look at me, you should try concentrating more on your own love life than mine." Drew flailed. Marti and Drew looked at each other unsure how to react. The noise from outside hummed in the background of the otherwise silent room.

"Look, Jane will be here any minute…" Marti stood and held the door open, then glanced at Drew. "I'm really sorry, pal, I didn't realise what I was doing." He sulked away into the living room, leaving Drew alone with his thoughts.

Drew, realising that Jane's arrival was imminent, decided to remind Marti of his promise to control her.

"Hey. Marti, remember to tell Jane…"

"Tell Jane what?" A chirpy voice followed as the door closed.

Marti had let Jane in, and as she went in to see Drew to assess the damage, Marti went and made her a cup of tea.

"Hi Drew," she said, closing the door slightly.

"Hi," he replied gruffly.

"Don't move - you could make it worse. Here, now relax and tell me where it's sore." Jane started moving her hands round the back of his neck and did some neck movements to find where the pain and stiffness lay.

"Right ok, I'll go set up while you get undressed." Jane turned and reached into her bag,

"Right, what? Undressed!" Drew's eyes flew open at the thought of getting undressed for her.

"Yeah - and put this gown on." Jane threw the pale blue gown on top of him.

She walked out with a grin, as Drew closed the door behind her so that he could get into the gown. He quickly changed and heard Jane and Marti talking quietly outside.

"He's still hung up on her," Marti told Jane as the kettle boiled. Drew heard the clicking noises of Jane's table being unfolded.

"Not if I have anything to do with it," she replied quietly.

"Now, I told you, Jane – don't do this now - I promised that I would have a word with you about this 'cause I've just got him talking to me again."

"Fine, but how long does it take to put on a stupid gown?" Just as she said that Drew appeared.

"You need to help me now, it's getting worse." He gingerly walked over to the bench and lay face down on it.

Jane moved over and began to work on him. Marti's mobile phone rang so he went out of the room, leaving the two alone.

"How does that feel?" she asked, pressing her fingers into his back, feeling for the painful areas.

"Yeah - in there... oh, it's really sore." Drew gasped in pain as she began applying pressure to the troubled areas. She began to massage her bony fingers into his back in all sorts of directions and areas, to help ease the muscles.

"Now I need to apply more pressure on your shoulder, so I'll need to climb on top of you."

"Do you heck?" Drew put his hand up to signal he wanted her to stop.

"Do you want to have a stiff and locked shoulder till Monday?" Jane folded her arms in a menacing way.

"OK - do what you have to do, but be quick." No sooner had Drew finished saying that and she was on top of his back and started to pull at his shoulder and more clicking could be heard. Drew tried his best not to scream in agony, but several moans escaped.

"Do you want a break?" Jane asked.

"No, just hurry and finish, please." A muffled response came as Drew gripped the table.

"Right - I need you sit up for me." Drew tried to lift his body from the table. As Jane tried to get off the table, the knee that was resting on top of a corner on his gown snagged as he turned to get up. Drew fell back which caused her to fall forward and the weight of the two falling caused the table to collapse with a crash. Marti came running in,

"Jane! What have you done? Mate, pull your dress down!" Drew pulled at his gown as Marti pushed Jane off him. When Drew tried to get up, he couldn't move. Marti hadn't closed the door to the dorm properly and a few other students passing in the corridor stopped and saw everything. Drew was mortified.

"I can't move," he yelled. "I need to see a real physio or a doctor, my back's really gone now."

"Hell! Right, go get the car, Jane." Marti threw his keys at her, but she didn't move and the keys fell to the ground as she continued to stare at Drew.

"She isn't coming with us," Drew cried.

Marti saw her lack of reaction so he picked the keys up and ran to the door. Luckily, Pete and a few of his mates were down the corridor coming out of another dorm, so Marti called to them.

They came running in and immediately picked Drew up, threw a jacket over him and carried him down to the car followed closely by a frantic Jane, The boys got into the car fumbled to get Drew in the most painless way possible and drove off, leaving Jane standing in the car park, crying over what she had just done.

In the car park, as Marti's car pulled out, Alex - who was heading back to his car from his meeting with his new boss - walked past and saw them driving off. He looked over to the front door to see Jane very upset, so he ran over quickly to find out what had happened.

"Oh, it's awful, I was trying to help by fixing his sore back and the table collapsed and he's really hurt his back now and..." She started to sob as another female student came over to take her back inside.

"Who is it and where are they going?" Alex asked the nearest student.

"It's Drew Matthews- they're off to the hospital," the student replied to him, Alex immediately recognised the name and rang Carla. He felt that she would want to know what was happening to her friend since they were all at the fair together; it was also a great excuse for him to call her...

*

Back at the shop Carla, Rachel and Paul were serving some customers when the phone rang. Rachel was closest so she picked it up.

"Hello, So Sweet. No, hold on and I'll get her - can I ask who's calling, please? Oh, hold on." Rachel covered the mouthpiece and called over to Carla.

"Carla, it's Alex." Carla went to the phone to leave Rachel to deal with the customer she had left midway through serving, Carla approached the receiver, brushing a few loose strands of hair behind her ear before speaking.

"Hi, Alex...what? Drew? Where? Right, I'm on my way." Alex offered to pick her up and take her round to see him: an offer she quickly accepted.

"What did lover boy want?" Rachel enquired.

"Drew's been taken to hospital," Carla told her, throwing her coat over her shoulders.

"What?" Rachel was stunned.

"Look, I don't have time to explain - Alex is coming round to take me up to the hospital."

"And why couldn't you walk? It's just along the road," Paul said, clearly irritated.

"First of all, my ankle is still recovering and second, he offered." She walked out the door, slamming it behind her.

"Why is she bothering with Drew, if she likes Alex?" Paul queried, shaking his head. He would never understand women...

"Oh, Paul - leave her alone!" Rachel retorted. "Drew has been a very good friend to her and to us, why shouldn't she care about him?"

Outside, however, Carla waited nervously and impatiently for Alex. After what seemed an age, he finally pulled up in a brand new, black Volkswagen Golf. Carla was oblivious to the lovely new car. She got in and they raced off.

At the hospital, Drew was sitting in an examination room waiting to be seen, when Carla and Alex came into the waiting area. Carla went to the desk and asked for Drew. The nurse looked at her.

"I know you."

"Do you?" she replied looking at the nurse wondering if she should know her.

"Yeah - you're the sweet shop owner."

"Yes, that's right – but could you tell me how my friend is doing, please?"

"Your mother was such a lovely woman, she was so kind and funny - I remember her serving me when I was at university, her baking was the only thing that kept me going through my studies."

"That's lovely, but how's my friend doing?"

"What's his name?" The nurse looked down at her list.

"Drew - ermm..." It dawned on Carla that she didn't know Drew's surname...

"We don't know yet, he hasn't been seen. But if you want to take a seat, I'll let you know as soon as we find out anything."

"Thanks," Alex said to the nurse. He realised that Carla was too distracted - she was looking up and down the corridor, looking for Drew, as Alex guided her over to the seating area.

"Do you want a tea, Carla?"

"What? Oh, yes, please..." Alex moved over to the other side of the large waiting area to the vending machines. It was then he spotted Marti sitting with all his friends, in the back corner of the waiting room, just as Marti spotted Carla sitting on her own...

Marti felt really guilty so he got up to walk over to talk to her when he saw Alex go back and hand her the tea he had bought. Marti now felt that she had betrayed Drew, so he sat back down again.

After half an hour of excruciatingly slow waiting, Carla began to pace the length of the room. Marti slid down in his seat to avoid being seen, then one of his friends spotted her.

"Carla - over here!"

"Oh - hi guys," Carla said, with a sigh of relief as she walked over to them.

"How is he?"

"Sore." Marti snapped at her, as the others threw him a dirty look.

"What happened?" Pete pointed to the empty seat beside him and began to tell the story. Carla listened intently as Alex sat down beside her, which no one seemed to mind but Marti, who slumped even further in his seat, listening but not making eye contact with anyone.

Now, an hour had passed since Drew had been taken in, then he appeared from the long corridor, shaking a man's hand. The group walked over and surrounded him but the boys allowed Carla through to see him.

"Drew - are you OK?"

"Carla - what you doing here?" Drew was surprised and embarrassed to see her standing there.

"I was told you were taken to hospital so I came straight up." Carla placed her hand on his back and gently rubbed it in a circular movement. Drew felt painfully nervous with his friends watching him, as she gave him a gentle hug.

"What were you told?" Drew suddenly panicked, hoping she hadn't been told an exaggerated version of what had actually happened.

"Just that someone was working on your back and the bench collapsed with you still on it... Are you OK?"

"Yeah, I am now, thanks to Doctor Maxwell here."

"You're welcome, but I want you to make an appointment to see the physio at your GP practice. .. You should only need a few sessions to keep a check on it. I'll let your doctor know you've been seen today."

"Thanks doctor," Drew said..

"Thank you, doctor," Carla said, as she put her arm back around Drew's back.

"Right you, you're staying with me and Paul, so that we can look after you." Marti and Alex became flustered with her suggestion but for different reasons.

"He's got a home, I can look after him," Marti said, through gritted teeth.

"Yeah - he'll be fine at his place," Alex agreed.

"But we have the room for him, and..." Carla couldn't understand why this was such a problem, when all she was trying to do was help him.

"No, look, Carla - I'm fine back at the flat, I just want to go home and sleep," Drew said, looking very tired. Pete started to walk him out to the car. Carla and Alex made to follow but Marti stopped them at the doors.

"I'll just get your painkillers," he called to Drew. Marti turned around and, with his face like thunder, he glared at Carla.

"You back off and leave him alone - he doesn't want you any where near him, get it?" Carla stood there shocked, unable to respond.

"Hey, there's no need to be like that!" Alex snapped back.

"As for you - moving in on someone else's girl, you make me sick! And the age of you compared to her." Carla still hadn't fully grasped what was going on.

"Wait, whose girl am I?" she asked. "I was never with anyone before I met Alex." Alex and Carla stared at Marti.

"Yeah well - if you had hung on for a bit, he would have asked you."

"Who?"

"You're pretty thick, aren't you?" Marti tapped his temple at her.

"Right - that's it, come on, Carla – let's go." Alex drew Carla away from Marti and made to leave.

"I mean it - leave him alone." Marti ran off, leaving Carla and Alex standing in the doorway of the hospital with a group of nurses and patients with front row tickets for the dramatic episode. Carla was deflated by the fact that Drew obviously no longer wanted her around. Though she couldn't imagine why.

Alex managed to lead Carla back to his car, as she was still in a daze wondering what she had done to make Drew feel like that towards her. In the car, Alex tried to talk to her.

"Carla, you alright? Don't listen to that moron."

"You're right, Alex, I don't know why he upset me so much. Well, Drew won't have that much time for us anyway, since he met that girl, Jane. He seemed to really like her."

Alex looked at her as they sat at traffic lights, with a look of worry. She was paying more attention to what had just happened than bothering about him. Carla, seeing his reaction, placed her hand on the side of his face and smiled at him.

"Drew has just been really good to me and my brother since I hurt my ankle," she explained. Alex smiled with relief - then he got beeped from the car behind as the lights had turned green.

Alex slammed the car into gear and drove off quickly. Pulling up outside the gates of her house, Alex let Carla out to press the security code into the keypad to open the large metal gates. She got back into the car and Alex drove her right up to the house.

"Thanks for tonight - I'm sorry you had to get involved. And thank you for defending me - it was very sweet of you." Carla leaned over and gave him a kiss on the cheek.

"You're welcome, Carla - I was happy being there for you." Carla reached for the door handle, stopped, looked out the window and turned slowly back to Alex. Both leaned in for a gentle kiss - short but sweet - then the kiss ended.

"So can I take it that you've decided not to go out with me?" Alex asked. grinning. They both laughed.

"You can take it as a yes - I'll see you tomorrow." She turned in her seat and got out. At the top of the front steps, Carla looked over her shoulder to see him watching her, having turned the car around so that the driver's side was in view of the front door to the house. She waved as she walked in doors then, and as he drove off, she watched him through the peephole.

Rachel and Paul were waiting for her in the hall.

"Well, how's Drew?" asked Paul.

"What? Who? Oh - right, he'll live." Carla said, vaguely, as Rachel and Paul looked at each other in bewilderment.

"Wow - that was cold," said Paul, amazed at Carla's lack of empathy for Drew...

"Yeah, Carla - what's wrong?" asked Rachel, sounding very concerned.

"Oh nothing. Never mind," she replied.

"No, there's something wrong - when are you so cold about someone especially after?" Paul began, before being cut off by Carla.

"After what?" Carla looked at him quizzically.

"Well, after everything that you two have gone through." Paul didn't like the way she was reacting to him asking questions: this wasn't like her at all.

"Well, after what I was told, not half an hour ago, it seems as though that doesn't matter any more anyway." Carla turned to hang her coat up.

"What?" the pair exclaimed in unison. Carla explained what had happened at the hospital. By the time she had finished, they were all in the front room and Paul had just handed Carla a large drink.

"I could thump that little moron," Paul said furiously.

"It's OK, just calm down, Paul." His sister frowned and rubbed her head pointing out that it was already bothering her without his moronic input.

"Calm down." Rachel mouthed silently to him.

"Well, thank God Alex was there to stop anything else happening," Paul mused, slumping down into his chair after handing Rachel her drink.

Carla began grinning again, feeling a warm tingling sensation all over. Rachel noticed this new expression and was intrigued to find out its cause.

"Ehh Paul, could you go check the dishwasher please?" Rachel asked sweetly.

"Why me?"

"Girl talk..."

"OK, you're right." Paul rolled his eyes then made his way to the kitchen and left the girls alone for a while.

Carla watched him go through the door, wondering what Rachel wanted to talk about. The door closed behind Paul,

Carla turned to look at Rachel to find her right in her face, and Carla jumped back and fell off the edge of the couch. Rachel looked down at Carla.

"Well, I *was* going to ask, have you have fallen head over heals for him? But I'll save that for later then!" Rachel began to laugh as Carla sat up.

"Oh yeah - real funny, Rach. Help me up." Rachel held out her hand and pulled Carla to her feet. Carla sat in the chair glowering at Rachel who was still smiling and trying not to laugh.

"Well, come on - what's going on between you and Alex?" Rachel pulled her legs up onto the sofa and tucked her feet under.

"What do you want to know?" Carla asked innocently, knowing exactly what Rachel wanted to hear.

"Hello - I want to know everything."

Carla was the most excited and enthusiastic Rachel had ever seen her as she talked about how great Alex was for trying to protect her from the mighty wrath of Marti, right through to how he made her feel.

"So have you kissed him yet?" Rachel asked, almost giddy with excitement. Carla grinned and nodded gently.

"Where? Don't tell me you kissed out there and I missed IT?"

"What - are you some kinda Peeping Tom or something? I don't watch you and Paul kiss - what age are you?" Carla couldn't believe that Rachel would have sat and watched them kissing, like a twelve-year-old.

"That's because he's your brother." Rachel smiled knowing that Carla couldn't argue with her.

"Fair point. Still…" Carla was confounded now that Rachel had provided the best reason to prevent reciprocation.

"So what happened after that?" Rachel pressed hard for more details.

"Well, he's asked me out to dinner."

"And what did you say?"

"No."

"What!" Rachel squeaked with shock,

"Yes, of course I said yes, what did you expect I would have said?" Carla laughed at Rachel's gullibility.

"Well, with you, who knows?"

"So he said he will phone me to arrange it."

"So what was the kiss like?"

"The truth?" Carla teased, as Rachel nodded, so Carla continued: "I'm not telling you."

"Well, aren't you the little minx?" The two began to giggle like little schoolgirls as they continued to talk. They talked for a little while about how life was looking up for both of them, having both found nice guys and their respective shops were doing well. They really had not been able to talk about this particular subject for a long time, which was why it was so much fun for them now. They were behaving like young girls again, though Rachel knew there was only so much she could talk about Paul with Carla, as it would have been just a little bit too weird for her. Actually, for both of them…

In the kitchen, Paul was emptying out the dishwasher, cursing Drew and Marti under his breath, when the phone rang.

Looking out to see if one of the girls was going to pick it up, he saw that the phone in the hall had been pulled out of the wall so they wouldn't be interrupted. After a few rings, the phone clicked onto the answering machine on the kitchen unit. Paul stood over it and heard Drew speak…

"Hi, Carla and Paul - listen, I'm not allowed to do anything for at least two or three days so that my back has time to heal. I'm sorry but I won't be able to help for a few days - I was just calling to let you know that I'm OK." Drew paused for a second.

"You'd better not come back at all, ya creep," Paul said to the phone. Then Drew spoke again: "Thank you for coming up to check how I was, Carla. Anyway, call me when you get this."

Just before Drew could finish leaving his message Paul deleted it and grabbed his mobile. Quickly, he began to type a message. He typed: "Drew, C says she don't need u 2 help anymore. No need to get in touch again – in fact, it's better you don't."

Putting his phone into the back pocket of his jeans, Paul stashed away the last of the dishes into the cupboards and decided to go to bed. He expected the 'girl talk' to go on for hours…

*

Drew was lying sleeping in his bed, having obediently taken the strong painkillers that the doctor had given him, when his mobile bleeped. Marti and Sarah, who were in the sitting area of the boys' dorm, heard it.

Drew had sat up for a short while after getting home: he had even managed to get out of his good clothes before falling asleep. So Marti quietly opened his bedroom door. He checked that Drew was still out like a light in a storm, then grabbed the phone and closed the door.

Sarah stood up abruptly.

"What are you doing? That's private!" she hissed quietly in case Drew heard.

"Oh, calm down - he's out cold. Anyway, we don't have any secrets from each other." Sarah didn't bother to argue - it was less hassle to leave him to what he was going to do, otherwise she would end up having her head bitten off. She sat back down and watched him reading the message.

"Well, well, Paul Devine - now we see your not-so-nice side," he remarked, still reading the message.

"What did he say?" Sarah looked on, worried.

"Telling Drew to keep clear of all of them - ha! So much for his new friends - and after everything he has done for them." Marti was still messing around with Drew's phone as he spoke.

"Why would he say that?" Sarah's worried expression deepened with anxiety.

"Don't know, they're all weirdos anyway and Drew doesn't need them. He'll have more fun and be much happier without them."

Sarah sat shocked at this declaration, while Marti reached for the remote for the TV.

"What's on tonight, then?" Marti asked, forgetting all about them as quick as he put the phone down.

"What are you doing?" Sarah asked in a high-pitched voice.

"What? Oh yeah - I should get rid of the message and their numbers to make sure - good thinking." Before she could utter another word, Marti had deleted the numbers from Drew's phone.

"Right, that's that sorted - so, what's on again?"

"Hey, wait a minute!" Sarah stood up with a very confused expression on her face.

"A), you have no right to take someone's phone and go through it," she declared. "B), you have no right deleting messages and contact numbers that don't belong to you and C), how are you going to explain to him when he asks what happened to them?" Sarah stood staring at the very calm, relaxed Marti who was looking at her as though he couldn't careless.

"Calm down, Sarah, let me deal with it; it's not that big a deal." Marti started flicking through the channels on the TV. Sarah stood looking around the room trying to come to terms with what he had just done.

"Not that big a...? Not that big a deal?" Sarah turned to look at him as he sat nonchalantly eating a packet of crisps.

"He was in love with that girl." Sarah rubbed her tired face, not knowing what to do now that he had deleted the contacts.

"Well, there are tons of girls round here that he can pick and chose as he pleases." Waving his hand dismissively.

"You chauvinist, misogynist, arrogant moron - we are not objects or disposable possessions to be picked up and discarded by the likes of you. I have known you since we were five years old and I knew that you were pig-headed sometimes, but this is really not funny. Marti, that poor guy is devastated that Carla is with someone else. You sit there thinking that, by deleting a few text messages and telling him to get a new girl, you're helping him? How stupid can you get?"

"Oh, Sarah give me a break!" Marti hadn't even looked at her the whole time she was shouting at him, but Sarah was shaking with rage as she grabbed her coat and bag and stormed off slamming the door behind her.

"That will be the door shut then!" Marti muttered after her. Then he went back to watching TV without giving it another moment's thought...

*

Drew slept right through until lunchtime the next day. Once he'd opened his eyes, he lay quietly before he slowly got to his feet to make a visit to the toilet. Walking through the sitting room he saw the TV was still on and that Marti had fallen asleep in front of it.

Drew walked over very slowly, reached for the remote in Marti's outstretched hand, turned it off and headed for the bathroom. Five minutes later, Drew emerged to find that Marti was still asleep, so he lifted the blanket that was draped over the back of the old couch and threw it over him.

He then spotted his mobile lying beside Marti, so he picked it up carefully, making sure not to over stretch his back again. As he walked back to his room, he was disappointed to find that there had been no missed calls or texts, having expected Carla to contact him to check how he was. Getting back to his bed he lay back down, placed the phone on the bedside cabinet and went back to sleep....

Chapter Eleven – Everybody hurts

Sunday turned out to be a great day, business wise, for Paul and Carla at the shop. Word of the shop's success had spread and visitors who had come to the city for the Fair went to investigate and to try the highly recommended confectionary for themselves.

The siblings had hardly any time to think, as the influx was immense and constant but it kept them amused. Some tourists, like the Americans, would ask if they could have a picture taken with them and permission to be able to take pictures of the shop. Carla was happy to oblige to a certain degree but it did slow things up a bit and customers were already spending so much time queuing outside waiting for their chance to sample the vast array of cakes and sweets.

In the afternoon, Carla had completely forgotten that Alex would be coming round to see her, as they had agreed the day before at the Fair. Customers' requests and orders had kept her busy and distracted.

Until, that is, she heard yelling outside and, leaving her post behind the counter, much to Paul's dismay, she went to the door. Looking out, she saw that a few people in the queue had stopped Alex; from passing all of them thinking that he was trying to skip the queue.

"Alex, come on - it's OK, he's with me, ladies and gentlemen - sorry about the wait, you will be served soon, I promise." She and Alex went back inside, squeezing their way through the crowd to the back room.

"Right…" she said to Alex as he took her hand and placed in it a single red rose.

"Oh, goodness - thank you." Carla swung her arms round his neck and kissed his cheek.

"Hey - you two! Hurry up, I haven't got eight arms!" Paul had opened the back room door which had been muffling the noise of the rowdy crowd then closed it behind him as he went back to deal with the madness.

"OK, listen - could you help me out here?" Carla asked Alex as she poured out a cup of water and placed her rose in it.

"Sure, what do you want me to do?" Alex asked, taking off his coat and draping it over the back of a chair.

"Well, first, wash your hands and put this apron on. Do you know how to work drink machines?" Carla asked as she washed her own hands and took out a fresh apron from a drawer to the side of the sink.

"Yeah, I worked as a waiter while I was a student." Alex was quickly washing his hands and began putting on his apron.

"Great - then you can manage the drinks counter then." Carla opened the door back to the shop.

"No probs - where do I find the prices?" Alex joined her out on the shop floor before making his way down to the right-hand side of the counters where all of the beverage machines sat.

"There are signs above your head and if you're not sure. just ask me or Paul." The pair then turned to join Paul and start making an attempt to clear the waiting customers.

The three of them worked through the crowds well and made the long queue diminish at a steady pace. Every now and then, Carla would go out with little samples for the crowd outside, to make sure they didn't wander off and also to thank them for waiting, which was deeply appreciated.

*

While the dynamic trio dealt with the crowd, Drew had decided to take a stroll – he was feeling much better and Marti was still asleep. He wandered round to the shop to see how they were doing.

Seeing the crowd outside, he panicked that they weren't coping so he walked across the road. As he got closer, he realised that, in fact, they were doing exceptionally well without him. This made him feel somewhat dejected. Upon reaching the window, Drew looked through and saw that he had already been replaced with Carla's new man. Good grief – they had only met the day before! Seeing their frequent exchange of looks as they passed each other, his heart sank deep into his stomach.

He moved off very quickly and discreetly in case he was spotted and went back home. Unbeknown to him, however, he had been spotted by Paul - who never let on to Carla that Drew had appeared...

As the last few customers in the queue came in, Carla stood having her picture taken with some more tourists.

Alex watched as the beautiful girl laughed and spoke to the many strangers, answering what seemed like a question a minute, which kept each one happy.

"She's always had that amazing skill," said a voice from behind Alex.

"Really?" Alex asked, without moving his head.

"Yeah - since she was old enough, Mum had her in the shop helping out, cleaning up and serving people. She was always able to connect with them on some level and read them very well." Both Paul and Alex watched Carla, as Paul dried two cups.

"She seems to love to talk and listen to them," Alex said, with a smile on his face as Carla talked to a baby boy sitting up in his pram.

"You bet - she loves it, but that's kinda why she's been so alone and never with anyone very long. The few guys that she has been out with always end up becoming jealous of her talking to others, when all she is doing is being polite and trying to encourage them to come back." Paul turned to place one of the dry cups on the shelf behind them.

"That's ridiculous!" Alex shook his head, breaking his stare at Carla to look in surprise at Paul.

"Yeah – well, you say that now, but just wait till a group of boys surround her, then you'll see why so many left."

"Why, does she flirt a lot?" Alex looked concerned over at Paul, who was wiping down the units.

"No, but they do with her and she is too soft to just walk away, unless they became vulgar towards her or anything."

"So they just got terribly jealous, her ex's?"

"Very - they would accuse her of being some kind of tease, which I can assure you now she is not."

In anticipation of orders to come, Paul moved back over to the other side of the counter to retrieve a bundle of paper bags, leaving Alex to watch Carla. As she finished talking with the group she made her way back to the counter where Alex was standing.

"Hi, you OK after that? You did really well."

"Yeah, fine, thanks - just amazed at being able to serve in here."

Carla laughed as she lowered the lid of the counter, then she asked Paul: "So how are you?"

"I think I have a grey hair," Paul joked, then he turned around to see Carla staring at his head.

"Oh yeah - I see it now, but think it's more silver than grey," Carla said, which made Paul turn to the mirror in the back room to check. After a minute or so, he re-emerged not at all amused with one eyebrow raised, to see both of them laughing uncontrollably.

"Yeah - ha, ha - hysterical, the pair of you."

"Listen, why don't we shut shop for half an hour now that the lunch rush is over so we can have a well-deserved break!" Carla suggested as she wiped a tear from her cheek. "We've made a whole day's takings already!"

"Well, I'll pull the blinds down and turn the sign if Alex gets the coffee and you get the sarnies."

"Aye, aye, sir!" Carla saluted him and turned to go through to the back room as she winked at Alex.

*

Back at the flat, Marti had eventually woke up and realised that Drew's mobile had gone. He immediately ran into his room to explain, only to discover that Drew was not there at all and, fearing that he had gone to speak to Carla, Marti belted out of the door, forgetting his own mobile and keys.

Flying down the stairs, he barged passed people to get down, causing a few angry yells.

At the bottom, he began to run again, heading in the direction of the shop. Jane and Sarah, who were heading back to Sarah's flat, saw Marti heading their way. They watched as he got closer and began smiling, thinking he had spotted them, but could only watch as he ran past them in oblivion.

"Hey, Marti, what's wrong?" Jane shouted after him. When he heard the shout, Marti swung his head round and lost his balance, tumbling to the ground, landing in a flowerbed and rolling into a bush of nettles.

"Aargh!" he yelled in agony as he got up, rubbing his leg frantically as the nettle stings covered his entire body.

"Stop rubbing - can you see a dock leaf?" The three looked around for a dock leaf. At the other side of grass lay another flowerbed, so Sarah ran over to check it.

"Why were you running like a flippin' madman?" Jane asked as she poured her bottle of water over some of the more severely-affected areas,

"Look, I have no time for this." Marti made an attempt to stand as Jane pulled him swiftly back down to the ground.

"Well, if you run off without treating that, it'll only get worse." Jane continued to use up the rest of her bottled water as well as trying to stop Marti scratching.

"Oh, really? " Marti looked surprised at the thought that his irritation could become worse than it already was.

"Yes, really." There was a pause as she lifted up his trouser leg to his knee.

"You shouldn't have been so nippy with her last night." Jane said sternly.

"Ow! Who?" Marti grabbed his leg, more concerned once again with his own wellbeing.

"You know damn well who I'm talking about! All she wanted to do is help you and look after you." Jane sat back and to have a quick glance back to check that Sarah could not hear.

"Yeah? Well, I don't need looking after," Marti replied in a childish fashion.

"Really? So you would have known how to treat a nettle sting? I don't think so." Jane voice dripped sarcasm.

"Well, if she wants to help. You can both help me find Drew." As Marti finished saying this, Sarah arrived back with a few dock leaves and heard the last comment about his need to find Drew.

"What about Drew? Where is he? What happened?" Sarah and Jane were both now rubbing his legs and arms, leaving him to rub everywhere else.

"When I woke up, both he and the phone had gone." Marti was rubbing the leaf he had in his hands trying desperately to relieve the annoying itch on his palms.

"What? I told you not to..." Sarah said in a raised voice. The girls helped Marti to his feet.

"Right, where would he go?" asked Jane.

"The sweet shop - if he's there, there is going to be a war," said Marti as they started to run towards the main road from where the sweet shop was only a short distance.

"What did I tell you?" Sarah kept repeating to him as they continued to run, stopping only to cross the busy road. Once across the road, the shop was so close that they could see that the blinds had been pulled down, to indicate that it was closed.

"I have never seen the shop shut at this time before. You don't think he's in there with them do you?" Marti wondered, standing on the opposite side of the street and facing the shop. He tried to think of what to do next.

"What are we waiting for? Just phone him." Jane said, feeling rather worried.

"No, we don't know what's been said - and anyway, what do we tell him when he comes out here, after having spoken to her?" Marti shrugged as he continued to stare at the shop door.

"Oh, I don't know, you could maybe try telling him the truth." Sarah shouted at him: she was truly angry with him now.

"OK, we get it, you were right."

"Hey, there's no need for that tone, Marti... Look, the longer we stand here and argue, the worse it could be getting for him in there." Sarah and Marti suddenly looked from each other to the door as they thought about what Jane had said.

"Well, go on, get in there, one of you." Jane put a hand on each of their backs and gave a gentle push forward.

"Wait!" Sarah said, grabbing hold of Marti's top to avoid him running off and making a big scene.

"When did the coach say he was posting the results of your football trials?" "Today..." Marti replied, unsure where she was going with this. Sarah pulled out her phone and searched through her contacts to find Pete's number.

"Hi Pete - have you seen the bulletin board today?" There was a pause. Marti and Jane remained confused about what Sarah was up to.

"Right, thanks." Sarah hung up and said: "Right - go get him now."

"What was that about?" asked Marti.

"Go tell him that he made the team." Marti and the girls went to cross the road when Marti stopped to ask: "What about me?"

"Oh - just hurry up." Sarah pushed him forward towards the door and he barged in without knocking.

Alex, Carla and Paul stood up in shock.

"What the Hell are you doing?" Paul exclaimed in shock at the noise and commotion Marti caused pushing the door open.

"Where's Drew?" Marti demanded, staring directly at Carla,

"Why should we care?" Alex said as he walked in front of Carla, Jane and Sarah stood shocked in the doorway at what he had just said.

"Have you seen him?" Marti forcefully asked in a panic.

"No, not since you told Carla and me that - wait, how did it go again we made him sick with the age difference! Ah, you told her to back off and leave him alone, that he didn't want her around." Alex said as Paul's head turned sharply to glare at Marti.

"Wait, that was you?" Paul's hand curled up into a fist and thumped Marti across the jaw.

"I'll teach you for talking to my sister like that." Paul approached Marti, who was on the floor with his mouth bleeding, tried to dab the blood away, thinking only of what Paul might do to him.

"Wait!" Sarah exclaimed as she stood in front of Marti to stop Paul hitting him again. She turned to look at Marti.

"Marti, tell me you didn't say that to her." Sarah pleaded.

From behind Sarah, Alex stepped forward and said: "He didn't *say* it, he shouted it so loudly the entire hospital waiting area and all the staff heard. He said that and a few more things too, before he told me that I made him sick, because of the age difference between us." Marti didn't respond - he was too busy watching Paul and what he was doing.

"Why would you do that to Drew?" Marti still could not speak to try to redeem himself; he could only look up at the group of faces from the ground. Paul and Alex walked menacingly forward towards Marti, forcing him to scramble to his feet and get out of the shop. They continued to walk out to the street, merely to get him out of the shop as the girls watched on... Alex was staying close to Paul in case he had to control him.

Carla did not step out of the shop: she watched from the window with the door closed so she could only hear muffled voices as they spoke. Then the clock in the shop rang, to let her know there was ten minutes before children would start arriving for their last chance of sweets before dinner.

"Paul, Alex, just leave it and come in," she yelled.

"But..." Paul said pointing over to Marti, who was nervously backing away across the street. Alex placed his hand on Paul's shoulder and pulled slightly to encourage him to do as his sister told him.

"He's been embarrassed enough - now come in and I wouldn't bother coming back here you three." Carla nodded at the girls, avoiding any eye contact with Marti.

Sarah walked up to the door of the shop and quietly said to Carla: "Jane and I had nothing to do with this - we only wanted to help Drew, I am so sorry for all of this." Carla looked at Sarah and could tell that she was genuinely sorry.

"Thank you - but now could you please tell Drew that we no longer need him to help out here? I'm a lot better now and can manage on my own from now on." Carla turned to Sarah. "You'd better tell him meaning Marti not to come here again as well," she said quietly. Sarah looked disappointed that Carla had to do that, but realised how difficult it would have been for them all to try and get on after everything that had happened.

"All right," Sarah said as she walked away from the door. Rachel then came charging across the road and ran into Paul's arms.

"What's going on?"

"Right - come on, let's get inside now," Carla said before she disappeared into the shop with the door closing behind her.

"I'll tell you later." Carla had to come back outside to help Alex bring Paul in. He was standing over Marti, shaking with rage. Carla walked up to Paul, looked at Marti then took her brother's arm and led him inside.

Jane and Sarah began to walk off on their own when Marti called out: "Hey, a little help, here..."

"Oh, you want help you selfish little..? I really should go and tell Drew exactly what kind of friend you are, but for his sake, I won't. You'd better pray that Paul and Drew don't meet in the corridor or you've had it." Filled with fury, Sarah verbally lashed out at him.

"All right, just help me, I'm bleeding." Marti touched his swollen, burst lip and looked at his finger that had a small amount of blood dripping from it.

"Help yourself and don't bother asking for my help again." Jane put her arm comfortingly around Sarah as they stormed off leaving him to get up himself and make his own way back to his dreary little room.

*

Inside the shop, Paul started explaining to Rachel what had happened, while Alex held Carla in a strong comforting hug, which Carla seemed to enjoy. As he held her close to his chest, Carla closed her eyes and breathed in gently to smell his aftershave, while she listened to his heartbeat, helping to ease her anxiety after Marti's visit.

Rachel and Paul stood in the doorway of the back room, watching as Alex gently rocked Carla from side to side and gently rubbed her head.

"She needs to get away from this mess," Rachel said looking on, as Paul hugged her tighter.

"Why don't the two of you go over to Ireland for a couple of days?" he suggested. "I'll look after this place."

"But what about uni?" Rachel lifted her head from Paul's chest to look at him.

"I'll get notes from a mate in the classes - don't worry about that, OK? Just you get her away for a bit and relax." Rachel gave him a kiss and smiled. She turned to Carla.

"Carla, can I see you a sec?" Carla reluctantly let go of Alex and followed Rachel into the back room. Paul sat down at one of the tables and asked Alex to join him.

"Listen, mate, thanks for taking care of Carla like that." Paul gave him a friendly pat on the shoulder and smiled.

"No problem - it's funny, I can't help feeling the overwhelming need to protect her." Paul smiled as he spoke.

"Just to let you know, Rach is in there telling Carla she's taking her away to Ireland for a few days to take her mind off things."

"That'll do her the world of good, getting out of here for a bit. Listen, would you like a hand in here while she's gone, as long as it is the weekend 'cause I wouldn't get time off my new job?"

"Yeah, that would be a great help, thanks." Paul felt a lot better knowing that he was going to have some form of help. "If you're sure it's not too much bother?"

"Not at all, I'm only too happy to help." They shook hands and drank their tea as they watched the door, as though it were a TV set.

In the back room, Carla watched Rachel as she paced up and down trying to tell her that she needed a break. Carla, who was getting slightly sick and dizzy from watching her move up and down across the room, grabbed her arm stopping Rachel dead in her tracks.

"OK, enough! Stop and sit... I would have said pace yourself, but I think you've overdone it already." Carla smiled jokingly as Rachel sat down beside her.

"Look, Carla, Paul and I think it's time you took a break – why don't you and I go to Ireland for a few days? Paul will look after the shop – it'll be great!"

Carla sat staring at Rachel for a minute or two in silence as Rachel stared back, willing Carla to say yes.

"Yes OK, fine - but it has to be over the weekend though." Rachel leaned forward and hugged Carla.

"Great – we'll leave Friday and come back Monday." Rachel said, determined to get longer than just a two-day break.

"OK."

"Well, you could try to sound happy about it." Rachel gave her a small nudge on the arm.

"I am, I'm just anxious about leaving Paul in charge of the business and the house." Carla stared up at Rachel who was smiling with excitement.

"He'll be fine," Rachel insisted. Carla drew Rachel a look that said 'Really?'

"What? He will." Rachel smiled knowing that Carla would still come with her as Ireland was her home away from home, having spent time over there with her mother as a child.

"Do you think if I asked Alex he would stay at the house and watch him?"

"You could ask, but you would have to make him offer, so Paul doesn't think you don't trust him."

"Yeah that would be one fight I could do without - and they seem to be getting on well."

"A lot better than he did with..." Rachel stopped, as she realised what she was just about to say.

"It's OK, he was just a friend and I have more than enough of those to keep me happy. Now let's see if they will take the hint..."

"Wait - are we talking about the same two men sitting in the shop?" The pair laughed as they opened the door to the shop. The boys were so deep in conversation that they hadn't realised that the girls were standing beside the table watching them with stupid grins on their faces.

"Hi, well - what's the verdict?" Paul asked as he tilted his head to look at Rachel and find some clue to the answer.

"We're going to go over for the weekend," Rachel replied, her eyes shining with excitement again.

"Great!" Paul exclaimed as he went over to the counter and picked up a bar of chocolate.

"On one condition - there are to be no parties," Carla remarked to test Paul's reaction.

"Right, sure." Paul sat back down, unwrapping the chocolate.

"Your mates are not allowed to stay over." Carla was making sure that she covered all angles of her rule, in case Paul found some kind of clause that she hadn't mentioned.

"Oh all right!" Paul reluctantly agreed as he took a bite of the bar.

"And no using the car," Carla continued. Paul turned and looked at her sharply.

"What?"

"I'm kidding, but only about driving the car - I meant everything else and I want someone to stay with you." Carla stood watching Paul's face contort, when Rachel tapped her in the back and whispered: "Subtle aren't you?" Carla and Rachel exchanged knowing looks as they sat down at the table, as Paul looked on in shock.

"I don't need a babysitter! C'mon, who are you going to get? And don't even think about asking Rachel's mum, 'cause that would just be weird." Paul flinched at the thought of his girlfriend's mother having to come over and baby-sit him.

"That's not a bad idea." Rachel then saw Paul's panicked expression and turned to Carla.

"You're sick, Devine." Carla tittered as Rachel tried to hide a cheeky grin from Paul.

"Well, if you want, I could stay with him." Alex offered as he looked at Carla, while Paul's expression turned to utter relief.

"Yeah - choose him, choose him, Carla." Paul pleaded with Carla, desperate to make sure Rachel's mother didn't spend the entire weekend with him. She would have driven him up the wall, treating him like a child. It would have also been severely weird for him, the very thought of her babysitting for him when he was dating her daughter! Freaky!

"Oh no! I couldn't ask you to do that," Carla said with a hint of sarcasm, which only Rachel picked up.

"No, really, it's no problem - I could sure use getting the inside scoop on some of the staff and pupils to watch out for," Alex said as the others heads turned at once to look at him.

"Staff and pupils?" Carla asked with a puzzled expression on her face.

"Yeah, did I not tell you? I'm a lecturer at the uni."

"You're not, are you?" Paul said, pretty impressed.

"Yeah, I am." Alex sat up straight as he answered Paul.

"What do you teach?" Rachel asked.

"English…"

But before he could finish Carla put her head in her hands and said:

"Literature." Her heart sank as she realised the implications.

"Yeah, but how…" Alex's brow furrowed as he looked at Carla leaning on the table.

"Drew is taking that course." Everyone fell silent.

"Well, that's tough shit." Paul muttered. Carla's head shot up and glowered at him.

"Paul, stop that language."

"Sorry, but who cares?" Paul then turned to Alex and whispered: "Give him a hard time for me." Alex smiled weakly at him, knowing that he couldn't do it,

"Paul, he will do no such thing," Carla snapped at Paul. "He has to be completely neutral when teaching and leave all prejudices at the door, treating everyone the same." Carla was becoming increasingly frustrated at Paul and his immature behaviour.

"She's right, pal, I'd get the sack before the end of my first day."

"Well, forget about him just now - how about a cup of tea and slice of mint marble each to celebrate Carla's first holiday?" Rachel stood up and collected the cups together to wash out and refill.

"Yeah, count me in," Alex said.

"Me too," Paul added as he stood to go over and help Rachel.

"I'll help Rachel - Carla, just you sit down and relax," Paul urged his sister back into her chair as he walked over to fill the kettle.

"Thanks for doing that," Carla said quietly to Alex as Paul's back was turned.

"Don't mention it. I know only too well what a young guy can get up to on his own."

"Have you got a younger brother?" Carla asked, realising that she knew very little about him, where he knew so much about her.

"No, I was left alone once when I was seventeen and – well, you could say my friends and I trashed the house." Carla looked at him in astonishment as Alex looked away sheepishly.

"Don't worry, I won't let that happen here - I'm a lot older and wiser now." Alex felt the immediate urge to defend himself, as he saw her instant reaction to his confession.

"Just how old are you?" Carla asked suddenly.

Alex laughed as Carla sat back not knowing how or why she'd had the nerve to ask.

"I'm thirty."

"You're what? No – really?" Carla laughed at what she thought was a joke,

"Yes, I am. Why - do I look older?"

"No, I thought you were younger." Carla felt a surge of embarrassment.

"Why - is that a problem for you?" Alex asked with a worried expression on his face.

"Not for me, I just wondered, that's all," she replied, hoping he hadn't taken her comments the wrong way.

Over at the counter, Rachel gave herself the laborious job of cutting the mint marble. She absolutely detested this task as, with every slice she cut, her longing to eat it deepened. A girl can have too much of a good thing!

"Right, here are your teas," Paul announced, as he walked over to the table carrying the cups on the large tray. He turned to see Rachel pretending to wash her hands, but she was, in fact, surreptitiously licking her mint marble-covered fingers.

"You OK over there, Rachel?" Paul asked sarcastically. Alex and Carla laughed as they watched Rachel's reaction at having been caught chocolate-handed.

"I think you could say that she's having a finger-lickin' good time," said Carla, making them all laugh anew.

"The Dark Side has taken her, hmm…" Alex said in his best Yoda voice, which sent the three of them into further fits of laughter. Carla had to fight back the tears as she made her way over to the counter, and gently rubbed Rachel's arm.

"You OK?" Carla asked, as Rachel had blushed but had also seen the funny side. She began laughing herself as she lifted the tray and walked over to the table. The cold, soft, yet solid rectangular block that melted in the mouth silenced them all as soon as they began to eat, only taking a break for a slurp of hot tea. The shop was quiet except for the gentle buzzing and humming coming from the different machines. Both of the guys sat back and eventually, as they finished the cake, the chatting restarted, first about the delicious slice they had just devoured, then on to the girls' trip to Ireland.

*

Back at the boys' dorm, Drew had returned to find Marti lying down on the couch with an ice pack on his face and a towel over his lip.

"What on earth happened to you?" he asked. Marti just lay there for a moment, contemplating his response, and then he quickly decided that a little white lie just now would be less painful for Drew to hear than the truth. And for Marti, for that matter…

"I was trying to find you to tell you that you've made the team and thought that you would have gone to the sweet shop. So I went over there and bumped into Paul, and he told me to tell you not to go back to the shop as Carla doesn't need you anymore, then the little tosser said something about you being useless anyway. The new squeeze, Alex, also said Carla told him that you were too in her face as well. I tried to defend you and - well, I got this for it..."

"Really? Paul said that and Carla said..?" Drew sat down on the arm of the couch as he stared bleakly at the floor.

"Yeah, hello, bleeding lip over here..." Marti said, his voice slightly muffled by the towel over his face.

"Are you OK?" For the next hour, Drew helped Marti to stop the bleeding and clean up the wound, Marti felt no remorse about the lie he had just told his best friend, just to get himself out of trouble.

"Right - so tell me again what he said that Carla said."

"Look, I told you, she doesn't want you round anymore and he thinks that you are useless. C'mon, get over it."

"Get over it? There was nothing there to get over, I'm just amazed that he hit you." Drew sat down on the coffee table in front of Marti, holding a bag of frozen peas to replace the now-melted ice pack.

"Really? 'Cause I'm not."

"Why?"

"Never mind - listen, I wouldn't go anywhere near that family again. They're barking. Could you get me a large drink, please?" Drew got up and went through to the kitchen without saying a word, leaving his mobile behind on the table. Marti saw his best and only opportunity, having been left alone with the phone, to convince Drew to remove the already-deleted contact numbers for Carla, Paul and Rachel, before Drew found out they had – actually – already gone. Looking at the phone, Marti called out to Drew.

"Hey, Drew – listen, I think you should get rid of their numbers from your phone - in fact, I'll do it if you want?" Marti in a slightly raised voice said as he picked up the phone. There was a moment of silence as Drew thought about it then he came back through to answer him.

"Yeah, why not? What do I need them for now?" As Drew walked back into the kitchen, Marti quickly pretended to delete the messages and numbers, before he had a chance to rethink his decision.

"No, in fact..." Drew came running back through, spilling some the water from the glass.

"Sorry, mate – all gone!" Marti shrugged then put the mobile back on the table, reached for the remote control and put the TV on.

Drew stood still then said: "It's OK, probably for the best." He looked a little saddened; those numbers were the last things he had left from their brief friendship. At least he knew where to find them if he ever needed them again.

"Yeah, it is - and on a lighter note, you made the team."

"Oh – right, good. What about you?"

"Actually, I don't know yet." Mari's face fell as he realised that he hadn't found out.

"Well, how do you know I made the team?"

"Pete phoned Sarah and didn't realise that I was there."

"Ah…"

"Well, let's celebrate!" Marti picked up the glass that Drew had just brought in and took a sip.

"Urgh, is this water?"

"Yeah."

"See, when I said drink, I meant alcoholic!"

"Oh, sorry."

"Listen, why don't we get Pete and the guys round to celebrate and get them to bring some beer round."

"Sure." Marti picked up his mobile to text Pete.

"What about Sarah?" Drew asked.

"Let's make it a guys night - I'm sick of her always hanging around." Drew was a bit shocked, but decided to ignore Marti's comment. Instead, he started tidying up to make the room semi-presentable for the guests who would be arriving soon so they could at least find a space to sit down.

Chapter Twelve – The morning after the night before.

Monday morning and the guys had major hangovers. Drew just made it in the door seconds before his first lecture was due to start. But the students were left sitting for five minutes at the start of the two-hour long class, before the principal of the department came in.

"Good morning class - I would like to introduce you to your new lecturer, Mr Alex Mulroney, who joins us from Stirling University." Drew's head popped up sharply at the name. He leaned over to his right, to try to get a better look at who was round the corner. Drew leaned so far forward that he nearly fell off his rickety wooden seat. Only a few turned to look at him as he fumbled to straighten up his desk: the rest were far too interested in seeing what their lecturer was like. Mr Clarke, their old lecturer, decided to take early retirement after his wife became ill, which caused the university a major panic to find a suitable replacement in a very short timescale.

"Now, I'm sure you will make him feel very welcome to our university. Mr Mulroney, please let me know if you need anything." The dean stood back holding his arm out as though to guide him in. Drew sat in his chair, repeating to himself: 'Please don't let it be him, please God, don't let it be him...'

Alex stepped more fully into the room and Drew's body sank back into his seat as he tried to hide.

"Thank you, Steven - right, good morning, I thought that we would pick up from where Mr Clarke left off, so take out your books please."

For the rest of the lesson, Drew hid behind his large textbook, hoping to be invisible and not to draw attention to himself and avoid being asked any questions. After what Marti had told him that Alex said about him, he was mortified in case Alex realised who he was.

Meanwhile, however, Alex had already spotted Drew, almost as soon as he walked in. Alex's game plan was to avoid any awkwardness, by deciding not to ask him anything. The rest of Alex's first two-hour-long lecture went off without any problems. He even made his students laugh a couple of times in an attempt to get them all to relax.

As soon as the bell rang, Drew made a dash for the door, unaware of having knocked down a pile of books until a voice called him back.

"Drew - come back here and pick up these books, please, would you?" Alex called to him down the corridor.

Drew went back very quickly into the room with his head down, picked up the books and ran off again, before Alex could get back to the doorway. Drew ran past Sarah in the corridor without realising she was there.

"Hey - Drew!" Drew looked round cautiously as though expecting it to be Alex or Paul. To his great relief and delight, he saw Sarah stare at him with a worried look on her face.

"Are you OK? You don't look great..."

"Yeah, well, no – what about you?" Drew's gaze seemed to wander, as he kept an eye out.

"OK, I guess... No - something's really up, what's wrong?" Sarah pushed him for an answer.

"I can't talk here," Drew insisted as he looked around.

"Well, why don't we go outside then?" Drew and Sarah walked outside into the bright sunshine and sat on a low brick wall. "Listen, why don't we go for lunch somewhere?" Drew nodded as the pair continued to walk down the street. They reached a small Italian restaurant. After examining the lunch menu, which was stuck onto the window, Sarah – still peering into the restaurant – exclaimed: "I think this looks great, Drew - and look at the price! Five ninety-five for two courses – brill." Sarah smiled hungrily at him.

"Yeah, c'mon before you begin licking the window!"

He took her arm and guided her in. A tall, dark and handsome man, whom Sarah almost actually drooled over, greeted them warmly. The waiter grinned as he pushed her chair in for her and handed over the menus, Sarah didn't realise that she was in fact holding the menu upside down when she spoke.

"Everything look so good, what would you recommend?" she gushed coyly.

Drew found this very amusing, to a point where he was momentarily taken away from thoughts of Carla and Alex.

Francesco – the waiter - brought over their drinks promptly. Sarah mistook this as his way of not being able to stay away, where really he was rushing to seat the next group that had walked in.

Later, during their main course, Sarah managed to pull her thoughts back to Drew, as he idly played around with his spaghetti bolognaise.

"Right - now tell me. Out with it!"

"You're never going to believe this…"

"Try me…"

"You know that guy that Carla's now dating?"

"Yeah - Alex?"

"Yeah – well, I just met my new lecturer."

Sarah sat back stunned. "Yeah and… Wait! No, it's not…" Sarah gasped slightly.

"It is… Imagine my surprise…" Drew's eyes dropped to stare at the ground. He realised that the awkwardness that he experienced those last two hours would continue unabated for the rest of the year.

"You're kidding…Oh no… So what are you going to do?"

"What can I do? Go to the dean and say "Please sir, he's dating the girl I fancy and I want him to leave?" Drew retorted, leaning heavily on the table.

Sarah sat up and looked Drew straight in the eye feeling guilty.

"Marti told me," Drew held her gaze right back.

"What - everything?" Sarah said dubiously.

"Well, he had no choice when I walked in and found him sitting there with blood gushing out of his nose." He lowered his head while running his fingers through his thick locks of hair.

"Was it that bad?"

"Yeah - wait, were you there?"

"Didn't he tell you?"

"No, he just told me what they said and did to him, when he only came to tell me I made the team."

Sarah sat staring at him for a minute, as he sipped his cold drink through the black bendy straw.

She asked herself, 'how much did Marti really tell him what happened?'

"Emm, so how did you take it?" she asked, examining his every move.

"Well, I was shocked, obviously."

"But what did you do?"

"Well, I went and got Marti a drink and he deleted all their messages and numbers from my phone for me."

"Oh, did he!" Sarah now knew that Marti had been messing Drew around with his own version of the truth, to allow him to justify deleting contacts from Drew's phone.

"It was just as well he did, because I probably would have talked myself into phoning one of them for some reason." A half-hearted smile crept onto his face and fell as he looked back at his drink.

"Yeah, just as well…" Sarah sat staring in the direction of the traffic, thinking about how Marti had deceived his friend and wondered if he had ever lied like that to her in all the years she had known him.

It seemed to Sarah that he was far too good at making up lies to save himself for it to have been his first time.

"So why haven't you been round lately? It's been weird without you…" Drew asked as he smiled and grasped her hand gently.

"Aww thanks, but I just felt that, with everything that's been going on, it was best just to stay out of the way and let your best friend help you." Sarah almost snorted at the idea of Marti even thinking that he was being a supportive and loyal friend to Drew, never mind a best friend.

"Hey - you're my best friend too. Try asking me next time if I need you or not." Drew hugged her warmly.

"Listen, just remember I will always be here for you, when ever and what ever," she told him. "I would never hurt you, you know that, right?"

"I know that," he said, squeezing her tighter.

"Why the long face?" he continued as they moved away from the hug.

"Just tired - didn't sleep well… Look, I have to go, I promised I would meet Jane and the girls." Sarah stood up and brushed herself down.

"Remember, anytime you want to talk… Oh, here there's a tenner for the…" Sarah scrambled with her purse.

"Look, I've got this after all you have sat here for half-an-hour, listening to me waffle on…and yes, I know you're only a phone call away!" he finished, nodding softly, as she leaned down and kissed his cheek.

"Thanks Drew…Listen, the next one's on me, right?" Sarah said, while walking backwards towards the door. As she turned to look where she was going, Sarah and Francesco bumped into each other. They both blushed and smiled shyly before trying to move round one another. As they attempted this, they both went in the same direction, narrowly missing another collision. Drew watched as the pair tried to move past each other several more times, before Francesco stopped and moved aside to allow her to pass.

"Signora…" He held his arm out as she passed. Once outside Sarah looked back in the window and mouthed the words 'Oh my God!' as she waved back to Drew, while continuing to walk on. Drew found this highly amusing and laughed quietly, though not quietly enough as near by customers tutted and shot him a variety of disapproving looks.

Drew sat in the now-busy restaurant thinking about the words that Sarah had used: 'I will always be here for you' and 'I would never hurt you'. He began to wonder why she would say these things. It was odd.

He looked around watching the world pass by; looking at people as they walked past; birds as they chased each other; and flowers as they danced in the breeze. He sat there for a full five minutes, before he realised he had to go back to pick up his football boots and a change of clothes for the first training session that afternoon…

*

That evening, Carla planned to cook a meal at the house for Alex and the two new love birds to celebrate Alex's first day in his job.

Alex remained unaware of the plans throughout the day as the trio had decided to do it for him once he left the shop the day before.

So he thought he was meeting everyone at the shop when, in fact, Paul was waiting to take him back to the house, where the girls were waiting.

Alex arrived at the shop just as Paul began locking up.

"Hey - where is everyone?"

"Oh, Carla just said come and have a cup of tea at ours so we can all relax. She told me to close up."

"That sounds great." But Alex sighed heavily, looking dead on his feet.

"The car is round here." The two headed to the car and, before they drove off to the house, Paul sent a text to Carla to announce their imminent arrival.

At the house, Carla's mobile bleeped to announce the arrival of Paul's text, Without looking, she shouted up to Rachel, who was hanging a silver 'Congratulations' banner over the banister.

"They've just left, so we have roughly fifteen minutes - let's get the bowls on the table."

"Just coming!" Rachel shouted back as she finished putting in the last tack to hold up the large banner.

Meanwhile, in the car, Alex told Paul about his first day and that Drew was one of his students. Though Alex didn't go into details about Drew, only about how tired he was though he loved the job and position, Paul couldn't help but laugh at the thought of Drew's face when he saw Alex.

Paul smiled inwardly the whole way home as Alex told him of how nervous he had been and the jokes he had cracked as he tried to make a good first impression.

As they got to the gates, Paul turned to Alex.

"Listen, we'd better stop laughing and not mention this to Carla, 'cause she's still kinda sore about the whole Drew subject."

"Really?" Alex said, unable to hide his disappointment.

"No - not like that! She just didn't like how it all ended. But trust me, the only reason she isn't dwelling on it is because of you."

"Really?" Alex replied, sounding pleased.

"Yes, really - is that all you can say?"

"Really!" Alex repeated.

"Mate, I will kick your ass if you do that again!" Paul drove up alongside the house and the pair got out.

Inside Carla had just started looking at her watch. She and Rachel had been hiding in the dark to surprise the guys when they came in, but it had been half-an-hour since Paul's text had arrived.

"Where the Hell are they?" said Rachel. "My knees are beginning to lock." She finished getting to her feet to stretch.

"I don't know, but if Paul has stopped off at the pub or anywhere, I'll kill him," Carla threatened.

Then a noise came from outside the front door and the pair ducked down again. Another couple of minutes passed without any action, so the girls made their way slowly to the door. Rachel took hold of Carla's hand as they edged closer towards the door, trying desperately not to laugh. The two were now within arms' reach of the door and Carla reached out her free hand to turn the door handle and gently pulled the door towards her to find the two guys standing there. She shrieked with fright, which triggered a chain reaction with Rachel who grabbed hold of Carla and both fell back in a heap on the floor. As they lay on the floor looking up at them, Carla turned to Rachel.

"What did you pull me down for, you idiot? It's just the guys, you maniac."

"I pulled you down? You screamed and backed into me."

"Did not."

"Did too."

"Did not."

"Hey Thelma and Louise - get a grip!" Paul shouted to be heard over their shrieking, and the boys burst out laughing.

"Oh, shut up and help us up."

Paul and Alex walked over and pulled the girls to their feet, then Paul went over to the wall and turned the light on.

"Surprise!" Carla, Rachel and Paul all shouted, and it was Alex's turn to jump. The others laughed, while he looked around to see that the place had been decorated with banners and streamers especially to celebrate his first day.

"This isn't all for me?"

"No - the Easter bunny was promoted to Santa Claus." Paul took Alex's jacket and hung it up for him.

"You shouldn't have done all this..." Alex said as he walked around the hall then into the lounge.

"Well, Carla did most of it, but I put up the big banner up there," Rachel told him, pointing to the banister. Alex walked over to her and gave her a big hug. "Thank you, I love it, all of it!" Alex exclaimed looking around.

"Well, if you like this, then wait till you see what Carla has done with the dining room!" Rachel took Alex by the arm and led him through. On entering the dining room, Alex gasped.

"Wow, this is beautiful, girls."

"So you like it?" Carla looked on nervously.

"Like it? It's great - no one has ever done anything like for me before."

"OK, stop kissing ass, we get it, you like it."

"No, I'm not kidding, we never had any money to pay for parties or celebrations of any kind. We grew up having to take care of our grandparents and we had to bring in home-helps to look after them when they were ill, Mum had to work two jobs and my father wasn't paid very much for being a handyman either."

"Oh, Alex I'm sorry." Carla walked over beside him and smiled gently.

"Don't be, I'm just so glad that I got this job, because it means I can send money home each month for Mum and Dad to help them out. They're still paying off the loans they needed to take out to look after us back then." Carla wrapped her arm around his.

"Look, let's sit down and we'll talk after dinner," Rachel said, trying to change the subject before they became too depressed to eat. Her main focus of attention was the new dessert Carla had made.

The guys sat down as the girls went into the kitchen to get the starters, which consisted of four different platters of appetisers that Rachel and Carla had made, found in an Italian recipe book that Rachel brought from the bookshop. As the platters were removed from the oven, the aromas began to waft through the house. Carla added a couple of sprigs of fresh herb garnish to each dish, before they carried them through to the dining room.

Once they had finished, Carla and Rachel disappeared once more into the kitchen and prepared the main course, opening another bottle of Merlot for the table. Taking the main course through to the dining room, Carla placed the dishes, gingerly down on the table.

Carla looked at Paul and Alex, who looked as though they were about to pounce on the food as their eyes widened with delight. The larger platter contained the steaming array of vegetables, carrots, sprouts, broccoli, baby potatoes with herbs scattered over the top of them; the other a joint of roast beef resting in gravy with all the trimmings.

"Well, this is what I call a home-cooked feast," Alex said, watching the plates.

"You'd think he'd never seen food before," Paul said with a grin on his face.

"Not like this I haven't," he admitted.

"Aw, thank you," Carla said, kissing the top of his head and heading back to the kitchen to bring in the last few bowls and the gravy boat. Carla cut the roast in front of them all and they helped themselves to the vegetables.

For the first half an hour, no one said anything because they were too busy enjoying their dinner. Carla would look up every now and again to check that everyone was all right and watched their expressions as they placed another forkful in their mouth. Their looks of utter pleasure warmed her heart, just pleased to be able to take care of her family.

At the end of the meal, knowing Rachel was desperate to taste the new dessert she had created, Carla decided to wind Rachel up for some fun.

"Right – well, why don't we move into the lounge for a drink?"

"What!" A high-pitched shriek emanated from Rachel, as she sat straight up leaning towards Carla.

"I don't know about you but I'm so full, I don't think I could eat another mouthful," Carla said winking at Paul.

"Try for the next twenty-four hours," Paul said, realising that Carla was winding Rachel up.

"What?"

"Yeah - I fancy a nice drink myself to round this off," said Alex and the three stood up to go into the lounge, leaving Rachel at the table, looking stunned and trying to work out what to say.

As they reached the lounge, the three of them began laughing quietly and decided to keep the joke going for as long as possible. On their way through, Paul announced his plans to go to bed in five minutes; Alex pretended to phone for a taxi and Carla began to bin the rubbish, all of them blithely ignoring Rachel.

As this was going on, Rachel sat at the table and built up her frustration to quite a head. Then she stood up and marched into the room and stood with her hands on her hips, staring at them in turn, which gave Paul his cue to make the first move of the plan.

"Right, night, guys." Paul walked over to Alex, patted his shoulder and said:

"Well done, mate, see you tomorrow."

"Night, Paul, and thanks."

Then Paul went across to Rachel.

"Night sweetheart," he murmured. He gave her a kiss on the cheek and walked towards the stairs slowly, trying desperately not to laugh.

"Well, I have an early start tomorrow, so that taxi had better arrive soon. I'd better call them again to make sure it's on its way..." Alex moved towards the phone.

"All right," responded Carla. Alex just smiled at Rachel as he passed her on his way out to the hall. Rachel stood with her mouth gaping. Then, as soon as he had moved to the phone, Rachel walked in, closed the large double doors and ran round the couch and sat down beside Carla.

"What the Hell are you doing?"

"What?" Carla asked innocently,

"Don't play games with me, Devine."

"Rachel, please tell me what you are rabbiting on about." Rachel sat staring at Carla, not at all amused. Carla continued to play the innocent so she didn't give the game away.

"If you think that I am going to wait any longer to taste this pudding, you've got another think coming."

"I'm really tired, Rach, and Alex needs to go home so can we do it tomorrow?"

"You're kidding me? After all I helped you with, you're denying me my right as your official taster!"

"Oh my God - now I really think you need help."

"OK, I admit it, I am an addict when it comes to your baking! Now please -make them eat it!"

"I can't make them eat it! Anyway Paul's away to bed and Alex is calling a taxi."

"We can be finished before the taxi comes."

"Look you go and call Paul and Alex and ask them."

"Fine, OK, is that you saying yes?"

"Only if they agree - you don't get to try it unless we all do." Rachel leapt up and ran to the doors and pulled them open, and found Alex and Paul laughing.

"You bunch of..." Before she could finish, they all began laughing as Rachel became all flushed with embarrassment.

"OK, you three go and sit at the table - I'll bring the plates in for you," Carla instructed. Without question or hesitation, Rachel, Paul and Alex rushed in and sat at the table. Carla had made beautiful mini strawberry-shortcakes in the shape of a pyramid, with slices of strawberries down each side, with a drizzle of strawberry and cream sauce and two mint leaves for decoration. Rachel's eyes were dancing out of her head on stalks as she watched Carla deliberately serve the guys before her to milk the moment. So much so that Rachel caved in, jumped up and grabbed the plate from Carla's hand.

"Oh, Hell, woman - would you stop doing that to me?" Rachel exclaimed, as the others watched on, hugely entertained by her behaviour.

Carla then brought out another surprise - for the first time ever, she had made her own vanilla ice cream from scratch and she placed a lovely round scoop on each plate.

"Well, don't just stare at it, tuck in!" she ordered. Hesitantly at first, not wishing to ruin the display, they all slowly began cutting through the beautifully-presented pyramid while Carla stood watching, waiting for their reactions.

"It's like feeding time at the zoo with you lot," she said finally, sitting down to eat her own bowl.

"Oh, Carla, this is great," Alex said.

"It's fantastic!" Paul exclaimed. "And you made this ice cream, too. Wow, what a talent…"

"No - you didn't, did you?" Alex asked, very impressed and amazed.

"Yes, do you like it? Really - tell the truth."

"OK, then - it's horrible," came the brotherly response from Paul. "Why would you subject us to this torture?"

"Shut up, Paul!" Carla laughed.

"Well… Alex?"

"I think it's incredible," he responded, as he took another mouthful.

"What about you, Rach?" No reply came from Rachel for a moment or two. Then, she slowly formed some words…

"You know, if I knew how good this tasted and you had made me wait another day to try it, I would have kicked your ass." Rachel finished off the last spoonful of the dessert, making sure she had completely cleaned the plate.

Alex, after sitting chatting for a while, decided that he'd better head off home.

"Wait - sit for two minutes." Carla stood up quickly and ran upstairs.

"What is she doing now?" Paul asked Rachel, who just shrugged back at him. Carla could then be heard coming back down the stairs at a tremendous pace.

"Right - close your eyes," Carla said, as she stood in the hall.

"Why?" Paul asked as Carla sighed loudly.

"Paul - I'm not talking to you! Alex, close your eyes."

"OK, my eyes are closed."

"No peeking!" She walked in with both hands behind her back and stood in front of him; Carla waved a hand in front of his face to check he wasn't peeking then slowly brought her hands around to the front.

"OK - open." Alex gazed down at her hands, which held a beautiful leather desk set, with two paper trays, a desk tidy, blotting pad and a very expensive Italian pen.

"Carla - what the..?"

"Don't start that I shouldn't have done it. I have and you are going to take it, so do you like it."

"Like it? I love it but that's Italian leather and – oh, my God, look at that pen! You shouldn't have!"

"What did I tell you? Now say 'Thank you, Carla'."

"Thank you, Carla," Alex repeated obediently as gave her a kiss.

"Now take the gift."

Alex took the parcel, out of her hands.

"Thank you. So much."

"You're welcome. Now you have something to look at to remind you of me," "Well, I don't really need these to remind me." Alex and Carla looked deeply into each other's eyes. Then Paul cut in, breaking the spell.

"Could you two get a room or give me a shot gun, please?"

"Paul!" Rachel hit him across the head, which caused him to yell in pain.

"What did you hit me for?"

"Oh, no, I've got brain freeze!" Rachel frantically rubbed her aching head as Alex, Carla and Paul began laughing.

"Well, you've just eaten an entire tub of ice cream, which I was going to take to the shop tomorrow and let the kids try, so obviously I will have to make a new batch tomorrow."

"That's not the only one you're making, is it?" Rachel asked, looking up to her friend, as she continued to eat the ice cream, regardless of the fact she had just had a severe bout of brain freeze.

"Right, sorry, but I now really do need to go call a taxi." Alex made his way to the front room door.

"Sure - use the phone in the hall, it has a taxi card beside it," Carla said. Ten minutes later, Alex had called a taxi and they were all waiting for its arrival when the buzzer rang.

"That will be the taxi - I'll open the gates." Paul went out to the hall and buzzed the gates open, as the taxi headed along the drive.

Alex made his good nights and hugged the girls, shook Paul's hand then walked down the steps ready to jump into the car. As the taxi drove up and stopped, Alex turned round and waved. As he did so, the car's door opened and the three standing at the top of the stairs stopped waving, wearing stunned expressions.

Alex swung round to find Drew standing there in front of him.

"Emm, hi Carla - could I have a word?" Drew asked, but before Carla could respond, Paul moved forward slightly.

"Does your pal want you dead or something?" he yelled, walking slowly down the steps.

"What?" Drew shouted back up to him, completely confused and bewildered.

"Didn't he tell you that I warned you never to come near my sister or have anything to do with her again?"

"Yeah, he did and I think hitting him was a bit out of order!"

Paul walked over and stood beside Alex, the pair stared at Drew.

"Look, guys, c'mon - arguing isn't going to get us anywhere, and it's upsetting the girls!" Alex finally spoke, pointing to the front of the house.

"Why did you hit him, was it because he tried to defend me?" Drew ignored Alex's plea.

"Is that what he told you?" Paul laughed sarcastically at Drew.

"That's what happened, right?"

"No, it is not." Alex said calmly, keeping a grip on Paul. "The night you were in hospital, he told Carla never to come near you again."

"He did not! Did he, Carla?" Drew asked, looking up at her forlornly, hoping she would contradict what Alex had just said. But she stood there uncomfortably as Rachel took hold of her.

"Go on, Carla tell him - tell him what that rotter said and called you." Paul insisted. Carla was unable to look Drew in the eye as she spoke.

"He did, Drew - and he told me that you didn't want me anywhere near you, that Alex and I being together made him sick because of the age difference."

"He didn't..."

"He did - and tell him the rest, Carla," Paul urged.

"Please - can we just forget about it?"

"No!" Paul exclaimed forcefully, as Drew's usually proud and tall stance melted into a slump. Alex pulled Paul away slightly to try to calm him down and whispered in his ear.

"Remember your sister in all this." Patting him on the shoulder, Alex loosened his grip.

"Fine then - the other day, he came barging in to the shop, and demanded to know where you were. When we told him we hadn't seen you since that night at the hospital, he went mental and didn't believe us, then Paul hit him and Sarah had to intervene to stop Paul from hitting him again." Carla spat quickly at them both, emphasising her frustration.

"Wait a minute - Sarah was there?" Drew interrupted, as his eyes widened in disbelief.

"Oh no - not another friend who doesn't tell the truth! You really know how to pick them, don't you."

"Paul, stop it!" Rachel shouted, but he continued.

"She had to ask Marti if it was true."

"So she didn't know anything about it?"

"It didn't sound like it - then she apologised and said that she was only trying to help you, she had no idea what he had done," Carla finished quietly, as Drew took a step back and lowered his head.

"So we have nothing more to say to you and want nothing more to do with you," Paul told him, as Rachel led Carla back into the house.

All the guys stood there, not wanting to move. At that moment, another taxi came up the drive. The driver of the car in which Drew had arrived ten minutes earlier jumped out.

"Look, am I waiting to take you back, pal, or can I go? 'Cause I could be making money here!"

"Yes, let's go." Drew said, opening the door to the cab.

"Right." The taxi driver sighed.

Drew's taxi drove away and the other moved forward to take its place nearer the steps to the front door.

"Hi, pal, I will be two secs." Alex turned to Paul. "Text me later and let me know how she is."

"I will do, thanks for that."

"No problem - anytime." Alex jumped into the car and the cab drove off.

Paul headed inside and found Rachel coming back down the hall stairs.

"Sshh, she's gone to bed."

"What was that guy like? I mean, honestly - she just got over that whole ordeal then to have it thrown back at her like that, tonight of all nights." He sighed and Rachel threw her arm round him.

"I know."

"All she wanted was for tonight to go well. she really doesn't ask for much - just as well you're both going away - that'll take her mind off things."

"Yeah, I'm sure it will… Look, I'd better go, too." Rachel grabbed her coat from the banister, but before she could put it on, Paul took it from her and helped her with it.

They hugged then Rachel headed for the door.

"Oh, wait…" She turned round and darted through to the dining room and came back with the tub of Carla's ice cream,

"I won't get anymore for a while." Paul just stood holding the door, shaking his head, laughing. She gave him a kiss on the cheek, walked down the steps, got into her car and, as she passed the stairs, she rolled down her window.

"Text me if either of you need anything," she told him.

"Will do, g'night." Paul closed the door, but watched her from the lounge window to make sure he could lock up the gates and house before going to bed.

*

When Drew returned to his flat, he walked straight past Marti without looking at him and locked his room door.

Marti assumed that Drew must be tired from training and left him alone without thinking too much about it.

Sitting alone in his room, Drew looked at the university booklet and started thinking.

"Well, nothing is keeping me here," he mused to himself. "All my family are in London, it makes sense, and I'll go see the year head tomorrow."

He looked over at family photos on his desk, lifting the small silver framed photo as he sat back on the bed. He would be better to transfer back down south for his last two years of the course: after all, he had said to his family it would only be for a year or two, before he transferred home to sit his final year, in order to graduate from the same university as his parents did.

Then his thoughts began to wander to the good times he'd had over the past few months since arriving in Glasgow. He started smiling, as his mind went over some of the most enjoyable and funniest moments, then he gradually fell asleep in his football gear.

Chapter Thirteen – Drastic Measures.

The next day, Alex sent a text to Carla to tell her that he wouldn't be able to take her out, as the dean had just put his name down to help a couple of students after hours, as part of a new scheme to aid students to better their grades on assessments. Paul heard this and decided to phone Alex.

"Can you talk?"

"Yeah - but for five minutes: the bell is about to go for next period."

"Right, well you have to tell Carla yourself and soften the blow with flowers or a cuddly toy but no chocolates, she ends up hating herself once she finishes them."

"Right, OK.."

"But will you be able to come to the airport to see them off?"

"What time is their flight?"

"Half ten in the morning."

"This Friday, yeah I can come I don't have a class till late that afternoon." "Right well I'll speak to you later."

"Right bye."

"Bye."

*

Drew came out of a meeting with the woman in charge of transfers, just as the bell rang for his next class.

Marti saw him walking past and tried to grab his arm. Drew pulled away as he reached for it and hurried into the class. Marti was now becoming slightly concerned about Drew and, as he walked off, he saw Sarah who also ignored him just as much as Drew had.

"What, do I smell or something?" he called after her. Without waiting for an answer, he walked off angrily.

As Sarah passed Drew's class and looked in, she saw that he looked terrible – tired, gaunt and pale - so she decided to wait for him coming out.

The hour passed slowly. Once the class began leaving, Sarah saw Drew heading for the door, but Alex called him back in and told him to close the door.

Sarah stood still outside the room, trying very hard to hear what was being said but without any success.

Inside the room, Drew stood away from the desk, Alex looked up to see his discomfort.

"Drew, please take a seat."

"I'm fine standing."

"OK, I called you back to say that Carla and the others don't blame you for what had happened. In fact, they feel sorry for what Marti has done to you."

"Thanks, can I go?"

"Just wait, I am involved in doing some night study sessions. Why don't you start coming to those? I'd like to help to make up for what's been happening to you - and it will benefit you in the long run."

"Thank you, but..."

"Well, look think about it, even if you want to see me after class to ask me anything - please ask. Honestly, that's what I'm here for."

"Thanks."

"Right, off you go and think about what I said." Drew walked out quickly and closed the door leaving Alex alone.

Sarah fell into step beside him and took his arm as they walked along the corridor.

"What's wrong, Drew?"

"Why didn't you tell me?"

"Tell you what?"

"About what Marti did."

"He still hasn't told you?"

"OK - I want you to tell me everything - now!"

Drew took Sarah out for lunch. Sarah decided that, as they were walking, it was about time he *did* know what had happened.

So she told him everything over lunch, as they headed back to the Italian restaurant, where they had had lunch previously... Though it made no difference to Sarah because she was so concerned about Drew, Francesco was not the waiter. It was a skinny fair haired young Glaswegian. Who was desperately trying to show he knew Italian, but failing miserably. The young man handed them both a menu. They quickly ordered, allowing the waiter to leave them to talk.

Once she had finished her tale, Sarah sat back in her chair and stretched out, her hand reaching across the table to hold Drew's.

"Are you OK?"

"I don't know," he responded, dazed.

"Please don't be angry with me. I wanted him to own up and tell you himself, but he's too much of a coward for that."

"Well, since you're so good at keeping secrets, maybe you could keep this one for me, since you're the only one who seems to care about me."

"Oh, Drew, please don't be like that!"

"I've just put in for a transfer."

"What to Caley - or to Paisley?"

"No, back home, where I should've stayed." Drew couldn't look at her.

"No, Drew! You're not thinking straight, you're upset, you should sleep on it," Sarah pleaded.

"I have." Drew stared at his wine glass, to avoid looking at her.

"Or give it a month?" She knew she was starting to sound desperate.

"Well, it'll soon be Christmas and I was hoping for a transfer then, but I was told it could only happen at the end of the academic year. I had only planned to stay here for one or two years of the course anyway, then transfer so that I could graduate down in London."

"Please - Drew, I beg you, please don't do this... Withdraw your transfer, just find a different flat, different mates – it'll be better..."

"No, I'll still be surrounded by the constant reminders of everything that's happened - and all my real friends and family are down there anyway."

Sarah felt as though she had just been slapped – she didn't know where to look.

"Hey - you know that you are the exception to that, right?" He assured her, aware of her distress.

"Thanks, but isn't there anything I can do to change your mind?"

"No - my transfer has been accepted and I want to do this."

"When does this happen?"

"After my last exam."

"What?"

"Please, can't you just be happy for me?"

"Well - you know me, I'm right behind you, whatever you choose. But I think it's a bit hasty."

"OK, I get it, but I want you to come down and see me as often as you can, and I will come up here to see you every now and again."

"You'd better. Well, I think, with this news, it's time we hit the pub."

"I agree." They paid the bill and went to the nearest pub, which they knew was one that Marti and the others didn't frequent. They stayed for a good while and the atmosphere between them mellowed as time passed.

Drew ended up very merry indeed and Sarah had to take him home. But no taxi driver would allow him in their car, so they had to walk the whole way back to his flat. When they arrived, Marti leapt to his feet when he saw Drew being helped through the door by Sarah.

"Where the bloody Hell have you been? I've been worried sick."

"See, I told you that he was like a bloody wife, demanding and possessive," Drew slurred as Sarah dragged him into his room and closed the door.

Marti stood waiting for Sarah to come out. When she did, she headed straight for the door without looking at him.

"Hey, why don't you talk to me? You're not responding to my texts or phone calls, you keep ignoring me."

"Do you blame me?" She stormed off, slamming the front door behind her. Marti went over to Drew's door and knocked.

"Hey, Drew - you OK? Look, c'mon, please talk to me." Marti kept talking to him, trying to get a response, but nothing happened. After ten minutes, he gave up, thinking Drew was too drunk to talk, so Marti went off to bed.

Chapter Fourteen – Escape

On the Friday morning, Alex and Paul saw the girls off at the airport and went back to the university and shop respectively to keep the money coming in.

As Alex arrived at the university, he bumped into Drew in the corridor.

"Hey, Drew, good luck for the game tomorrow, in case I don't have a chance later today."

"Oh, thanks. Listen, can I get some more notes on that assignment that's due on Monday?"

"Sure - come round to my room after lunch and I'll give them to you. If you need help with them, please tell me."

"Will do, thanks." Drew headed to the library to study. After lunch, Drew went round to pick up the notes and knocked on the door.

"Come in." Alex's yelled. Drew walked in to discover his lecturer and the person in charge of transfers staring at him.

"Close the door, please, Drew." Drew closed the door and hoped they weren't going to try to convince him to stay.

"Drew, it's not true is it?" Alex looked worried. "Jennifer has just told me…"

"Yes, it is. Due to certain circumstances in my personal life which are distracting me from my studies, and I can't afford to let happen, I've asked for a transfer." Alex tried to act innocent as to the reason.

"Really, it can't be that bad? Is it girl trouble?" Jennifer asked sympathetically as both men shifted nervously.

"It's a bit more complicated than that." Drew's head fell in embarrassment, he felt as though he was talking to his mother about a problem, as she would always relate it to women problems.

"Well, if you've made up your mind and there's nothing we can say or do..?" Alex asked, genuinely concerned.

"Nothing," answered Drew.

"Well, I tried," Jennifer said, shrugging slightly. "It was nice to meet you, Alex. and Drew - if you change your mind, you know where I am." As she walked out the door, Jennifer turned slightly behind Drew's back and gave Alex a cheeky wink. Alex sat bolt upright and looked down at the floor until the door had closed.

She left the two men alone in the room, giving Alex the space to quiz Drew further.

"C'mon, Drew, is it really that bad?" Alex gestured to one of the chairs in front of his desk, so Drew courteously accepted the invitation and quietly sat down.

"Yes," Drew answered, unwilling to venture further into an explanation.

"Talk to me, mate - what has happened that has caused you to take such desperate action?"

"Alex, I really don't want to go into it."

"Drew, anything you say here is strictly confidential."

"What, even from Carla?"

"Especially from Carla."

Drew considered his options for a moment or two. Then he shrugged.

"Well, I found out that Marti had concocted this whole mess." Drew put his head in his hands. Alex saw how distressed he was and pulled his own chair over and sat down opposite him.

"So what did he do?"

"Marti was jealous that I got close to Carla."

"And when you say get close..."

"Like friends, talking and getting on without it being anything more than that." He reassured Alex, though not understanding why he did so.

"Right... So what has he actually done?"

"He began to get bitter towards her, because I was spending a lot of time round at the shop with the three of them, so he was making snide remarks about her."

"Go on..."

"And when I told him that I would spend more time with him and his mates, the first time was at the trials, everything was great, till Carla showed up to surprise me with Paul and Rachel, then Marti turned again."

"Right, but you are allowed to have other friends apart from him."

"See - that's what I said, but anyway, we got to the barbecue and he was in a foul mood, until Jane thought that I was interested in her, because Marti had wound her up, so she threw herself on me in front of Carla."

Alex sat back, realising that Drew really did feel more for Carla than simply just friendship.

"Then at the hospital, when he said those things to you both about me and how I felt, that was him talking, not me."

"We know that now."

Drew smiled and continued. Once he had finished explaining what had happened, Alex sat forward.

"Well, really, I can't argue with your logic about wanting to move, but I need to make sure that you really want to do this. I mean - is there nothing I can do?"

"It's OK, Alex, thanks - but that would just make things worse. Having to go through another year with that would be unbearable, trust me."

"You can't let your life be run by someone like this, Drew – he's just not worth it. He's shown his true colours as a friend and you need to get him out of your life and move on. But you can do that without leaving your course midway through."

"No, I need to get away – this has been a nightmare for me and I want to move to clear my head of these distractions, they aren't doing my studies any good."

"OK, then - but please take me up on the extra help at least."

"OK, but only with notes. I just want to pretend that nothing has happened, so that Marti doesn't suspect anything. There's been enough fighting. I've no energy left for any more."

"Sure, well - I'll copy my notes for you that you can pick up at the end of each class."

"Thanks. Listen, I need to go, last practise before the game. But thanks."

"Right, good luck."

Drew walked out and headed off to the pitch, while Alex pottered around the class tiding up and gathering his things. He couldn't help but feel sorry for Drew, with everything that had happened to him in such a short space of time.

*

Meanwhile the girls had landed in Ireland and collected their bags in the arrivals hall, before heading towards the car hire centre.

At the desk Carla handed over her details to the young man on the other side of the desk, who was very thin with shaggy dirty blond hair (a mullet!) and who couldn't take his eyes off Rachel.

"And how many drivers?" he asked Carla in a thick Dublin accent.

Carla was just about to answer when Rachel piped up: "Two." She smiled at the young man, who smiled back and began typing again. Carla turned to her and shook her head.

"No way - you're not driving in Ireland, Rach, no way."

"Why not?" she squeaked slightly with indignation.

"You're scary enough at home without taking to the wheel over here."

"That's not fair!"

"Right, well tell me how you would get to Dun Laoghaire from here." Rachel stood staring blankly at her, as Carla and the young man looked on. Carla decided to ask an easier question to prove her point.

"OK, something simple, which side of the road do the Irish drive on?"

"That's easy, the right." Rachel smiled feeling very proud of herself when the man behind the desk let out a small chuckle. Carla turned to him, leaned in closer and asked: "Right, so how many drivers then?"

"That'll be just the one, then, miss. Here is your set of key's the number is on this declaration which I also need you to sign, then you're good to go."

"Thanks..." Carla read his name badge. "...Shaun." The girls reached the car and Rachel climbed in as Carla walked around it. She wanted to check for any bumps or scrapes that hadn't already been listed, so that she wouldn't be charged for them. Rachel jumped out of the car, impatient already.

"What are you doing? Can we get going now?"

"You sound like a five-year-old - get in, we're going now."

On the road Carla sang along with the radio, to old familiar Irish folk music until Rachel began to change the channels.

"Hey, I was listening to that!"

"No, you weren't - you were screeching to it. Here's something we can both enjoy." The station had been changed and the Corrs came on with a song the pair used to dance to when they had sleepovers, so the two of them were at least both screeching to the same song as they passed through Dublin's busy town centre.

Rachel soon fell asleep and Carla began to wonder if she could survive Rachel's incessant snoring all weekend.

Chapter Fifteen – Just for the weekend.

As they drove into Dun Laoghaire, they passed the harbour where they spotted many families and couples - young and old - walking to take in the clean fresh air. Then they drove up through the town centre, passing the large church on the right with the shopping centre on the left. Carla was amazed at the development that had taken place since the last time she had visited. As they meandered up the small narrow streets into the quiet residential area of Dun Laoghaire, Carla was reminded that she was always amazed how busy the centre was, but as soon as you took a turn up a side street, any side street in any direction, there was not a soul to be seen.

The car turned yet another corner into a large square filled with tall terraced houses, all with exactly the same number of concrete steps leading up to large, heavy-looking wooden doors. On the left, as they came into the square, they saw a children's home on its own, looking rather lonely and depressed, as children played outside.

Yet it still managed to dominate the large quiet square, with a long patch of fenced grassland surrounded by tall trees. Circling twice round the square, Carla had to settle for a space in front of the house next to the B&B.

Then getting out of the car, Carla went to the boot to take out their small bags they had brought for the few days they would be there. Rachel stood in the middle of the quiet road and stretched with a loud yawn.

"Well, that wasn't as bad as I thought it was going to be," Rachel observed.

Carla stood up sharply and stared at her best friend, as she went back into the boot pulling out more heavy cases, Carla began muttering to herself.

"She's your best friend, she's your best friend!"

Inside, a lovely older woman showed them to their room on the top floor, which was the largest guest-room in the house, overlooking the park and their car. Carla went to check out the view from the window, but when she turned back round, her so-called best friend was lying on the double bed, stretched out face down and was snoring again.

"The single bed for me then is it? Thank you, Rachel you're too kind." The landlady saw and heard the noise of Rachel's snoring and turned to Carla.

"Right, well - so you'd be having the room next door then!" Carla looked over and gave a look of relief as she followed her through to the next room.

"Well, there's another guest on the other landing who will be here for tonight only and gone very early in the morning. Then it's just the pair of you until your last night, when a party of six young girls from Liverpool come, then I need you to go back and share your last night together, if that's OK."

"Oh - that's no problem - and thank you so much for this."

"Oh, my dear, it's not a problem! My late husband used to snore like your friend, so I completely sympathise. Right, I'll let you get settled then."

"Thanks again." The woman closed the door as Carla put down her bag and gave a great big sigh, before she collapsed on the bed and closed her eyes.

After what felt like only a few moments later, she heard the hurried patter of feet outside her room then silence. Then there was a knock at Carla's door and Rachel walked in.

"Oh, thank God - here you are, I thought you had gone out without me! Did you fall asleep?" Rachel said accusingly.

"Oh, Rachel - shut up and go have another sleep," mumbled an exhausted Carla as she turned to face the wall.

"I wasn't asleep," said Rachel, shocked at the accusation, her eyes still heavy and her hair all dishevelled as if to deny her.

"What do you call that foghorn noise that came out of you, which was so loud it made that poor woman give me this room, so that I could get some peace and quiet?" There was silence as Carla sat up finding Rachel standing at the bottom of the bed with her mouth wide open.

"Don't know what you're talking about! Look, why don't we go to the shops, then have something to eat before we phone the guys to let them know we are here, OK?" Carla got up from the bed and made her way over to the dressing table to brush her hair. They grabbed their coats and bags, and then headed out, deciding to walk down to the shops instead of taking the car, as it was such a warm, bright day.

*

Later that night, after work, Alex headed for the sweet shop, carrying his suitcase for the couple of days he would be staying with Paul. As he arrived, Paul was waiting for him and was clearly not very amused.

"Hey Paul, how's it going then?"

Paul said nothing, so Alex walked in and closed the door.

"What's up?" Paul looked up displaying an angered expression.

"Do you want to sit down?" Alex sat down, unsure of what could possibly be wrong.

"Just before five today, I served three girls from the second year in the uni, who came in talking about you."

"Oh, for God's sake, don't tell me one of them fancied me and thought I felt the same way." He found this rather amusing, but Paul didn't.

"No," Paul answered sternly.

"Well - what?" Alex's amused expression fell to one of confusion and panic.

"They came in talking about you and the woman in charge of the transfers and how the two of you seemed very friendly." Paul's face was twitching slightly as Alex sat upright in his chair in shock.

"What?"

"They saw the both of you going into your lecture room." Paul watched intently as Alex's face flushed a pale pink.

"We were talking about a student, who has asked to be transferred to another university - one of my students."

"Oh like who? Drew - I wish." As Paul said this, Alex went quiet and sat back looking at the far wall.

"Tell me it isn't true," Paul said, almost laughing at Drew.

"Hey - lay off Drew." Alex said, very seriously, and stared Paul dead in the eye, agitated slightly.

"Yeah, yeah, so what's his reason?"

"I can't tell you that!" Alex raised both hands to show he was going no further with the conversation. This slightly annoyed Paul.

"Fine, then."

"Paul, although Drew has a thing for the girl I happen to be dating, who is also your sister, I am still his lecturer and need to look out for his best interests. So do you accept there is nothing going on?"

"Sure, fine - it just sounded suspicious when they were talking about it." He shrugged, feeling embarrassed of having accused Alex wrongfully, without talking to him first.

"Of course it would, they probably know that I'm dating Carla and that she's your sister just to cause mischief. Now let's go and order a curry, I'm starving! So how was your day?" Alex asked as he picked up his briefcase.

"See that madwoman, Mrs Betty? Everywhere I turn, that woman was in my face, smiling at me, wanting to know where Carla was, even after I had told about forty million times, then insisted I put a candle in Mr Betty's muffin for his birthday." Paul paused, as he flipped the last switch off at the wall.

"All I want to do is punch the space where the old man is apparently standing and tell her that he died a decade ago. She belongs in the nuthouse, along with her equally-mad old gossipy friends, who are never done telling me that Carla is much better at making tea than I am. Aaargh! She infuriated me so much today."

"Well, glad I asked. Let's forget about them and hurry up - I need food now." Alex walked out the door as Paul finished locking up. They went to the nearest take-away, picked up their order and headed back to Paul's house for the rest of the night, to watch the football...

They had just walked in the door when the phone rang.

"It'll be Carla!" Paul yelled and dived for the phone.

"Hello," Carla said before launching into a series of twenty questions.

"Yes, Carla; no Carla; oh three bags full Carla! Calm down, I'm only having you on, everything's fine. Are you both enjoying it, what's the weather like?" Paul then started his own series of twenty questions.

Meanwhile, Alex walked into the kitchen to start putting all the food onto dishes. Alex was still thinking about the conversation he had with Paul earlier, hoping that his suspicion had gone completely from his mind. As he thought more about it an image of Jennifer consistently washed in and out of his thoughts. A wicked smirk rose on his face.

He admitted to himself that he found her very attractive - she was well dressed, he remembered, thinking about her again. Though the thing that attracted him the most was that she noticed him. The wink that she gave him as she left his room earlier, gave him a cold chill down his spine, a good one. There was a sexy danger about the way she made him feel, as though they were going to be caught, but for doing what? Nothing.

The answer disappointed him because he was yearning for more affection and attention from Carla. He did feel something for Carla but was now questioning what exactly it was. He was, after all, in his thirties and Carla in her very early twenties – there was no question, he wanted more intimacy and time alone with her. Though he knew deep down that the odd cuddle and kiss was as far as it was going to get between them.

Alex remembered bumping into Jennifer at lunchtime. She had insisted that they have another chat about Drew. Jennifer had only been able to tell Alex about him wanting to leave before Drew actually walked in the room.

Jennifer and Alex had sat in her office and discussed many things, only briefly turning their attention every now and again to Drew.

Alex had remembered asking himself why she was taking such an interest in Drew, but believed it to be simply her nature. Alex, somehow, left the meeting with her mobile number, he couldn't remember how, but it was something to do with ideas about Drew – something to that effect anyway.

As he recalled images and thoughts of her in the office, laughing and talking to him, sharing stories, every now and again, she had either reached to hold his hand, or grinned at him wickedly. Whatever she did, Alex would become flustered, not knowing if he was shying away because of Carla or if it was actually because he was enjoying it…

A text message from Jennifer suddenly broke his train of thought: she was asking him to join her for a drink, to discuss Drew's situation. Alex became flustered again, as it now occurred to him she was deliberately making excuses to be around him and that she was trying to get him on his own now out of office hours. He panicked.

So he replied back, saying: 'Sorry staying with girlfriend's brother this weekend'. He hoped she would get the message with him having mentioned his girlfriend, so he went back to unpacking the food, when his mobile beeped for a second time.

"Oh, for…" He then mimed the end of the expletive he was going to say, then reached for his pocket and pulled out the mobile to reads the response: 'She's away then, u can come out, I really need 2 talk 2 u.'

"No, you stupid girl," he said quietly to the phone, then frantically texted back: 'No 2 busy, don't have time 2 talk 2 u about that anymore, he has decided, so best leave him alone.'

As he sent the message, Alex couldn't help but feel bad that he had been so abrupt with her and as he began to type an apology, another response came in:

"Oh God, please don't let her have taken this badly," Alex said as he opened the message on the phone: 'Well that's good, because I wasn't really wanting to talk about that.'

"Oh, Hell." Alex decided to cut the conversation off by stopping her innuendoes. 'Please don't take this the wrong way, but I don't want to go out to meet you, good night.' He locked his keypad on the phone, put it away in his jacket pocket then took through some dishes to the dining room.

Alex had forgotten that Carla was on the phone when Paul shouted through to hand the phone to him.

"Hey - Alex, come here! Carla wants a word." Alex ran through with a smile on his face and grabbed the phone.

"The food's on the table."

"Great, ta." Paul walked through to the dining room, but before Alex could say anything to Carla, Paul jumped back out to the hall.

"Hey, could you tell Carla once you guys have finished, that I want to talk to Rachel?"

"Err....Sure." Alex managed barely to sound relaxed.

"Ta." Paul disappeared back into the dining room.

"Hey, sweetheart." Carla then began asking her twenty questions of him

"Everything's fine, yes, I'm sure, so you're enjoying yourself? Good, right – well, I'll text you tomorrow because Paul is champing at the bit to talk to Rachel. Night, honey."

Alex placed the phone down on the table in the hall and was about to head into dining room to tell Paul that he could talk to Rachel, when he heard, his mobile going off in the kitchen.

"Oh shit... Paul, that's Rachel for you," Alex shouted as he ran through to get the mobile.

Closing the kitchen door, he waited to hear Paul start to talk, he quickly looked at the message: 'Well what she doesn't know won't hurt her and I need 2 see u and don't pretend there is nothing between us.'

"Urgh!" He_turned to pace towards the door when Paul came through,

"Hey – dinner's getting cold and... Wow, what's up with you?" Paul asked, taken aback by Alex's expression.

"What? OK, fine, listen I need to pop out for a bit." Alex picked up his jacket from the table.

"But what about your dinner?" Paul asked, startled.

"Put it in the kitchen for me, I'll heat it up when I get back. Can I take the car?"

"Yeah, but what's wrong?"

"I'll tell you when I get back."

Paul tossed the keys towards him.

"Thanks, I won't be long - lock the doors."

"I'm not a child." Paul groaned.

"Right, sorry - I'll only be half an hour to an hour tops." Alex ran out the door.

*

When they finished their shopping in the town centre, Carla and Rachel decided to walk back to the B&B - Rachel thought that it wasn't far back and that she could easily manage it. But it was a different story when she realised that, with her heavy shopping, it was much further than she had remembered.

Half way back to the B&B, Rachel decided that she couldn't possibly walk any further.

"Let's find a taxi," she pleaded with Carla. "I can't walk another step – my feet are killing me and my arms are dropping off with the weight of these bags – please? Or could you walk back and bring the car down? I'll sit here on the verge and wait for you..."

"You must be joking! You decided that we were going to walk it, after dragging me round every shop in the town and then expect me to go get the car to come back down here to pick you up? Are you out of your tiny mind?"

Rachel sat on the verge in front of a large stone house,

"No way, missy - up you get." Carla tried to pull Rachel but she wouldn't budge.

"Rachel, I'm knackered, too."

"Yeah, but you can still walk."

"So can you, how are you going to cope when we go walking in Dublin, cause I ain't carrying you back, just like I ain't gonna now, so get up - or I'll see you back at the B&B."

"You wouldn't dare!" Rachel said defiantly, smiling as though daring Carla to abandon her.

"Try me!" Rachel stayed on the ground, rubbing her aching feet, looking up at Carla and trying to work out whether Carla was having her on as usual, or if she meant it. Then Carla picked up her bags and walked off, removing any doubt in Rachel's mind that yes – she really did mean it!

"Remember, I'm going out tonight," she shouted back to Rachel from thirty yards away. "So if you wish to join me, you'd better be ready by six o'clock." Carla kept walking and didn't turn around again.

Rachel remained seated on the ground, surrounded by loads of shopping bags, as she watched Carla turn the corner and disappear out of sight.

"Ahh, she won't leave me here by myself for long - will she..?"

Back at the B&B, Carla was fuming with Rachel for the scene she had created out in the street, but was getting ready to go to dinner, despite the fact that Rachel still hadn't returned yet.

Once she was dressed, Carla walked into Rachel's room to find she still wasn't back.

"Maybe I was too hard on her," Carla thought to herself. "Maybe I should go back for her…"

Then she looked out of her bedroom window and saw Rachel walking very slowly towards her, the bags almost dragging on the ground.

Carla ran downstairs down to meet her.

"Are you OK?" Carla asked as she took some bags from Rachel.

"Yeah, I'm fine, I'm sorry I was such a prat."

"That's OK – I'm used to it," Carla replied. They both burst out laughing and hugged each other.

"Right - are we still going out?" Rachel shook herself and stood up properly.

"Well, I'm not exactly in my pyjamas, but I think we should phone the boys before we head out, I'll go ring them just now," Carla decided as they walked back to the house.

"Right well, I'll be half an hour tops - call me when Paul's on the phone. Well, come on then," Rachel said from the top of the long staircase.

Carla stood at the bottom of the steps, smiling up at Rachel.

"Well, would you come on? I need help if you want to go out for dinner tonight," Rachel urged her with a grin.

The girls went back inside and finished getting ready before calling home.

Carla didn't talk long to Alex, mainly because the two love-sick puppies wanted to tell each other how much they missed one another and loved one another: it was starting to make Carla feel slightly sick and headachy. And it was a bit weird with her brother and her best friend.

Then they left for dinner. Carla drove to a nice hotel nearby - she had been there as a child, she remembered. The exterior had been cleaned up since she had last visited and had been completely re-decorated inside.

The restaurant itself was beautifully laid out - so fresh and vibrant, with a new feature fireplace providing just the right amount of heat and homely atmosphere to the place, encouraging everyone to relax.

For the rest of the evening, Carla and Rachel spent relaxing and talking, enjoying each other's company and forgetting problems that remained at home. Which had been the entire point of the trip in the first place. Even the skirmish earlier in the day had been forgotten and they felt completely at home in each other's company again.

They got back to the B&B late that night, rounding up their first day by going to sleep with a smile…

*

At the pub Alex walked down the stairs and, with each step he took, he could feel himself becoming angrier for having let Jennifer blackmail him into going out to meet her. Reaching the last couple of steps down into the pub, he looked over the mass of bodies, readying himself for what he was going to say. Suddenly, Alex spotted Jennifer, sitting at a secluded corner table, just as she got to her feet and waved eagerly over to him. Immediately, Alex felt his manner change - he made himself stand up straight and walk very tall and strong. But as he got closer, his anger and determination began to waver as he looked at her gazing at him.

Reaching the table, Alex remained standing and looked down at her.

"Right, what is so important that it couldn't wait till Monday?" He was aware he had to shout over the noise in the pub. Jennifer smiled at him.

"Hi, have a seat," She said, gesturing to the seat next to her.

"Look, can we hurry this up? I still haven't eaten," Alex told her sternly.

"Come on - one drink?" Alex sat down reluctantly, but refused a drink.

"I'm not staying long."

"OK - look, I have to be honest here, I quite like you and I know that you like me," the young woman said confidently, causing Alex to sit up and stare at her with a furious look on his face.

"What?" Alex exclaimed, but he felt that his stern expression was fading the longer he sat with her.

"Hear me out - I've caught you staring once or twice and you haven't exactly tried to stop the flirting, have you?" Alex sat back and listened.

"Well, it hasn't gone unnoticed by other members of staff, you know, and I think that we would be good for each other." She smiled, batting her eyelids at him.

"So are you trying to ask me out? I have to tell you you're wasting your time - I'm in love with another woman. So please - don't try this again," he said, getting to his feet.

"Why don't you sleep on it? You and I could have a little fun - what she doesn't know won't hurt her." Jennifer grabbed his hand and gripped it tight. At first he didn't struggle to pull free, but just stared at her hand holding his. Then he remembered where he was and the vast number of people that were around and, with one mighty pull, he freed his hand.

"Do you honestly think I find it fun being dragged out of my girlfriend's home when I was about to have my dinner? We may and I mean, *may*, have had some innocent flirting but it was all a bit of…"

"Fun!" She cut him off, raising one eyebrow. He found this look very attractive and had to fight hard not to lose his train of thought.

"Look, you and I can't happen – alright? There's just no way!" He was scrambling for words; Jennifer had thrown him he couldn't think why he couldn't be with her.

"Are you two married?" she asked in a matter-of-fact way.

"What - no! Of course I'm not." He scoffed, then realised how he reacted opened his mouth to speak but Jennifer beat him to it.

"Well then - it should be simple enough to just end it, I mean does she honestly make you happy?" Jennifer sat back and absent-mindedly stirred her cocktail with its long, black plastic mixing stick. Alex stood rooted to the ground - she had just read him like a book. Everything that he had been thinking about before the series of text messages between them, she had correctly pointed out to him. She reached for his hand again and held it in one hand and stroked it with another. Alex closed his eyes for a second. The loud sound of the pub drowned his thoughts as he sank into the feeling of Jennifer's exquisite touch. Then he came back to his senses, his eyes shot open then he stormed off without a backward glance.

*

Unbeknown to Alex, Sarah and Jane were also in the pub and had been watching the exchange between him and Jennifer since he walked in.

Sarah was not at all happy with what she had been witnessing. She decided to ask Alex what was going on and rose out of her seat and moved towards him.

"Hey, Alex!" Sarah yelled as she caught up with him, so he would hear over the noise.

"What? Oh, hey," he shouted back, awkward at the thought of being caught with Jennifer.

"Hi, are you here with someone?" Sarah asked innocently, pretending to be unaware of having seen the pair together.

"Yeah – just the Head of Transfers," Alex replied, his face flushing hot with embarrassment.

"What was going on with you two?" Jane asked nosily, not really caring that she had seen them together.

Alex shrugged wearily.

"She has this weird, deranged idea that she and I belong together," he said unable to look at them as he turned to check that Jennifer wasn't on her way over.

"What - are you dating her?" Sarah demanded forcefully.

"No, I really can't stand her," Alex said rather quickly - much too quickly for Sarah's liking. She got the distinct impression that he was trying desperately to get away from them as he moved closer to the stairs beside them and placed one hand on the banister.

"We saw the whole thing!" Jane admitted, as Sarah stood staring inquiringly at Alex.

"She threatened me!" he said defensively as they moved closer to the pair to avoid being overheard.

"She didn't?" Jane said, as Sarah looked at him, surprised.

"She did - look." He whipped out his mobile to show the text messages.

"The bloody idiot! Well, you definitely have our support, Alex," Jane said quickly, despite not having consulted Sarah. But then, she had her own agenda - she saw her opportunity to encourage things to go badly for Carla because she knew that Drew wanted Carla and not her.

"Thanks. Listen, I have to get back, so I'll see you later." Alex slid his phone back into his pocket and turned to go up the stairs. Then he stopped and took a quick final look around.

"Bye then," Jane said, as Sarah stood watching him run up the long staircase, wondering how much of what he had told them was the actual truth.

For the rest of the night, Sarah sat thinking about what she had seen and heard from Alex. She believed that Alex was not being totally honest with them. After all, she had seen Alex sit with Jennifer for so long then allowing her to hold his hand for a few moments before he reacted by rather ostentatiously pulling his hand away...

*

At home, Paul had been waiting up to find out what was going on with Alex, when he heard a knock on the front door. He moved quickly to the door, opening it to find Alex on the doorstep.

"Right - what's going?" Paul demanded, as Alex walked in and hung his coat up.

"Look - sit down." They went into the sitting room, where Alex explained what had happened, much to Paul's disgust.

"She has been kind of stalking me." Alex didn't dare look at Paul as he explained for fear of being caught out. "You see, she has been using a student case to provide her with excuses to be around me. I went there tonight to put an end to it and also stop these threats she was going to falsely accuse me of... She asked me to leave Carla and... obviously, I said no...." Paul cut him off.

"So she got the message then?" he asked forcefully, making sure Alex hadn't given this woman any hope of him leaving Carla.

"She better have. Anyway I have two witnesses, just in case she tries anything." Alex sat rubbing his tired eyes wearily.

"Who?"

"That girl and her friend who was with Marti at the shop the other day."

"Who? Jane and Sarah?"

"Yeah, that's them. They saw everything and can back me up."

"Well, we better not tell Carla or Rachel, it would only upset them."

"Carla has had enough to deal with lately. Listen, mate - I'm knackered, I think I'm going to take my supper up to bed," Alex said, slowly getting to his feet.

"I'm going to bed too - see you tomorrow." Paul went upstairs and closed his door, as Alex headed for the kitchen. As the microwave oven was heating his meal, Alex sat at the large wooden table shaking his head, thinking about the mess with Jennifer. Alex had just lied through his teeth and gotten away with it. Lying to Paul was much easier than he expected.

He began to wonder how he was going to be able to cope at work with her constantly wandering around. Then, as the smell of food began to fill the kitchen, Alex decided that he wasn't hungry anymore. He turned off the oven, scraped his food into the bin and went to bed with a headache.

*

The rest of the time the girls were away over the weekend, Alex and Paul fell into a predictable routine. Paul would go to work at the shop, while Alex would sit in the house, pretending to work until Paul called and asked for help. Then Alex would head down to the shop and help as best he could. On closing the shop, they would go home with a take-away of some sort.

But when Alex tried to sleep, closed his eyes or had even a tiny moment to himself, he would start to think about Jennifer, as the statements she had made that night in the pub kept spinning around in his head.

"Just a bit of fun…"

"What she doesn't know won't hurt her…"

Alex found it increasingly hard to concentrate, but not wanting to give in to her somehow made it harder for him to stop the thoughts getting louder.

He began to imagine what it would be like being with her, exchanging looks in the corridor, sneaking around to spend a few minutes alone with each other. These thoughts began to excite him, although he would always be reminded by something that he was meant to be with Carla, for now anyway.

Alex gradually realised that when he was reminded of Carla, he never felt the same energy and excitement for her as he did for Jennifer. With Carla, he felt comfortable and safe, and he started to wonder who he should, in fact, be with – a troubling thought for him to bear.

But for the time being, he decided to see what he would feel when Carla got back…

Chapter Sixteen – Coming home

Monday morning finally arrived and the girls were due to return home from their break. For Alex and Paul, not a moment too soon.

Paul had begun to get thoroughly sick of the sweet shop, because he was too lazy to make his own lunch, and resorted to eating cakes and sweets from the shop, which were – literally - making him feel sick.

Alex was going back to work for the first time since Friday, when he would, once again, be in the same building as Jennifer. This brought back all the temporarily- suppressed thoughts about Jennifer, which didn't help his mood towards the students.

*

Drew, on the other hand, had had the best weekend he had experienced for a long time. Marti had been too busy to bother him all weekend and he also managed to do more studying, as well as catching up on some overdue essays. The only fly in the ointment was Jane. He met up with Sarah most nights at their new local pub, but Jane was joining them more and more often, making sure that her flirting was stepped up to the next level.

Drew let her flirt with him and he even flirted back, as it actually made him feel quite good. It was better than feeling rejected, lonely and worthless, he thought, but flirting was as far as he would let it go.

At the start of Alex's third lecture of the day, Drew ran in and took his seat, noticing quickly that everything was not at all well with his lecturer, who clearly didn't have his mind on the topic and rambled incoherently at times. Shortly before the end of the class, Alex told the students just to hand in their essays and take their next assignment off the board and leave.

Drew took his time so that he could hand his essay in last. when he got to the front of the room, he checked he was alone with Alex.

"Are you OK?" he asked Alex quietly.

"Look, Drew, I'm sorry but I'm not in the mood today."

"What's wrong?"

"Drew, just leave it, please! Just hand over the essay - and here are your notes for the next two lessons. Now go, please." Alex put his head in his hands, as Drew left his documents and picked up the plastic folder with his notes, before heading for the door.

Reaching the door, Drew looked back.

"I think you need to go home," he said, "or take something for what ever's wrong with you." He walked off, closing the door sharply behind him. At that moment, Jennifer passed the door and stopped to stare in at Alex, sitting with his head in his hands.

She knew very well why he was having such a bad day, and she smiled to herself, confidently aware that he was struggling to think of anything else but her.

Sarah came round the corner and spotted Jennifer staring into Alex's classroom, so she walked straight over to her.

"What do you think you are you doing?" she demanded in a take-no prisoners kind of way.

"What? Er - nothing! I was wondering if it was safe to go in, why? What is it to you, anyway?" Jennifer asked, realising that she was, in fact, being spoken to rather vulgarly by a student.

"Why wouldn't it be my business? I'm a friend of his." Sarah almost winced at the thought of Alex being a friend of hers.

"Ahh, so you're a friend of his... Is that because he's your lecturer or because you have a crush on him? I don't have to tell you what I'm doing." Jennifer looked Sarah up and down with an indignant look, before she turned to stare back into the lecture hall.

"Well, sorry to disappoint you but he's not my lecturer and I don't have a crush on him," Sarah answered, folding her arms.

"You think he regards you as a friend?" Jennifer's eyebrows were now raised as she turned back to face Sarah, folding her arms in response to Sarah's open hostility.

"I don't care whether he does or not, but you should care, because I have seen the text messages you sent him and what happened at the bar the other night. So tell me, what have you to say about that?"

Jennifer's eyes widened, as Sarah continued angrily: "Leave him alone or this whole place will know what you are trying on here."

"That's all well and good, but you didn't hear his responses, did you?" Jennifer replied, smugly.

"No, but..."

"But nothing. He wants me and it's only a matter of time before he gives in." Sarah stood in shock, as Jennifer walked off down the corridor, humming a soft tune and taking an odd glance to smile back at Sarah before she disappeared from view.

*

Alex had no teaching commitments for the last few hours of the day and was able to pick up the girls from the airport - Paul was too busy minding the shop to accompany him.

On the way back home, Carla could see that something was wrong and tried to quiz him on it. But he wouldn't be drawn and remained tense and quiet, which worried her. He had been very distant at the airport and didn't even smile at her when they appeared through from the departures gate. He dived for the bags as she made to hug him. They made brief pit stops at both the sweet shop and Rachel's mother's bookshop.

Carla saw how well Paul had done, selling the cakes and sweets, but he hadn't ordered any more stock, so while Rachel ran over to see her mother, Carla went into the back to place a few orders, leaving the boys in the shop alone.

Alex started to try some of the testers and Paul watched him, noting that Alex's facial expression didn't change, even for his favourite mint marble squares. Paul went over quickly.

"Alex, Alex what's wrong? You look dreadful," he whispered,

"I didn't sleep."

"Fine - you didn't sleep, but Carla's back and you should be happy, not looking like it's the worst thing to have happened." Paul gave him a small but friendly shove.

"I'm fine, Paul, honestly - it's this whole mess with Jennifer," Alex murmured, rubbing his aching neck.

"Listen, forget about her! Just now, your girlfriend's back, so move on."

"OK – I'll give it a go."

From the back, Carla had overheard the last few comments the pair had exchanged. She was now extremely puzzled, wanting to know who this girl Jennifer was and what she was to Alex.

'She's probably his sister or cousin,' she thought and walked out of the backroom into the shop.

"Paul, by the way - I know you've done well, but how much of it did you actually sell and how much did you eat?"

"What? Do you think that dealing with that stuff all day, I would want to eat it?"

Carla just leaned against the door, and raised an eyebrow quizzically.

Paul cleared his throat.

"What?" he demanded indignantly. "But I didn't... Oh, what's the point? you'd never believe that people want to come and buy from me rather than you."

"Oh. so it's like that, is it? Well, how about you take the sweet shop and I will go do your uni course?"

Paul flung his arms round his sister.

"OK, OK, don't do that please, I beg you. But I swear - I didn't eat the stuff, I only took some boiled sweets now and again."

"Paul!" Carla stared at him with an 'I don't believe you' look.

"Fine - twice, I had a cake for lunch, but that's it, I swear."

"That's all I wanted to hear." She was smiling for the first time since she got off the plane, until she turned and saw Alex's expression, which wiped her happy beam clean off her face.

"Right - well, I want to get home and unpack."

"Did you bring me something?" Paul asked, eagerly.

"Yes, do you think I would go away and come back without anything for you?"

"It had better be big."

"Sure it is - do you want it now?"

"Yes, please!"

"Close your eyes, then – and no peeking." Paul obediently closed his eyes and Carla put her hand into her back pocket and pulled it out and held it out in front of him.

"Right - open!"

"What? I thought you said it was big!"

"Oh, shut up and watch my hand." Paul leaned forward and stared hard at her hand. She opened it quickly, then used her other hand to slap his forehead.

"Oww!"

"That's for being impatient! Right, I'm off - Alex are you able to take me home?"

"What? Umm, yeah, no problem..."

"See you tonight, Paul, and could you bring me the supplies I've just ordered? So I can start making more tonight?"

"Fine, " he replied, still rubbing his head.

Just then, Rachel came belting across the road from the bookshop and reached the car. Alex had turned the engine on and was waiting for the pair to get in when Rachel pulled Carla back.

"What's up with him?"

"I'll tell you later." They got in and headed home.

*

On arriving home, Carla ran in and checked every room for accidents or cover-ups and was pleasantly surprised that nothing significant had apparently happened. Washing had been done, dishes cleaned and put away, the place looked as though it had actually been vacuumed and polished.

"Well, looks like I will have to leave those two on there own more often." Rachel started to laugh as Alex brought the last case to the door.

"Right, that's the last of it, what the Hell do you two have in these bags? You were only gone for three days," he said as he straightened up.

"Well, I am going to take my case upstairs and take out Paul's present before I go." Rachel headed upstairs. As she heaved the heavy bag up the stairs, she let out one or two groans to accompany the massive thumps as the case hit each step.

"Well, I'd better go start unpacking -half of what's in my case is hers anyway." Carla looked tired as she walked over to the bag.

"So do you want me to go?" Alex muttered.

"No, you need to get your present first." She picked up her suitcase and headed up the stairs, Alex saw she was struggling, so he ran after her and grabbed the bag.

For the first time since she got home, he gave her a smile, which made her feel a lot easier, after what she heard earlier. Alex walked into Carla's bedroom and put her bag on the bed. He walked over to the window and sat in her window seat, watching her as she opened her bag.

He couldn't see into her case as the lid leaned against a side of her bedpost. Then, after pulling out most of the contents of the case, she triumphantly pulled out a plastic bag.

"Ahh here it is." she exclaimed, then walked over to Alex and handed him a duty-free bag.

"It's just a small thing," she assured him, watching him carefully.

"Thank you," he replied in a low voice. But before he could open it, Carla gently grabbed his hand.

"What's wrong?"

"Nothing, really."

"No, I don't believe you. Look, I heard something about a girl called Jennifer. Please, I want to know what's going on, you can tell me."

Alex sat there unable to look at her.

"Oh my God, you've been seeing someone else!" Carla's faced dropped as she pulled her hand away from his.

"No, I swear," Alex said quickly, grabbing her hand back.

"Well, then - tell me she is your sister or something?"

"She's not my sister." He sighed then took a deep breath before continuing:

"She works at the uni and she's in charge of transfers." He couldn't look at her.

"Are you being moved?" Carla asked, with panic in her voice.

"No - she's been involved in a case with a student of mine, and has been using that excuse to come see me." Alex sat rubbing his hands awkwardly.

"Right…"

"So last Friday, Jennifer told me she wanted to see me after work, but Paul and I had already picked up our dinner, we were about to sit down and eat when she sent me another text."

"So what did she say?" Carla took his hands to stop them distracting him, pulled him closer then held his arm tight.

"She told me that - well, not in so many words, but implied that she didn't care whether I had a girlfriend or not and what you didn't know wouldn't hurt you if we *were* to see each other." He looked away again, having repeated the words that had been bothering him all week.

"Oh, she did, did she?" Carla sat up straight. "Really? Well, she's met her match, messing with you." Carla leaned over and kissed his cheek, she lifted her right hand and gently turned his head to face her.

"Now you listen to me Alex," she said quietly, "don't you ever keep anything from me again because we tackle things together, OK? We are stronger together, she will never get her way if we stick together, right?" Alex grabbed her and held her tight, until she pulled away to look him in the eye.

"By the way, Paul mentioned something about a Hallowe'en Ball coming up - why don't we show her just how close we really are!"

Alex began to laugh

"I'm so glad you're back." After a few minutes of talking, Rachel barged into the bedroom, and rudely interrupted them. She had bought a ridiculous leprechaun toy and let it walk through the door. When it came to a halt, it began to laugh hysterically with a very high-pitched screech causing Alex and Carla to fall off the window seat laughing. Rachel also fell to her knees laughing, because she had also been recording their reaction on her new digital camera.

"Oh, that was so funny! Do it again, I think I missed Alex's reaction, could you do that face again?" Rachel tried to copy the contortion in Alex's face. By this time, Carla and Alex were now on their knees, leaning on the bed laughing as the leprechaun fell over and started going round in circles as it tried to walk.

When Paul finally got home, they all sat down to a bought in Italian meal and the boys sat and listened to the girl's stories from their holiday, taking great delight in each one. Then Paul asked Rachel which side of the street the Irish drove on.

"Erm, the left," Rachel answered sheepishly as Carla choked.

"Excuse me! You said the right, and the guy behind the desk decided you weren't safe to drive."

"OK, I admit it - it's true." She hung her head in shame.

Once she had confessed, there was complete silence and Rachel brought her head up from staring at the table to find the three of them buckled in their chairs looking as though they were about to explode.

"It's not funny – how was I to know?" she said with indignation, and then the three of them erupted with laughter.

"Well, it's not…" But the more she protested about the serious nature of the story, the worse they became. This lasted all the way through the evening with random attacks of giggles breaking out all over the place before Rachel became too tired to care and began laughing herself.

Eventually, Alex decided to go home so he and Rachel left at the same time, tired but in a happier frame of mind.

Chapter Seventeen – Torn

Two weeks before the Hallowe'en Ball, the university was filled with a buzz of excitement. Students had just finished the first set of assessments, so it was a chance to let off steam.

Paul ran round to Alex's lecture room and knocked on the door.

"Come in." he heard Alex yell, so he walked in.

"Right, the tickets are on sale now and there's a limit, do you want me to go round and get ours?"

"Calm down Paul - I got them this morning."

"How on earth…?"

"Hey – I work here, I get first priority," he joked.

"Great - well, it looks like the girls have got the ideas picked out for our costumes."

"Oh deep joy - if I have to be a pirate or clown or something, I'm not going."

"You and me both, pal - I'm off. Listen, do you want to have lunch in here today?"

"Sure, and it means You-Know-Who can't come in."

"Fine - I'll meet you in the canteen then."

"Sure." Paul walked off to his next class. Later on, Alex was coming back from the office heading to his room when he bumped right into Jennifer, and dropped his rucksack in confusion.

"Oh, watch it." Jennifer stood watching him, as he scrambled to collect all his scattered belongings. She bent down and grabbed his hand.

"Come on, why don't we go out for lunch and we can talk about this like adults?" Alex crouched down looking at the floor, wondering what to do. Impulsively, he replied: "Right - but I choose where."

Jennifer smiled as he stood up and tried to hold his arm, but he walked faster, making her lose grip as they walked to the restaurant of Alex's choosing.

But what they didn't know was that Sarah had seen them and had heard their conversation…

She was shocked at Alex's decision to accept the proposal of lunch, proving that Jennifer had been right - Alex *was* struggling with his feelings for her.

As Sarah was about to walk off, Paul appeared, on his way to have lunch with Alex. The pair stood staring at each other, not knowing what to do, until Paul decided to break the tension.

"Hi," he said awkwardly, as Sarah smiled back.

"So what are you doing here?" Paul asked as he looked at Alex's room door. Sarah didn't respond as Paul walked over to the door and peered in through the glass window.

"Do you know where he is?" Paul asked, as he looked back to her. But Sarah looked away awkwardly.

"I'd better be going - I said I would meet emm…Jane - in the - emm…" Then suddenly, Sarah walked up to Paul and said quietly: "I would watch him if I were you."

"Who?" Paul asked, very confused.

"Alex - he's not the kind of guy you think he is," Sarah replied resolutely, and she tried to walk off before Paul grabbed her arm. But Paul kept up with her.

"What do you mean?" Paul was now very curious and desperate to know why she would say such things.

"Let's just say - he's made plans with someone for lunch that he shouldn't have." Sarah's eyes lowered as she walked away, leaving Paul none the wiser about what she was talking about and she headed off in the direction of the canteen.

*

That night, Alex and Paul had both received texts from the girls, asking them to come straight up to Carla's to find out their fate for the ball. The pair stood at the door of the house, taking deep long breaths as they tried to prepare themselves for what lay on the other side of the door,

"Ready?" Paul asked Alex.

"Are you?" Paul didn't answer. Finally, Paul walked forward and pushed the door open, the lights came on and the theme tune to Andrew Lloyd Webber's 'The Phantom of the Opera' came from the front room speakers and the hallway lights revealed the costumes. The girls stood grinning as the guys walked in.

"Well, what do you think?" Carla asked, smiling widely.

"Who is the Phantom?" asked Paul, his eyes wide with shock.

"Alex," said Rachel.

"So Paul's the fat one," Alex remarked, causing the girls to laugh.

"Yes - and Rachel is the Prima Donna, I'm Christine." Said Carla, Alex walked over and gave her a hug.

"I must admit, we're definitely going to be noticed in these get-ups," he replied.

"So you like the choice? Because it's either this or we go as characters from 'Pirates of the Caribbean'," Rachel said.

"No, this is fine." Paul said, as he examined his costume in more detail.

"But why is he the Phantom? Why not me?" They all began to laugh as Paul posed, in front of the Phantom's costume, believing he would look better.

"Well, you would have to then go as your sister's date because I couldn't get into the Christine outfit; it was the only one we could find."

"I'm fine with this." Paul grabbed his costume, with an expression like a child, fearful of having it taken from him. Paul, by this time, had forgotten about the events at lunchtime, having convinced himself that if there had been a problem then, of course, Alex would have told him...

*

Sarah had bought three tickets for the ball for herself, Jane and Drew. She believed that if it was an enjoyable night, it could possibly help make Drew rethink his move back home.

Sarah decided to go as Tinkerbell; Drew had reluctantly agreed to go as Peter Pan; Jane, therefore, was destined to be Wendy.

When Marti discovered that they were going, he tried to get a ticket, but found that they had completely sold out, and that there was a long waiting list for getting in. This infuriated him. He was aware that Drew, for a long time. had been avoiding him and had not been involving him in any social activities - or even talking to him except for when he had to.

Sarah also secretly hoped that Alex would make a decision on which of the two women he really wanted. She hoped that, if he chose Jennifer, then Drew could ask Carla out, giving him another reason to stay...

Chapter Eighteen – At your side.

The night before the ball, everyone was putting the finishing touches to their costumes when, all of a sudden, Drew had a dramatic change of heart and ran down to the fancy dress shop to swap costumes. However, he forgot to let Sarah know what he had done...

The night finally arrived and, as the guests started to arrive, Sarah and Jane anxiously awaited Drew outside the hall, both desperate to see him in tights as Peter Pan. When he stepped out of his taxi, though, it was as Captain Jack Sparrow and Sarah and Jane were less than impressed.

"What the heck are you wearing?" Sarah asked bewildered.

"Yeah - where are the tights?" asked Jane, bitterly disappointed.

"What? You don't think this looks better? And it's much more topical." Drew stood with one hand on his hip and the other holding the plastic sword, camply tossing his beaded hair.

"That's not the point, there was a theme going on here and you've ruined it."

"Calm down - it's about having fun! Let's get in - it's freezing out here." Carla and company arrived just as Drew and the girls walked in. They got out of the taxi as a crowd gathered outside for sneaky cigarettes, and they turned to watch as the quartet walked up the steps into the main reception area.

Inside, everyone was welcomed with a glass of champagne, as they were encouraged to mingle before being seated for dinner.

Alex hadn't really said anything since they had left the house - he was positively riddled with guilt about taking out another woman to a nice restaurant. This was something he hadn't even yet done with the woman who was meant to be his girlfriend.

This was coupled with the fact that he and Jennifer had also shared some intimate time at the table, flirting with each other, occasionally touching each other's hand, as well as a single kiss.

At the ball, Carla and the others all managed to be seated at the best table, with the dean and his wife as well as the assistant principal and her husband, which could help Alex in his quest for being kept on after his one year provisional contract at the university.

The only flaw was that Jennifer was seated opposite Alex at the table.

During the meal, there was a great buzz and everyone was laughing and enjoying the great food that was presented to them on beautifully decorated plates.

Carla had found common ground with each one of them involved in the university.

Anne, the dean's wife began quizzing Alex and Carla over how they met. Carla insisted that Alex told them, as she felt that she had done enough talking, that it was his turn to talk about something which he knew better than anyone else. Besides, she had never heard him talk about that day, and she was intrigued to hear his account of it all.

"Well, it was like this…" As Alex started telling the story, Paul was doing his utmost to make Alex laugh or stutter while telling the story. But the others at the table found it interesting - and especially Carla, whose head was resting in one hand as she listened to his well-modulated, almost posh, voice. This was obviously the Alex that his students were used to but neither Carla, her brother nor her best friend had ever heard it before.

Jennifer sat opposite, staring at him pretending to gag, at the most sentimental parts of the tale, to which everyone else was 'oohing' and 'ahhhing'.

Then Jennifer started to raise her eyebrow like she had done that night in the pub, as he struggled to finish. As Alex ended his detailed account of the event the dean began to clap,

"Well done son, I couldn't have done it better myself." Winking at Alex then his wife belted him in the shin with her heel,

"Oh - ow, I meant explaining the tale so well my dear, I could never better you, my sweet." He remarked still rubbing his shin,

"Hmm, I should think so," she muttered indignantly, as the others tried not to laugh, this was the first sign of how much alcohol that the dean, his wife and the others at the table had consumed, as the noise level proceeded to get louder as the night wore on.

Carla sat rubbing her aching feet beside Alex, who hadn't spoken since the meal, nor had he asked her to dance once, leaving Carla to dance with complete strangers most of the night.

"What's up, honey? You OK?" she asked, looking into his glum expression.

"Yeah, I'm fine." Carla noticed that his eyes didn't move from one particular spot on the dance floor, so she followed his gaze. He had been watching Jennifer dance with one of the other teachers, dancing in a very un-lady like manner.

"Alex, is that her?"

"Yes," Alex replied sheepishly.

"Has she said something?" Carla's eyes were transfixed on the blonde.

"No," he answered sternly, almost as though she had accused him of something, causing Carla to turn and face him.

"Why won't you talk to me?" she asked quietly.

"Oh, Carla, leave me alone!" Alex snapped, shirtily.

Carla, upset at the tone in his voice, decided to go get some drinks, to give him some space. The truth was he was jealous that she was deliberately dancing in view of him with other men, as if to show him what he was missing.

The rest of the night was spent dancing and laughing, for everyone except Alex who sat miserably alternately watching Jennifer dancing with other men deliberately to upset him, or disappearing for long periods of time, which went unnoticed by everyone except Carla, Paul and Sarah.

When Carla returned to the bar to order more drinks for the table, Captain Jack Sparrow joined her at the bar.

She didn't recognise Drew with the full regalia on, though he had recognised her.

She stood next to him humming along with the music, in a long white dress and curly, dark brown hair, though it was still very obviously her.

"Hi!" Carla exclaimed in delight. "I love your costume, Captain Jack. Your hair is amazing!"

"Thanks" Drew grunted, so he didn't let on his true identity.

"How long did it take you to get all that on?"

"A while," he said, trying to mask his voice, as the other bartender asked for his order. Then Drew forgot to disguise his voice when he spoke, and Carla stood up straight and looked at him. Then she looked more closely and began to make out his features underneath the costume, braided hair and make-up.

"Drew?" she asked with a half smile, but he didn't move.

"Oh, I'm sorry." Carla walked off to the table, having noticed that she had embarrassed him... But before she had gotten too far away, Drew called out.

"Hey Christine, fancy a drink?" Drew immediately felt like an idiot - all the time he had spent thinking about her and that was the best he could come up with!

It wasn't embarrassing but it was a bit lame - if he had really had time to think about it, he could have complimented her outfit. To his pleasant surprise, Carla turned back and smiled - as she went to walk back to the bar, their eyes were locked to each others.

His heart was beating fast in his chest, his hands were clammy and he began to think rapidly of what to say when she reached him. People walked past them and neither broke the stare. Until, that is, Paul called out from over at the table.

"Hey Carla are you gonnae get those drinks over here anytime this century?" The table erupted with laughter as Paul sat down then received a thump on the arm from Rachel. Carla's steady pace slowed till she had stopped, Drew began saying under his breath: "Don't look away, don't walk away, pretend you didn't hear them....please!"

An instant after he said this to himself, she looked down at the tray of drinks and when she brought her head up again her face was full of dismay. Drew's heart sank as she turned and walked off to the table to raptures of applause as she handed the tray to Paul. Sarah witnessed this from her table - she saw the connection, thinking furiously: 'if that stupid pain in the backside brother of hers had shut up, then Drew would have proof she still wanted him'.

"Bloody fool!" Sarah said aloud.

"What?" asked the young man sitting next to her, somewhat put out.

"No - not you! I was talking to myself, eat your pudding!" Sarah knew just by watching the pair that hope was not lost. Carla did want to talk to him and he desperately wanted to talk to her. The only problem was to get them together which was going to be difficult, and it certainly wasn't going to be tonight...

Later that night, just before the end of the ball, there were award presentations for Best Male and Best Female costumes and Best Couple.

The finalists were announced; Carla and Alex were nominated for the best duo, along with Zorro and Elena as well as Beauty and the Beast. Rachel had been going around with a camera all night taking pictures. The DJ kept them all waiting for a number of minutes after announcing the nominees, then all of a sudden, the theme tune of the Phantom of the Opera blared through the hall, much to the delight of the crowd. Alex and Carla went up to collect their prize to the raptures of applause and cheers.

"You'd think you lot weren't pleased with your winners - come on!" the DJ urged them all on, as volume in the hall grew louder. Carla and

Alex made their way back to the table, where the others at the table were on their feet applauding them.

The winners of the Best Female and Best Male costumes were Lara Croft and Captain Jack Sparrow, which embarrassed Drew so much, he ran to the toilet as his name was read out as a nominee, which left Sarah to collect his award on his behalf.

At one thirty, Carla and the group decided to call it a night and headed home. As they walked out to grab a taxi, they found that Drew, Sarah and Jane had had the same idea. They all stood at the side of the road, looking round, trying desperately to avoid eye contact with each other. A taxi pulled up after five minutes of uncomfortable silence.

At that moment, the silence was suddenly broken by the dean as he teetered out of the main entrance, singing one of the explicit songs the DJ played before they left, much to his wife's mortification, who was already walking away from him.

Both groups allowed them to take the first taxi, to save his wife any further embarrassment.

When the next one came along, both groups began offering the taxi to the other, and it took so long that eventually the driver had to get out and almost ordered one group of them to get in.

Drew told them that they were going into town: "Look, you guys have longer to travel, so you take it."

"Thanks, Drew," Carla said, smiling warmly at him as the others got into the taxi. Paul sat in the front and Rachel in the back with Alex and Carla.

Driving away, Carla smiled again at Drew, but he turned his head away in embarrassment as the car went round the corner.

By this time, Sarah was livid with Alex. His behaviour all night had been appalling but had provided no conclusive sign as to which girl he wanted to be with. Which threw her great plan of reuniting Drew and Carla before it was too late into complete disarray, yet hope still lay with Sarah getting them on their own.

Chapter Nineteen – Secret life

For the next couple of days, the hype from the ball was still buzzing, although they were all feeling the after-effects from the exciting event. Photographs of the night had been posted online and were being shown around. Someone had also made copies for Alex that included everyone at his table.

He would sit, as his classes read or studied for tests, flicking through the pictures and, having seen his expressions in almost all of the photographs that he was in, Alex realised just how rotten he had been, especially to Carla after he snapped at her.

Alex sat thinking about what Carla must have thought of his behaviour and presumed that she would have put it down to either tiredness or stress. At lunch, he went to the lecturers' lounge and found more pictures of that night lying on the coffee table. He stared long and hard at each one, sometimes even laughing out loud, remembering what happened when they were taken as well as his mood at that particular moment.

A week after the event, Jennifer and Alex had been meeting up after work and going for long drives together or having dinner when he had actually told Carla that he was marking up assignments. Their carefully planned meetings were giving Alex the thrills and excitement that he had been desperately wanting from Carla.

"Hi, Alex," Jennifer whispered into his ear.

"What did I tell you about doing stupid things like that here - what if someone sees us?" he responded, talking through his teeth with a forced smile,

"Even you have to admit it is fun! Anyway I need to talk to you," she said, looking round hastily to make sure no-one was watching.

"Not here! Look I'll come and see you later, OK? Now don't come after me." Alex walked off and went to his class to finish his lunch.

About ten minutes before the end of lunch the dean walked in.

"Ah, Alex, I hoped I would find you here. I thought you ate your lunch in the staff lounge."

"I do, sir, just wanted some quiet time, that's all."

"Quite right, I don't blame you... Anyway, my wife and I enjoyed your company so much, we would like you to come round to ours for dinner very soon." Alex looked up from the tray of food that he had been playing with for the past ten minutes.

"Really? Thank you, I'd be delighted to join you and your wife for dinner." Alex paused for a beat. "When you say I'm invited, do you mean..?" he asked warily.

"Well, you and that remarkable girl, of course."

"Great, sure, just tell me when and we'll..."

"Well, how about next Friday?"

"Oh, that soon?"

"What - too early for you?"

"No, it's great, I'll tell her tonight."

"Good,- oh and Alex... neither of you are vegetarians are you?"

"No, sir. Both carnivores!"

"Good. Well, see you then, OK?"

"Thanks, sir." The dean left Alex sitting alone, smiling with delight.

"Oh, Carla - you beauty..."

*

That night, Alex went straight over to the shop after work, filled with excitement about telling Carla about the dinner invite they had received. When he arrived there and burst in, Carla was busy serving a young family of four.

"Carla!"

"Hi, Alex! I'll be with you in a minute, I'm serving..." Alex, by this time, had run around behind the counter, and grabbed her by the waist.

"I really need to talk to you." The parents told the kids to go and sit down as Carla pushed Alex's hands away from her waist and threw them to his sides.

"Would you go and sit in there? I will be with you in a minute."

Alex reluctantly went into the back room, leaving Carla to attend to her customers.

"I'm very sorry, he's worse than a child." The couple weren't hugely impressed by being interrupted so they took their order and left the shop with out a thank you.

Carla felt a little perturbed by their attitude – and by Alex's behaviour – so she went through to the backroom, keeping the door open slightly just in case a customer needed her.

"Right - what is it, you Muppet?" Carla said, as she walked through to the back room. Alex jumped to his feet and grabbed her by the arms and kissed her tenderly on each cheek.

"OK, OK!" She pushed him away.

"Oh, Carla, you beauty! We - sorry, you - impressed the dean and his wife so much the other night he wants us to have dinner with him again."

"Great - when?" Carla tried to act pleased but inside she could hear herself scream 'No!'

"Next Friday."

"Wow, that's soon, isn't it."

"I thought so too, but who cares? If you keep this up, I could get a contract extension."

Carla turned to put the kettle on and felt her heart sink as she realised what she felt was as though she was being used. But maybe it was worth it to make sure he wasn't moving to another university far away.

Suddenly, Mrs Betty began rattling her bony knuckles on the counter in the shop, to attract Carla's attention for service.

Carla emerged from the back room, relieved to have a valid reason to leave Alex alone with his thoughts.

"Yes, Mrs Betty - another tea, is it?" Carla smiled gently.

"No - well, yes dear, but how is that young man of yours? I saw him arrive… Carla heaved a large sigh.

"Yes Mrs Betty, he's fine, thank you."

"Oh dear, I'm not prying, I just wanted to know."

"Yes and..?" Carla said impatiently.

"Serious, is it?."

"Serious? Oh, I don't know…why would you think that?" Carla said surprised, as she turned her head to look at her.

"Oh, dear. it was Mr Betty that came to the conclusion; I was merely asking to stop him talking about it." Carla turned her head back round and put the kettle on, cursing under her breath.

"Interfering old bag."

"Dear, are you talking to someone?" Mrs Betty asked, looking around.

"No, Mrs Betty, I'm not."

"My dear, if you are talking to yourself, I would go and see someone about it. These types of problems don't go away on their own, the problem only escalates."

Carla rolled her eyes, before saying in a hushed tone: "Hmm, look who's talking!"

"What, dear?"

"I said - one muffin or two?"

"Oh, right - well, Mr Betty's put on a bit of weight, best just make it one just now, thank you." Carla placed the two cups on a tray then scooped out one of the muffins from the display cabinet onto a saucer. Mrs Betty handed over the money for the items, but as Carla was collecting her change from the till, Mrs Betty couldn't help but antagonise Carla further.

"So are we going to hear wedding bells, then?"

Carla heard Alex in the back room, coughing and spluttering into his tea as he heard the last statement.

"Oh - um, er - not for a while, Mrs Betty, there's too much happening just now."

"Right you are dear." Mrs Betty winked at her then walked off, as Carla began to think about the prospect of being married to Alex, which for some strange reason didn't feel right at all.

She had never dreamed of Alex proposing to her - she also began wondering what her answer would be if he did ask her.

This one throwaway statement by a dotty old lady troubled Carla for days. She started to obsess about people looking at her left hand, waiting for a ring to appear as they purchased confectionary from her.

Rachel found the whole story hysterical and told Carla to forget about it, as she believed that Alex lacked what she called the 'commitment gene'.

"Some men have it, others just don't," Rachel told Carla knowingly. "Alex soooo doesn't."

The trouble was, Carla couldn't see herself married to Alex in any case; the thought had never crossed her mind. Sure - she wanted to get married, but in all the time that she had been dating Alex, he had never once taken her out, except to the ball, and Rachel and Paul were there, so it didn't count. He had never made an attempt to be alone with her, or do anything special for her, especially after all the things she had done for him. Carla felt as though a tiny warning bell had started to ring...

*

Friday night - and Alex arrived to pick Carla up for the meal. Paul opened the door to let him in and saw instantly that Alex looked stressed out of his mind.

"Bloody Hell, Alex, what's wrong?"

"Where is she, is she ready? We're late."

"OK, calm down, go sit down, and I'll…"

"No, I can't sit, just go get her!" Alex responded, sounding irritated. He started to pace the hall while Paul ran upstairs. Alex would stop and look up the stairs from time to time, for some sign of her arrival, but quickly went back to frantically pacing. When Carla came flying down the stairs, she grabbed Alex.

"Hey - you OK?" She tried to hug him, but he pulled away.

"Calm down, honey, we have plenty of time," she said, taken aback by his reaction to her.

"Wait - are you wearing that?" Alex asked indignantly, to Paul and Carla's shock.

"What? Don't you like it?"

"You think that a black suit would impress them?"

"OK, I'll go change." Carla turned to go back up the stairs when Alex took her by the arm.

"No, there's no time, it'll have to do. Come on."

Paul just stood watching everything happening, as Alex gripped her by the wrist and pulled her towards the door. Carla barely managed to grab her bag from the table beside the door as Alex dragged her out the door.

"G'night, Paul, don't wait up," she called out. They got into the car and drove off as Paul watched them in complete shock.

In the car, Carla spent the whole journey staring out the door window worrying what kind of night she was going to have. All of a sudden, as they were nearing the dean's house, Alex spoke.

"Right, look, I'm sorry about my behaviour back at the house, I'm just so nervous and you look lovely," Alex said, his voice quiet but stern and abrupt.

"It's OK, I know." She leaned across to kiss his cheek but he pulled away again, she sat back in her chair and closed her eyes.

"I want you to calm down and remember to relax," she urged him.

"This must be it." He ignored her last comment, preoccupied by looking for the house as he parked on the kerb. Getting to the door, Alex turned to her again.

"Right, remember to keep him laughing at all costs. He likes you." He rang the bell, as Carla looked about wishing a taxi would drive by so she could jump in and go home again.

"And don't go on about that shop." The door opened before she could speak and the dean welcomed them in. They were led into the sitting room and invited to sit down on the beautiful red suite, in front of the large coffee table that had a selection of nibbles on it.

The dean started off his conversation, about things that he personally loved about her shop and what had happened at the ball - or what he could remember of it.

Alex, however, was less than impressed as he turned his back to Carla, hoping she would get the hint to change the subject. As she was being quizzed about the shop, Carla stared at the back of Alex's head, wondering what she was meant to do.

She decided very quickly that her best plan of action was to just be herself. 'Sod him,' she thought, as she began to respond to her hosts' interest in her shop.

Alex thought that they were being gracious by appearing to be interested in 'her stupid wee shop'. His mind wandered into thoughts of Jennifer, before he snapped back to the conversation.

"Carla, they aren't that interested," he said without looking at her.

"No, we are really interested - do let her finish," the dean said.

"No, he's right, it's rather boring anyway. Is there anything I can help you with in the kitchen, Anne?" Carla asked, desperately looking for a way out.

"No, my dear - you are our guests, so please relax, Anne has it under control, don't you dear?" His wife stood up and said: "Actually yes, there is, we could have a nice little natter and leave these boys to talk."

"Great!" The two women walked off into the kitchen, where the clatter of plates and a gentle hum of talking could be heard. Suddenly, the two men were left without anything to talk about, as the dean clearly needed his wife to inspire a funny story, and Alex realised that he had no idea on this earth what his boss was interested in…

*

Ten minutes later, they were all gathered round the table filling their plates with the delicious food prepared for them.

"This is beautiful," Carla said, as she spooned some vegetables onto her plate.

"Thank you," Anne replied, beaming with genuine delight.

"What did you put in the sauce?" Carla asked as she added a little extra to her meat.

"Don't ask her - she paid a woman to come in and cook it." There was an uncomfortable silence then Anne added:

"And you can bet it wasn't your mother!"

Carla dropped her head down to stare at her plate with embarrassment, as Alex kept eating.

"Leave my mother out of it." The dean was too engrossed in his argument with his wife to remember that he had guests sitting opposite him.

Anne smiled weakly at Carla who returned a half-hearted smile of her own as she put another piece of meat in her mouth. The dean looked across to see Carla and Alex now both sitting very quiet and resolute with what had been happening.

"We have guests, not now, James." Anne leaned over to Carla, when her husband wasn't looking and said: "He should be careful, with what he says to the woman who makes his meals everyday."

Carla pulled away and displayed a confused look. Carla smiled rather awkwardly and went back to eating, as Alex watched every movement of his boss, to pick up any indication of how the evening was going, but never got so much as a sniff of a hint.

James involved Carla in so much of the conversations with him and his wife, while Alex sat stern-faced, silent and unengaged.

"I would love to come and watch you bake one of your delicious cakes," the dean said, very excited.

"I would be very happy to have you both round and I'll make you a batch of your favourite cake."

"Really? You would do that?" Anne asked, as Carla nodded her head.

"Yes, of course I would - what's your favourite?" Carla asked.

"Mint marble." Carla grinned – it was everyone's favourite, it appeared. Alex became increasingly frustrated as hardly any of the conversation had involved him at all.

"Well, I would just like to say thank you, James, for giving me the chance to work for you and the university. I have enjoyed the past few months and hopefully many more to come." Alex lifted his glass and took a sip.

"Good, I'm happy for you," James responded vaguely. He then went back to talking to Carla, but this time about football.

Alex put down his drink and sat back in his chair with his arms folded, glaring at Carla, wishing he could pull her out of her chair and take her home. The rest of night continued on in a similar vein.

At quarter to ten Alex stood up.

"I'm sorry to be a party pooper, but we have to make tracks," he announced to the astonishment of the others.

"Oh, Alex - please its early yet," Carla said, tugging at his hand encouragingly, but he quickly withdrew from her grasp.

"Sorry, Carla, I have an early start tomorrow," he replied through gritted teeth as he stared down at her. The dean was now on his feet, with one hand in his pocket.

"Oh - what are you doing tomorrow? You do know it's Saturday?" The three of them stared at Alex, as he struggled to find an answer.

"What? Oh, yes - er, I help out in the shop when I can, you know, being the supportive boyfriend and everything." Carla looked at him astonished. He took her hand and pulled her to her feet.

"How about we come to see you tomorrow?" Anne asked, inviting herself.

"What, to the shop?" Alex asked too quickly.

"Yes, that's a good idea, dear - how's half past eleven for you, too early?" The dean's wife rolled her eyes, then looked away as Alex spoke: "Nope, fine, great, OK - let's go, sweetheart." Alex took Carla by the arm, moving her to the front door. Taking her jacket he put it on her, then picked up his own.

"Thank you for a fantastic night, sir, and it was great to see you again, Anne - thank you for the beautiful food." Before Carla could get a word in, Alex whisked her into the car and drove off...

The car ride home was worse than the journey going - the whole way, Alex was yelling at her.

"What were you doing? I told you not to rant on about that stupid wee shop, you selfish woman" Alex's ears were scarlet, Carla sat silently, hoping that he would stop at a set of traffic lights and she could jump out. She was sick of him.

"You are an attention grabbing, self obsessed shop assistant, you never let me speak and when I did manage to say something, that old git of a dean thought that I had cut across you. Tonight was my night, not about you or that bloody shop." Alex slowed down the car as he neared a set of red traffic lights. "Honestly... I hope you didn't bore that woman stupid in the kitchen, did you?"

That was the last straw.

"You absolute shit," Carla said as she hit his arm. She saw her chance at the traffic lights and jumped out of the car then slammed the door. Alex put the handbrake on, jumped out after her, leaving the car parked on the road as he raced towards her.

"What are you doing? Get back in the car!" he shouted angrily at her.

"Not a chance - go to Hell." Carla continued to storm off, followed closely by Alex.

"Look - get in and I'll take you home."

"Get lost and leave me alone."

He grabbed her arm, swung her round to face him.

"Come on!" he yelled.

"No!" she cried, struggling to get loose. The two kept arguing, as the drivers of cars sitting behind Alex's car began beeping their horns.

Alex had stopped his car at a set of lights, which had now turned green, but he just ignored them. It began to rain and the pair were getting soaked as they argued, when Alex felt a tap on the shoulder.

Three men had come out of a pub near by and witnessed the argument.

"Are you OK, hen?" one of the large men said to Carla, as he held Alex's soaking shirt to pull him away from her.

"I'm fine, thanks - I just want to get home." One of the other men waved down a taxi.

"Right - get in there and get yourself home," he told her. "We'll take care of this idiot."

"Yeah - I don't like woman-beaters, pal."

"I'm not a woman-beater, shit head! Who asked you to intervene?"

The large man pulled back his hand made a tight fist and was about to throw a punch at Alex in reply, when Carla jumped in front of him.

"Stop please, he wasn't beating me," she yelled. " We've just had our first fight. Please – he's upset, please just don't hurt him."

"Are you sure he's not hurting you?"

"Yes."

"OK - well, if he ever does, you come to this pub any night and get us." Then he turned to Alex and pushed his finger into Alex's chest.

"And if you do anything to her, I won't miss you next time," he growled.

"Thank you, guys," Carla said. "Now, Alex, go back to the car and go home. I'm getting in the taxi." Carla kept her distance from Alex who was preoccupied with the threatening man standing over him.

"I'll call you tomorrow," he said, as he turned to walk off.

"I think you'd better leave it for a bit, think about what you said before you do that," one of the men advised him. The trio were still hovering round Alex to make sure he left Carla alone. Then, as she got into the taxi and drove off, they walked him back to his car. Before he could close the door, the largest bulky man grabbed the car door.

"Remember - if you do anything to her and I hear about it, you've had it, pal." Alex suddenly shivered as he realised he was alone with three rather bulky, scary men without Carla to stop him being pummelled to smithereens.

Alex closed the door and drove off, watching in his mirrors all the way home in case they followed him. For the rest of the night, he was scared to move in his own apartment, left alone to contemplate what he had done earlier and how he had behaved to Carla. It was completely out of character for him. He began to feel sorry for himself and had nightmares all night about losing both Carla and his job...

He sat up in the early hours and began to text Jennifer who was slightly miffed at him also for not going to see her the other day. But Alex managed to smoothe things over and explained about meeting the dean and how he wanted Carla there. They finished texting each other after an hour, then he turned over and went to sleep.

*

The next day, Carla received a call from the dean who was apologising for him and his wife not being able to show at the shop: his mother had taken unwell. Carla found herself so relieved that he was unable to make it after what had happened after she and Alex left last night.

"I'm very sorry to hear that, James, but there's something I feel I need to tell you." Looking at the back of Anne's head, Carla pondered for a moment whether or not to tell him that his wife was actually sitting in the shop. She decided to leave it.

"Well, go on Carla - what is it?" he insisted politely.

"Oh – er - well, Alex and I - we split up last night." Her voice faded to a whisper as she turned away from the busy shop, to avoid anyone overhearing.

"What?" he gasped. "You mean - after the meal at our house?" He sounded confused and upset.

"Yes, but it was nothing to do with you or your wife. I suppose it had been building up for a while." Carla found it strange to talk to him about it as she hadn't yet told Rachel or Paul.

"My poor dear girl, is there anything I can do?" James asked empathetically.

"No, it's OK, thank you, James, I'm already moving on," Carla said, smiling as she poured water into the kettle.

"So no hope for a reconciliation then?" The dean fished none-too subtly to hopefully make amends.

"No, not that I can see, but anyway - you and Anne are still very welcome to come round to the shop anytime," Carla insisted, while she took another glance at the dean's wife, who was reading a book near the window.

"That's very kind of you, dear – well, I'd better go."

"Yes, same here, the shop's getting quite busy now, so do take care."

James hung up, Carla felt bad because he will probably think that last night had something to do with their split.

Turning back to face the crowded shop, she was startled by the sight of Mrs Betty hanging over the counter, who had not realised the conversation into which she was attempting to eavesdrop had ended.

"Mrs Betty, what on earth are you doing?"

Mrs Betty scrambled to get off the counter, while Carla waited for an answer with her arms folded tapping her foot. Mrs Betty mumbled an inaudible response.

Carla leaned over the counter.

"Mrs Betty, were you listening into my private conversation?"

"No, my dear, I wasn't." There was a pause, the whole shop now agog as they watched the drama unfold.

"Well, what were you doing?" Carla asked calmly.

"I was checking that you didn't have mice."

"I don't have mice, Mrs Betty: you know how rigorously I clean my shop."

"Yes, sorry, dear." Mrs Betty sheepishly turned to walk away.

"So sorry to hear about you and Alex, you know I never liked that man."

"How may I ask, would you know about Alex and me, if I hadn't told anyone?"

"Oh, er..." Mrs Betty looked as though she was going to choke with embarrassment.

"Yes, Norma, will that be one cup of tea over at the window then?" Carla looked down at the old woman, who nodded her head before shuffling off to her usual seat. Carla stepped into the back room for a minute to calm down. 'Oh my God, I just knocked that Norma Betty right off her high horse, Rachel's gonna love this!' she thought to herself. Carla never heard another peep from her for ten glorious minutes, until the rest of Mrs Betty's elderly posse walked in. The noise level returned to its usually loud pitch, which was a lot better than the deadly silence that had followed the episode with Mrs Betty.

*

For two weeks. Carla refused to talk to Alex. If he appeared at the shop or at her house, as he would occasionally in contrition, she would close and lock every door until he left.

Paul and Rachel became worried about Carla, as she became a recluse as soon as she was out of the shop and she hardly ever spoke to them about it or him. She was constantly being badgered by Alex on the phone as well. Carla would just let the answering machine pick up all calls. Alex believed that Carla was the key, somehow, for him to secure the permanent contract with the university. This did not go down well with Jennifer because she felt that she was still having to compete with Carla for Alex's attention.

Carla was winning and Jennifer knew it.

*

Two weeks after the fight, Alex decided to make one last attempt to make it up to her and apologise for his behaviour. At lunchtime one day, he phoned the shop and pretended to be a new delivery driver to check that she was there.

Carla fell for it and he went round the back door to wait for her. When she was finally able to close the shop to bring the new stock in, she opened the door and was too busy pushing a large box away from the doorway to see Alex straight away. Then he stepped forward, took her hand and kissed it. Carla jumped back, startled.

"What the Hell are you doing?" she said furiously, as he moved closer to her.

"Please, Carla - hear me out."

"I think I heard you just fine the other night." Carla reached for the door to slam it shut, but he put his foot in the way to block it.

"No – please, Carla, just listen, all I ask is that you hear me out, then decide." Although she was absolutely furious with him, she couldn't say no.

"Fine, but what ever I decide goes, right?"

"Thank you." They sat down and, as she listened to him explain, Carla could see he meant every word.

"What I'm trying to say, Carla, is that I am so sorry. The way I behaved was atrocious and really out of character. I don't know what came over me, other than I've been really worried that my contract won't be renewed. I know that's no excuse but I've been so worried that I may have to move so far away that we could no longer be together - please believe me." Alex put his head in his hands, while Carla stared at the top of his head, her hand reached out to caress his head but pulled back slightly. Then she took his head in both her hands and kissed him softly.

"As long as you understand that I will not take that abuse ever again and you will only get one more chance."

Alex lifted his head, tears in his eyes.

"Yes I understand - I promise it'll never happen again."

"It had better not. No matter how bad you're feeling, you have to talk to me, don't yell at me, and then we can sort it out together. All right?"

He sat up and looked at her, pathetically grateful for her forgiveness.

"I love you. " Alex opened his arms and held her close, pulling her tighter to his chest. Sitting there for a minute in his embrace, Carla realised that she still had doubts over Alex and a tight knot in her stomach told her she might still be making a mistake by trusting him again.

But Carla took him back, hoping that he had learned his lesson…

Chapter Twenty – The decision

Christmas Day was spent at Carla and Paul's house – they were joined by Rachel, her mother, Alex and even his parents, who had come to Glasgow for the holidays.

Everyone was excited at the prospect of a large get-together, especially Carla, who had almost forgotten what a family Christmas was. And they weren't disappointed. The weather got colder, the fire roared in the hearth keeping them all warm, helping to circulate the sweet aromas of mulled wine and cinnamon round the house.

On Boxing Day, after everyone had given up hope of a white Christmas, they woke to find that every square inch of the outside world had been covered in a glistening blanket of snow, lighting the entire landscape in an almost-blue glow. The blanket had only been disturbed by the footprints of the garden birds and some snow, which had fallen from the trees…

*

Drew had gone home to London for the holidays. The trip made him realise just how homesick he was, proving to him that his decision to leave Glasgow to return home after his first year exams was the right one.

This was further confirmed when he found out that so much was happening with his parents and his sister. He was missing it all, which upset and frustrated him.

He would find it difficult returning to university in the new term, with his mind very much on returning home for good…

By the time Drew came back up to Glasgow, Sarah had already formulated a plan. Her flatmate had moved to Italy with her best friend for a year, leaving her bedroom in the flat empty. The flatmate had paid for the next few months rent to cover the costs in case Sarah couldn't find a room-mate quickly enough. So Sarah offered the room to Drew on the basis that he could use it to escape Marti whenever he needed it, giving him the spare key. Drew now had a place to hide that Marti wouldn't know anything about or come anywhere near because he and Sarah were still not talking.

Drew's grades began to pick up, now that he had found somewhere quiet to lock himself away to study. It also helped that Sarah was in the year above him, having already taken the course.

*

Suddenly, it was Spring and the first year exams were just around the corner. Alex was up to his ears in revision for his students - as was Paul. Which made life difficult for Carla, as only she behaved normally.

Alex had his year review coming up with the dean and that meeting, coupled with the grades his classes got, would determine his longer-term future with the university too.

He was, as Carla put it, 'stressed up to the gills' and he began to get nippy with her again, but she ignored it.

Paul, on the other hand, was the exact opposite as he would begin laughing nervously every time he thought about his exams. The pressure was greater than he had felt at school and he needed to pass them to progress to the second year of the course. This actually became rather amusing as he would suddenly burst out laughing at the most inappropriate moments possible: during seminars; at dinner; when he was meant to be helping in the shop. But funniest of all was when he tried to give Rachel a kiss. Every time, without fail, just as Paul leaned in, he would spontaneously burst out laughing hysterically and would be completely floored, knowing how much it upset Rachel. He tried desperately not to laugh, which inevitably made the laughter worse. Rachel eventually saw that he also did it to Carla or when saying hello to people he knew in the streets or in the shopping centres. Seeing that it was nothing personal, she soon came around to the fact he did it all the time and, like the others, she too saw the funny side.

Carla and Rachel tried in the best way to assist their men through their very stressful time, as the exam results mattered greatly to both of them....

*

Drew was also beginning to crack under pressure, but he was grateful he had Sarah to help him out with his revision.

She was sitting her second year exams in English Lit. so he had the added bonus of not just having his lecturer's revision notes but also

Sarah's entire knowledge of the first year course to go through. The two studied together for hours, managing to aid in each other's revision. As well as enjoying some chill-out time with a drink or two in the flat, Sarah was trying desperately to think of what to do to keep Drew from making rash decisions and leaving the university.

*

Things with Alex and Jennifer had subsided, mainly due to work and Alex's reluctance to confront things, not to mention stress levels rising. But Jennifer always managed to distract and meet with him on her own when she could manipulate it, which raised a lot of eyebrows from students and staff alike.

*

Two weeks before the exams began, many of the students decided to take breaks at the weekend to go home or go camping or caravanning to elevate themselves from the depths of the dark depression that was revision.

One Saturday, Alex decided to take Carla away for the day to Loch Ness for a picnic, to go sight-seeing. Alex and Carla arrived at the picnic area by the waterside and sat down under a tree on their large throw, as they spread out the sandwiches and drinks.

The entire picnic had been made by Alex's fair hands, to treat his girlfriend, as he had realised how annoying he must be to Carla in his current state of revision madness.

Once they had finished eating, they leaned back against the tree and looked at the beautiful landscape around them. Carla had brought the camera she had bought Paul with her, so when Alex had dozed off, she began taking pictures of the loch and the surrounding mountains.

As it was early in the afternoon, there were a few boats out on the loch, as the water was calm and glistening. The air was cool, but the sun blazed down with tremendous light, enhancing the landscape's wild beauty.

The hills and trees were so stunning to behold that she would often stop and look at the area she had just captured, then breathe in deeply, taking in the fresh country air.

Once she was quite content with the pictures she had taken, Carla turned to walk back to the tree and found that Alex was still sleeping soundly. As she walked towards him, she spotted something sitting on his nose. Moving closer, she crouched down just beside his hand and brought the camera up slowly,

"OK, little ladybird, just one sec - this won't hurt, just wait." She took a couple of great pictures of it, then it prepared to fly off. But before it could, Alex's hand flew up and smacked it dead.

"Alex!" she yelled, but he was still asleep. Carla felt responsible for the poor thing's untimely death and occasionally, she threw Alex a dirty look as he snored, oblivious to the murder he had just committed.

"Well, isn't this romantic?" Carla sat back and snuggled into him, resting her head on his chest and listening to his heartbeat.

Carla smiled to herself and looked up and saw the way the light shone through the trees, casting little shadows of leaves onto Alex's face.

She turned to pull out the camera again and quickly switched it on. Focusing on him, looking through her viewfinder, Carla could see three people further up the hill, glimpsing them through a parting in the tree's branches, above Alex's head.

Taking the picture, she suddenly realised that she recognised one - if not two - of the group of three people laying out their own picnic. She zoomed the camera in as far as she could.

Carla gasped - it was Drew and Sarah and the other girl: Carla had forgotten her name but remembered her vividly.

Drew looked round to enquire where the sudden human noise came from, but he saw only a pair of long legs beside the tree, so he turned round and finished helping to lay out the picnic.

For ten minutes, Carla sat leaning up against the tree, as Alex continued to sleep, watching the three of them enjoying their day out, laughing and joking.

Why had they come here? Was it deliberate? Had they known she and Alex would be here? All these thoughts raced through Carla's head.

Drew, once he had finished his lunch, began to eat an apple then whipped out a book to start to read, as the girls went down to the water's edge to dip their toes in its icy coldness.

Carla looked over at the girls every now and again to make sure they could not see her, as she couldn't help but be fixated by watching Drew read. Which was making her skin go all goose pimply and she didn't know why.

"Drew!" one of the girls shouted, causing Carla to fall into full sight of the girls. Luckily, though, they were too interested in the fact that he was reading, which contradicted the reason for their day out.

The girls ran at him as Carla quickly but quietly got to her feet. She hunched down and shuffled over and squatted down at the side of the tree, watching the three clown around, the girls trying desperately to grab Drew's book to throw it away, as Drew clung on to it for dear life, laughing as he did so. Carla found this very entertaining – more so than her own day out which had been quite the opposite of their lunch.

As she watched on, Alex suddenly stirred and Carla looked down to check he didn't wake up. But he just curled up into a ball, wrapped his arms round Carla's leg, leaving her pinned to the spot, then continued to sleep. She tried quietly to break free of this grip, but couldn't move. Forgetting that she had been watching Drew and company, she suddenly realised that their screaming was getting louder and closer. Carla looked up and there they were – right on the other side of the tree, feet away. She couldn't move for fear of being seen and prayed that Alex didn't snore or wake up.

The three of them each had a hold of the book which they began spinning round pulling in all directions. When they let go, it flew up into the air and landed beside Carla's leg. Carla's blood went cold, as she heard it land with a thud.

'Oh shit!' She slouched down to hide herself, using Alex's body as a shield. Drew ran round to the other side of the large tree and, as he bent down to pick the book up, he spotted Carla straight away.

Neither could move as they stared at one another, then Drew looked over and recognised the draped body lying over her as his lecturer. He became very flustered as he tried to move away. The two girls came from around the tree shrieking excitedly as they saw Drew's face and walked over beside him to investigate.

Standing beside Drew, they looked down to see a very embarrassed Carla, as she tried desperately to wake Alex. But he was sound, so she wriggled free and rose to her feet. She quickly dusted herself down and straightened up, trying to regain her composure.

"Hi," she said to them all.

"Er – hi," replied Sarah. Jane just glowered at her and Drew didn't know where to look or what to say.

"Lovely day, isn't it?" Sarah said to break the silence.

"Yes, it is - seems great minds think alike," Carla responded, with another grunt coming from Jane to meet her reply. Carla looked puzzled, not knowing why Jane – that's her name, she remembered now - was reacting like that to her.

Then Carla turned to Drew, took his arm and squeezed it slightly. She was about to ask him a question when Jane jumped between them, prising them apart.

"Right, well," she said, "we'll let you two get back to whatever it was that you were doing. Come on, Drew." Jane pulled Drew away. Sarah, who was very embarrassed by Jane's actions, smiled meekly at Carla, looked at Alex then ran off after the pair, leaving Carla alone with her sleeping beauty...

Sarah ran up behind Jane and Drew.

"Drew, I heard an ice cream van," she announced. "We'll just go get some cones, be back in a sec."

He didn't respond, but sat down staring at the tree from which he had just been dragged,

"But I didn't hear..."

"Come on." In the same way Jane had done a few moments previously, Sarah pulled Jane as she walked faster with a tight grip on her arm, refusing to let go.

*

As they went behind a few parked cars, Sarah pushed Jane behind a van. Looking round to check that no one was around, Sarah then tore into Jane.

"What was that all about?" she exclaimed in a hushed tone.

"I could ask you the same thing!" Jane replied, rubbing her arm frantically.

"I mean, about the whole pulling Drew away, when you knew that Carla was going to speak to him."

"I didn't know! Anyway he didn't look comfortable."

"He looked fine till you started dragging him."

"He just seemed as though he didn't want to be around her, that's all."

"Ahh."

"Ahh, what?"

"Ahh, you're jealous!"

"Jealous? Ha, I'm anything but jealous of that little tart - did you see her lying there?"

"Yeah, so what? Are you trying to tell me that you haven't done or wanted to do that and that doesn't make her a tramp, it's not like they were..."

"So she's still a tramp!" Jane snapped.

"At least she had the decency to talk politely to us unlike your grunting responses, if you can call them responses."

"She deserved it."

"Why does she?"

"Just because."

"That's not an answer." Sarah threw her arm against the van to stop Jane walking away mid-conversation.

"Yes it is - and so what? He's a lot more relaxed now that he's away from her - look." The two peered round the side of the dirty white van to check on Drew. Finding that he was still staring at the same tree, they both felt a flush of guilt pass over them as they looked at each other.

The pair went for a short walk to cool down. Sarah told Jane about what had been happening between Alex and Jennifer. At first, Jane couldn't care less - she even tried to turn the discussion around to Sarah and how she used to have a huge crush on Marti.

Sarah quickly pulled her back, explaining what Marti had also done to Drew. This latest news appalled Jane and she now understood completely why Drew had been avoiding Marti.

"You know we are trying to change his mind about going back home to London ," Sarah told Jane. "And the only way we can do that is to somehow heal the rift between Carla and Drew."

"I'm sorry, but she looks to be quite settled with Alex Thingy." Jane didn't try to hide the fact that, although she did not want Drew to be unhappy, she also didn't want anyone else to have him.

"Maybe so, but we have to keep Drew's hopes up. think about it – they've been fighting on and off, then they actually split up and then got back together only a few months ago."

"So what? You think that Carla will find out about Jennifer and that she will dump Alex and Drew will step in and save the day?" Jane guessed in a dramatic voice, to show how stupid she thought the whole idea was.

"Well, it wasn't quite what I had in mind, but that would work - she's our only hope of keeping Drew up here."

"Really!"

"Oh, stop with the jealousy, you idiot, and listen to me - do you want to see Drew happy?"

"Yes, of course."

"And you agree that he still loves her?" Jane looked away.

"Yes, you obviously do, so you also agree that we either have to tell Carla about Alex and about what Drew plans to do after his exams or hope that something just happens between them and Drew can finally tell her how he feels - the latter option is a bit random so we have to take control. It's the only way."

"Fine!" The pair saw an ice cream van drive into the car park.

"I thought you made that up?"

"I did. Well, we can't go back to Drew with out anything - quick." The pair made a run for the van...

Carla, feeling like a complete idiot, sat back down beside her snoring boyfriend, and stared out at the water thinking about what had happened. She wracked her brains, trying to figure out why the conversation had ended so abruptly.

She sat there for quite a while, thinking about Drew. She hadn't realised that a smile had crept on to her face and her eyes were gleaming.

Alex started yet another bout of horrendous snoring as she looked down at him. She asked herself if she really loved him or was he only the guy she wanted to distract her from Drew.

He woke up and looked up at her, watching her staring out onto the loch.

"Hi."

"Oh! Alex - I thought you were still sleeping."

"I was sleeping?"

Carla laughed.

"What?" he asked, as he sat up.

"Nothing, it's just..." She burst out laughing again.

"You should see your hair. You have bed head." Alex looked at one of the metal cups then ran his fingers through his unruly hair. They began to laugh and he slumped back down.

"So, what were you day-dreaming about then?"

"Oh, nothing... It's getting cold, I think we should head back now." Alex tried to hide his disappointment, as Carla cleared up. Shortly, they headed back in the car.

By the time Sarah and Jane headed back to talk to Carla, she had already left and they began to panic, as they didn't have much time left to sort out the Drew problem...

Chapter Twenty-One – Time running out

The first year exams were now underway: Alex was extremely busy marking papers as well as helping students revise, and making trips to Jennifer's office for a break.

Carla found she had a lot of time on her own in the shop to think about her situation with Alex. She couldn't help but feel a pull towards Drew for some strange reason, even though she still cared for Alex.

But the fact was she only cared for Alex - she didn't love him, which is why she was constantly thinking about Drew.

There was also the mess with Drew's friends not liking her much, so she didn't know if she could ever have had a relationship with him at all, which complicated the matter even further for her. Why did life have to be so confusing and difficult?

Once Alex had completed the marking and grading process for the exam papers, he began paying a lot more attention to his job situation, still paying little attention to Carla.

He had become more distracted and distant recently as he tried to work hard to extend to his contract with the university. He began to revert back to his past ways, hinting to Carla to help keep the dean sweet. He kept suggesting he could have to reapply for another job somewhere else and move away to another part of the country, which tested her patience.

He began phoning and making unexpected appearances, especially when Paul was trying to study, which didn't go down well with either Paul or Carla. Rachel had been warned to give Paul some space for a certain amount of hours a day to avoid distractions.

Carla knew that his hints were becoming more obvious and deliberate, the more panic-stricken he became about the time he had left before being reviewed. However, she didn't want to intervene because she felt as though she again was being used, as she was able to find common ground with the dean. Carla was shocked one day when the dean - whom Carla had been thinking about - walked into her shop.

"Oh, James, hi, how are you?" Carla was startled, having turned to find him standing in front of her.

"Carla, I'm well, my dear, thank you for asking. Listen, I wanted to ask you a favour."

"Yes, James, ask away."

"Well, knowing how much everyone round here enjoys your cakes and sweets…"

"Uhuh…"

"I was wondering if you would make some of your cakes and especially the mint marble for the End-of-Year Ball, as I would like to have some kind of different feature in the hall this year. Anne thought that getting some of your cakes in would go down a treat. I would pay you, of course."

"Yes, sure, no problem - just let me know how many are going to be there and I'll pull together something. But someone will have to pick them up on the day of the ball."

"I'll pick them up," the dean volunteered quickly. Carla chuckled a little. She then asked, as he was in a good mood, about Alex and his job, but his response did not encourage further enquiry.

"Now, Carla, I can't say much - that issue is out of my hands. I have made my recommendations, but it is up to the council whether or not to keep him here." Carla was very embarrassed by the comments.

"Oh, I'm sorry, James - I didn't meant to stick my nose in."

"Don't worry about it, Carla, dear, I would do the same if it were me in your shoes. Now I must be getting back - lovely to see you, my dear."

"OK, well, just let me know how many I need to cater for and I'll call you."

"Thank you so much - I do hope Alex knows what a precious gem he has."

*

Carla had Rachel come across to watch the shop for her as she headed to the university to speak to Alex. She walked across the car park and spotted two people standing by the cars. Not paying much attention, Carla kept walking supposing it to be students, but it wasn't.

Carla did a double take over to them and recognised it to be Alex and Jennifer. She immediately ducked down beside a car and scuttled round the cars to get closer to hear what they were saying. As she approached, Carla realised that Alex was talking softly to her not sharp or dismissive. Carla was now on the opposite side of the car to the pair and was listening intently.

"How has your day been?" Jennifer asked Alex as they each stood with a small stack of books in their hands.

"They are all panicking like mad: it's making my head spin. Not to mention that three of the second years have been flirting with me during lectures."

"Oh, have they now? Well, just as well you're devoted, hmm?" Carla saw in the reflection of the car window beside her that Jennifer had one hand on Alex's chest and then fixed his tie.

"So am I going to see you tonight or is *she* already got you booked?" Jennifer said snidely.

"Well, to tell you the truth, she's doing my head in, Jen. She's become very selfish lately. To be honest, I've been a bit distracted by a certain member of staff lately anyway." Alex grinned, looking round. He pulled her closer to him.

"Hmm, I wonder who that could be." Jennifer leant in for a kiss but a group of boys passed and made whistling sounds at them.

"Alright boys move on!" Alex said before moving in for the awaited kiss.

Carla had seen and heard enough about her boyfriend's infidelity. She decided it was time to make her presence known.

She walked round the car then stood behind Alex facing Jennifer. Once they had finished kissing, Alex dropped a book and watching him pick up the book, Jennifer remarked:

"What a stupid bitch she is thinking that you want her for anything other than to get this job..." Jennifer then turned as Alex was standing up. She immediately saw Carla standing there.

"Carla!" Jennifer said, aghast. Alex looked confused as Jennifer stared at his chest. Alex was unable to shake her trance so he turned to where she was looking and his mouth dropped open in shock.

Alex also dropped his books on his toes as Carla stood in front of him, both eyebrows raised.

"Hi honey, it's your stupid bitch here- sorry, did I embarrass you?"

"Err, I'll leave you to it, Alex," Jennifer said trying to slink away.

Alex didn't even flinch as he was still in state of utter shock. He watched Carla staring at him waiting for his reply, then he smiled and tried to laugh it off.

"Oh Jennifer - I think you might want to stick around for this, I won't be long I promise!" Carla's gaze never flinched from Alex's.

"Honey, look - I'm sorry, it's just..."

"It's just what?" Carla demanded, her eyes narrowing at his inability to tell the truth even though he had been caught red-handed.

As they stood there, a large crowd began to gather, which in turn attracted the attention of passers-by.

"Well, I'm waiting, what was it exactly? I'm intrigued to know what you have to say about that entire conversation then that kiss, and don't you dare tell me she fell on you!" Carla was fuming, her rage tangible to everyone watching.

Jennifer, who was lurking a foot or two away from them, surreptitiously looked around at the crowd and realised there was no way to resolve this quietly - some people were even cheering Carla on!

"I - urrm… well, you see - listen, can we go somewhere quiet?" he pleaded pathetically, having caught sight of the waiting crowd.

"Not a chance - I want you to admit to what you have been up to." Carla had no expression on her face - but she was trying her best to suppress the urge to lamp him one on his ugly big chin.

"C'mon honey - not here…"

"I am not your honey!" The crowd applauded her statement. "You have been coaxing me to talk to the dean to convince him to let you keep your lousy job, while you're sleeping with this dame and treating me like utter shit!" The crowd filled the sharp air with 'ohhhhh's.'

"No - it wasn't like that…"

"Well, then explain it, 'cause we're all dying to know!" Carla gestured to the crowd. She didn't care anymore that she had been humiliated for months, had been taken for a ride and completely used. Carla was ready for him - and his bit on the side, too.

"Carla - you and I, you know we weren't working and you just didn't want to be… well…" He leaned forward to whisper and the crowd copied the movement to hear. "Intimate."

"Intimate, intimate!" Carla shrieked then laughed. "Well, there's a joke - you take me on a picnic and fall asleep for two ruddy hours then wake up and decide because you were feeling in the mood that something was going to happen." The crowd erupted.

"At the ball, you didn't dance with me once, you sat staring at her the whole night.." Jeering from the crowd followed as Carla pointed to Jennifer who tried to escape the crowd. The dean appeared in front of her, forcing her back inside the now nearly-complete circle.

"I was going to tell you!"

"Oh yeah - when? Huh? When you had got the job and shacked up with – with _that_." Carla saw the dean arrive but didn't care. She was in full spate.

"Well…" Alex raised his hand to the back of his neck and rubbed it trying to mouth 'stop it' to Carla.

"You mean, miserable asshole – you know, I have to admit that, at first, I thought you were a kind, sweet man. But the more time I spend with you, the more I realise you are a self-obsessed, arrogant, shallow, pathetic, ignorant weasel who only helps others if it helps him."

The crowd gasped - some even cheered Carla on further.

"Listen, can we move this inside?" Alex leaned forward, and grabbed her arm.

"Don't touch me! Don't you ever come near me again, you moron!" Carla shouted at the top of her lungs.

"Please - don't do this!" Alex began, pleading with her as they stood staring at each other for a moment. James then moved forward and beckoned Jennifer to follow.

"What's going on here?" he demanded. Carla smiled at Alex, turned on her heel to face the dean and the crowd.

"I just realised what a scumbag this idiot is and, by the way, he thinks you're a drunken old buffoon. Goodbye, James - and sod off, Alex."

The dean stood on the spot, shaking with rage at Alex as Carla stormed off, She felt quite happy with herself for putting the dean straight about Alex but, at the same time, she was upset at how everything was unravelling…The crowd cheered as Alex and Jennifer were taken inside by the dean. The crowd dispersed and the cheering died out.

*

Paul had finished his exams and was looking forward to his End-of Year Ball. Carla had virtually locked herself away in her bedroom since she split up with Alex.

Rachel and Paul were quite worried about her, as the shop was suffering. It would be shut for a good part of the day before one of them could spare the time to open it for a short while. Carla went to the shop after a day or so to restock and then would only be able to get up to open it after the morning rush, which would be less than profitable. Then she would close the shop for a break but end up drifting off and forget to re-open.

Rachel would sometimes look out of the bookshop window to see the mass of customers gathered outside the shop, staring at Carla through the window, forcing Rachel to go over with a spare set of the shop keys. She would to go through the back door to open up the shop, making Carla snap out of her trance and move into automatic pilot. Even a few of the customers became concerned enough to ask questions about Carla, which Paul and Rachel had to say she was fine, just tired.

Carla preferred to occupy herself with making cakes for the shop as well as the Ball, which kept everyone away from her. She liked peace in the kitchen when she baked.

Chapter Twenty-Two – Is it too late?

The day of the Ball dawned. Carla was up early to finish checking and wrapping the cakes, and then she phoned the dean to arrange for him to pick them up. She went for a drive before she could face the shop.

Almost two hours later, she arrived at the shop and opened up. Carla sat at the table beside the window and relaxed, watching the world go by. After half an hour of staring at the walls, she decided to go for some retail therapy, but just as she went out of the front door of the shop, Sarah ran into her as she hurried along the street.

"Carla - I'm so sorry!"

"It's OK, Sarah - oh, your hair's lovely."

"Thanks! Listen, could I talk to you?" Sarah seized her chance to tell Carla everything about what had happened and what Drew was about to do.

Carla opened the shop door again and the pair sat down, pulling two chairs down from the nearest table.

Sarah went through every detail of everything that had gone on within the past few months - she told Carla about how Drew felt about her; how depressed and lonely he was after the fall out; how he *really* felt about Jane. Sarah then started on Alex, and what he had been doing; that she had hoped he would have made a decision before anyone got badly hurt. Carla was shocked as she finally heard the truth; it made sense to her now.

Carla then told Sarah about how she thought that Drew actually fancied her and only saw Carla as a friend, which they both found extremely funny. Then Sarah fell silent.

"Drew is leaving to go home and finish his last two years in London."

"What?"

"It's true - and you're the only one who can stop him from leaving! Oh, please – Carla, I'm begging you. You've got to do something!" Sarah moved forward and held Carla's hand.

"What do you want me to do? What can I do?" Carla asked, completely at a loss.

"Go talk to him, make him see sense! I know that you feel something for him, I saw it that day at the loch." There was a silence as Carla looked away while she thought about it.

"Carla, tell me you don't feel anything for him and I will leave you alone!" Carla stared at her with tears in her eyes. Sarah knew that, at last, she was getting through to Carla.

"I'm not sure what I feel!" Carla said quietly.

"Well, isn't it better to find out while you still have the chance, than to find out when you can never do anything about it?" Carla felt a big fat tear spill out of her right eye and tumble down her cheek. Then she smiled at Sarah.

Sarah grinned.

"What are you waiting for? Come on!" The pair jumped to their feet.

"Right - where is he?" Carla asked.

"He should be in his flat, that's where he told me he was going to get something." Carla ran out the door after Sarah, locked it then quickly got into the car. Carla and Sarah then drove off, heading for the student flats...

*

Ten minutes later, having struggled their way through Traffic Hell, then tried to find a parking spot, Carla and Sarah ran up the stairs of the building where Drew lived. They spilled out of the stairwell and turned the corner to face the front door to Drew's flat. Carla battered on it frantically.

Marti opened the door.

"What do you want, bitch?" Resting one hand on the door Marti moved his body over to block the view of the flat, which was obviously a mess.

"Shut it, Marti, where's Drew?" Carla demanded, trying to see over his shoulder.

"I ain't telling you unless there's a kiss in it for me?." Marti said puckering his lips and leaning forward. Carla stopped moving then leaned forward, grabbed his shirt.

"I'll give you a bloody fat lip unless you tell me where he is!"

"No way am I telling you!" he countered, when he remembered how her brother hit him and he didn't want to take the chance that she might have taught him. So he stood motionless in the tight grip of Carla, as Sarah stepped forward.

"Tell her now before he leaves!"

Marie Clare Friar

"What are you talking about?" he asked, without breaking his eye contact with Carla.

"He's going home."

"Bull!" Marti said, as Carla let him go. She walked into the flat looking around the living area blankly. Sarah now had become just as angry as Carla and grabbed Marti.

"Bull nothing - you stupid, pathetic excuse for a friend - he's leaving because of you and your interfering, so tell us before it's too late." Marti could see that Sarah meant every word and was very angry, more than he had ever seen her before, as he felt her grip getting tighter. He decided that two angry women were two more than he could safely handle on his own.

"Aargh, I honestly don't know, Sarah." Sarah didn't care what he said; she was ready to ring his neck. From behind Marti, Carla suddenly reached for a white crisp clean envelope addressed to Marti.

"What's that on the table?" Carla asked looking from Marti to Sarah.

"Dunno, thought it was for him," Marti replied croakily, having now been let go and on his knees massaging his neck. Sarah made her way over to Carla, who was standing, running her fingers over the writing.

"That's Drew's handwriting," Carla said very slowly.

"Wait - that says my name! Give it here …Ow!" Sarah swung her arm back deliberately and knocked Marti back down to the floor.

"Carla, open it!" Carla ripped it open under the watchful eye of Sarah. She read the note, which simply said:

> Marti, I am going home. I have left my key on the cabinet in the bedroom; let's hope you don't do to your next roommate what you did to me.
> As for Carla, I loved her and will never forgive you for what you have done to us. Tell Sarah I'm sorry for not telling her I was leaving today, but I wanted to get away before she tried to stop me.
> Drew.

As Carla finished reading the letter, slowing slightly towards the end as though to keep it from ending, Marti jumped to his feet, to be knocked to the floor again by Sarah, with another sharp swing of her arm.

"Are you trying to kill me? I'm trying to tell you…"

"What?" The girls chorused in unison as he lay on the floor, his arms raised for protection.

"He's must have gone to the airport - I saw a ticket the other night but reckoned it was a ticket from the last time he went down to see his family - he is pretty sentimental you know," he explained.

"We know!" they barked back. Marti lay back down to avoid being hit again.

"What are we standing here for?"

"Come on!" Carla and Sarah ran to the door

"I'm coming too!" Marti said, clambering to his feet, clutching his sore neck.

"No way!"

"I wanna help Drew."

"Don't you think you've done enough of that already?" Sarah asked snidely. Just before the pair could argue with each other anymore, Carla gave a large whistle, stopping them in their tracks.

"Look, we're wasting time - if he's already checked in, I can't get through to him, unless I have a ticket and a passport. One of you needs to go to my house and get *my* passport."

"I ain't going - Paul would kill me before I could open my…"

"Your big trap," Sarah finished for him.

"Oh, shut up."

"Make me."

"Hey - Twiddledum and Twiddledee - shut up! Marti's right, Sarah."

"I can't drive either of your cars because I'm not insured to and mine's in the garage getting an MOT," she said helplessly.

"Fine – I'll go," Marti capitulated. "But I mean it - if I get killed I'd better be forgiven for helping him." The girls had already run out of the room by the time he had finished spluttering away. They were driving off as Marti got to the car park - he quickly jumped into his car and sped off in the other direction, heading for Carla's house and feeling more than a little apprehensive about the reception he might receive.

*

At Carla's house, Marti pulled up the driveway - the gates were already open. Jumping out of the car, taking a deep breath as he reached the door, he raised his hand to knock on the door when Paul swung the door open and made a fist.

"Are you stupid or do you get a thrill out of being thumped?"

"Before you maul me, I'm here for the Common Good and for Carla's passport!" Marti said, nervously waiting for a punch as thanks for his heroics.

"Excuse me! Are you missing a chromosome? You think I'm gonna give you my sister's passport just because you asked nicely?"

"Look, call your sister and check, but give me her passport - quick!" Marti remained a few steps away from the door, to give him time to run in case Paul went for him.

Paul paused for a second, analysing the way Marti was acting. This puzzled him. He saw Marti's genuine desperation so he shouted back into the house: "Rachel, could you phone Carla quickly, please?" He turned back to watch Marti, as Rachel dialled his sister's mobile phone.

Rachel asked Carla what was happening and Carla explained very briefly but effectively. Rachel immediately yelled at Paul.

"Paul – get her passport." Paul spun round and she pointed with her finger stabbing at the air to the stairs before turning back to the phone.

"Oh, Carla, that's so romantic…"

"Why? Who's being romantic? Why does she need her passport?" Paul stopped his way upstairs to shout back down.

"Just do it - and hurry." A few minutes later, Paul came leaping down the stairs and handed it to Marti.

"Give it here, you lopsided, lovesick moron." Then Marti ran for dear life, realising what he had said out loud and drove off, leaving Paul and Rachel standing talking at the door. Mart let out a massive sigh of relief, having escaped, for the time being at least.

*

Carla and Sarah ran frantically into the airport and made their way first, to the airline desk. On seeing the queue, Sarah stopped.

"He'll have gone through by the time they get to us!" Sarah sounded defeated as Carla grabbed her hand.

"Like Hell - I'm waiting in this one, come on." Carla stepped out of the line of passengers holding Sarah's hand then made her way to the available check-in attendant, much to the other passengers' chagrin.

Carla asked the very surprised girl behind the airline desk if the London flight had already boarded.

But the poor girl couldn't hear for the rabble, so Carla swung round to face the queue, who were all barking at her.

"Ohh, would you lot shut up," she yelled in an un-Carla like fashion. "I am trying to find out if the man I love has boarded his flight yet, so I can stop him leaving and tell him I love him. Is that OK with you lot?" The entire Glasgow airport terminal went quiet.

"Thank you. Right - now has he checked in? The name is Drew Matthews, bound for London Gatwick, I think."

"Yes, he has," the very scared, young check-in girl answered.

"I need to get to him - is there anyway I could..."

"Well, you won't get through security without a ticket or a passport..." the girl told her quietly.

"I have someone coming with my passport," Carla said, looking around for any sign of Marti. One of the waiting passengers standing behind them started shouting to the back of Carla's head: "Hey come on, lady - move, will ya? We have a flight to catch."

Carla turned back to the check-in girl who was frantically typing. Carla and Sarah leaned over the counter to see what she was doing.

"There's one seat left on another flight, but it will get you through to the departure lounge. But this will only work if you get the passport here in the next few minutes, because his flight is due to board in ten minutes." Carla and Sarah looked at each other in complete panic.

At that very second, Marti came into the airport waving the passport in the air, he ran straight into one of the security fences and winded himself. Sarah ran over to get the passport.

"Give it here!"

"Hey - aren't you gonna at least help me here?"

The two women ran through the airport to the security point to the departure lounge, Carla didn't even stop to say anything to Sarah: she ran straight through.

"Bring him back!" Sarah shouted to her.

When she cleared security, Carla ran like the wind, frantically reading each of the gate signs, then she spotted the flight destination on a large screen at the end of the lounge.

The passengers were already lined up, ready for boarding and she realised that it must be that one Drew would be leaving on.

She ran up to the desk in a desperate state, looking all dishevelled and out of breath from running the entire length of the lounge.

"Trust my luck for it to be down here," Carla muttered to herself, as she gasped for each breath, to muster up enough strength to speak.

"Excuse me, Miss, but you have to queue like the others," a flight attendant told her.

Carla suddenly realised she hadn't done anything but collapse on their departure gate desk, straightened up still very breathless and said,

"Could you please help me? I'm looking for a passenger who's due to board this flight."

"What's the name?" The two crew members were now looking down at Carla, as they tried to work out if she was intoxicated with alcohol or not, due to her appearance.

"Drew – err..." Carla panicked; she had said his name not five minutes before. She began rubbing her forehead making it redder than it already was.

"Wait – it's Drew Matthews." She gasped again. "Yes, that's it."

Carla was now clinging to the desk, knowing that if she were to let go her body would fold up and collapse in a heap on the floor.

"We've begun boarding now, Miss, but I can put a call out for him if you want," the short English woman said.

"Thank you." Carla stood clutching her chest as she looked around. The announcement asking for passenger Mr Drew Mathews to come to the flight check-in gate was called out over the Tannoy. Five minutes later, the announcement was made again. Carla's heart began to sink as she realised he wasn't coming...

Then from out of the crowd, Drew appeared with a puzzled look on his face. Carla ran up to him and pulled him aside to a seat away from the prying eyes and ears of the other passengers, but obviously not far enough. They all took a large side step to get closer.

Drew spoke first.

"What are you doing here? Did Sarah send you?"

Carla smiled gently at him.

"Sarah told me you were leaving, but it was my choice to come here."

"Well, what's wrong?" he asked.

"I don't quite know how to tell you this..." Carla said, fidgeting with one of her now-broken nails.

"Carla, really - you have to hurry because my flight's boarding."

"Don't go!" she cried, which made the onlookers gasp as Drew sat back in the chair.

"What? Why?" Drew was more confused and worried than ever. Carla looked towards the line of passengers which had seemed to have doubled since she last looked, before Drew shook her.

"Tell me, Carla - what's going on?"

Carla mumbled her response.

"Carla, I can't hear you," Drew insisted.

"Drew - I'm in love with you." Another gasp came from the crowd as Carla's eyes filled with tears. Drew sat staring at her, his mouth gaping in shock.

"Well, son, come on - we haven't got all day," a lady from the crowd blurted out. "I ain't boarding till you answer her." The rest of the crowd unanimously agreed with her.

"Aye, pal, if you don't want her, I'll happily take her off your hands." another passenger piped up.

This amused everyone except Drew and Carla. Drew, who hadn't taken his eyes off Carla the whole time, stood up.

Chapter Twenty-Three – All the love in the world.

Rachel was still in her nightdress, pacing the floor. she hadn't stopped pacing since she put the phone down on Carla forty minutes earlier, except to tell Paul how to tie his bowtie.

Paul left her to pace, so he could go and get ready. Rachel, he had discovered, always paced the floor when nervous or trying to think: it was her way of dealing with things. Paul had also learned the hard way that it was best not to bother her in that state and to always keep a distance.

With an hour to go until they needed to arrive at the ball, Paul had tried to guide her towards the stairs. As she climbed to the top, she turned into the bathroom and began running the shower. A short time later Paul ran upstairs at a tremendous pace as she had already done her hair: the only thing she had left to do was put on her dress and coat.

Finally ready to leave, Rachel had snapped out of her trance when she realised that Paul had paid for a limo to pick them up.

As they headed to the car Rachel suddenly gasped.

"Wait no, we can't leave yet!"

"Bloody Hell, why not?"

"'Cause Carla would be upset if she didn't get to see us off, maybe she's on her way back."

"Carla would be upset if we missed tonight waiting for her. Now come on, Rach - you can phone her when we get there." Rachel reluctantly got in and the whole way to the ball, she had her face pressed against the window, convinced every car that went past was Carla rushing back to see them.

*

Arriving at the ball, Rachel dug out her mobile from her bag and dialled Carla's number, which was speed dial number one. Paul saw what number Carla was and turned to Rachel.

"Hey - wait, if she's number one, what am I?" Rachel didn't look in his direction, as she hadn't put him on speed dial at all. She marched quickly inside to avoid the question, then putting one finger in her ear to stop him repeating it. Paul hung up their coats as Rachel continued to try to raise Carla on her mobile. However, the more she had to keep redialling, the more uptight she became. Eventually, Paul grabbed the phone and put it in his pocket.

"Hey - Paul, give it back, I need..."

"You need to have a dance with your boyfriend. She'll be fine, I'm sure that she will ring as soon as she can, when she sees how many hundreds of missed calls her best friend has left. Now shall we..?" Offering his arm, Paul waited as Rachel took a deep breath, linked her arm through his and walked in with him to the function room...

The meal began almost immediately after they had arrived and was enjoyed by everyone there in a swell of chat and laughter. After an hour and a half, the meal was complete and the dancing and merriment began.

Rachel had actually relaxed a little, but had transferred her panic over to Paul, who began checking the mobile in his pocket every couple of minutes.

Then, as they were dancing, Paul received a tap on the shoulder.

"Carla?" He wheeled round to find a very scruffy and untidy Alex in front of him.

"What, is Carla coming?" Alex asked excitedly, his eyes heavy.

"Get lost, ass..." Before he could finish, Rachel had covered his mouth, as she had noticed other members of the faculty were watching.

"Please, Paul, I need to talk to her, I'm..."

"Dying, by the looks of you." Paul said unsympathetically as Rachel gave him a sharp elbow to the ribs.

"The staff are watching us Paul, smile, please," she said through gritted teeth. The three smiled, which allowed the other members of staff to turn back to the bar.

"Do you think I would let you anywhere near my sister, after what you did?" Paul demanded through his forced smile and narrowed eyes.

"I know - and I'm so sorry for that, I really didn't mean to hurt her. It just happened, I didn't want it to - I hate myself for it." Alex pulled on his scraggy hair, as though to prove he was punishing himself.

"Yeah - after you tried to convince me that this Jennifer woman was delusional and that she'd got the wrong end of the stick! Well, I think she may have got the right end." Paul poked Alex sharply in the chest, with his index finger.

"Paul!" Rachel gasped.

"Why won't you let me finish this guy?" Paul didn't turn his head, still sporting the forced grin.

"Let's leave him to drink away his sorrows, Paul - I need a seat." Rachel tugged on Paul's new dinner suit.

"Yeah - I need a good stiff drink." Alex was left standing, slouched in the centre of the dance floor, alone, humiliated and ashamed. As he moved away to go back to his seat, he could see Jennifer heading over to him, so he dived under a table causing people to stare. Jennifer stood at the side of the table waiting for him to come out.

Paul was now getting into trouble for his behaviour, when suddenly the people on the dance floor stopped moving. Paul and Rachel couldn't see over the mass of bodies, so they stood up on their chairs to see Drew walk in the door looking round nervously.

Rachel and Paul look at each other in amazement then made their way over to him, stopping just in front of the crowd to see Carla walk in behind him. Sarah and Marti closely followed them into the hall. Marti was now sporting some interesting bruising across his neck, where Sarah had grabbed him earlier.

*

The crowd watched as the newly-arrived couple walked forward and took a spot on the dance floor beside Paul and Rachel, smiling adoringly at each other. The couples began to dance - they even swapped partners for fun - but Drew and Carla stayed together most of the time.

Then Rachel grabbed Carla and they began dancing together and took the opportunity to quiz Carla about the day's events.

"So what happened?" Rachel demanded eagerly. While dancing with her best friend, Carla started to explain about how she bumped into Sarah coming out of the shop, then about being told about Drew and what he was about to do.

"God, so what did you do?" asked Rachel. Carla continued to tell her about getting to the flat and the argument she and Marti had before Sarah stepped in and began to hit him, which amused Rachel immensely.

"So what's happening now?"

"Well, he's going to see the person in charge of transfers tomorrow and is going to stay up here with us after all." Carla looked round and smiled, as she saw Paul and Drew talking in a corner, laughing and enjoying themselves.

"I'm so happy for you." Rachel wrapped her arms around Carla and hugged her friend tightly…

Carla had been receiving compliments all evening for the display of cakes and sweets that she had created. She had also sent along her chocolate fountain, with some of her mint marble melted down into liquid form, which had become hugely popular. Everyone had lined up to try it, with mixtures of fruits on cocktail sticks to dip in. This became such a big success, the supply began to run out and two trays of the solid mint marble were taken to the kitchen to be melted down, which pleased some and angered others who liked the solid form and didn't believe that there was enough of it in the first place, but that was sheer greed talking.

Later on in the night, Carla decided to go to the bar for a last round of drinks for the group, when she felt a hand rub her arm. She looked round quickly and saw Alex standing there, looking even worse than when Paul and Rachel had seen him earlier that evening.

"God, Alex - you look awful, have you been attacked?"

"No." he replied, confused as he tried to tidy himself up.

"Oh, sorry – it's probably just the light in here." As she talked, she couldn't help noticing that both Drew and Marti were having to hold down Paul to keep him from coming over to put Alex's lights out for good. She turned back to look at Alex, who muttered something about being sorry and being a major fool for what he had done.

"Look, I think we have said everything we could say to each other," Carla told him quietly.

"Please - could you forgive me? I was a prat, I know and..." Alex took her arm and gave it a squeeze, but Carla shook him off.

"What's different this time from the last? Alex, I'm not interested in the 'us' anymore. Drew and I are together, as we should have been in the first place." she announced. "I should have listened to my heart in the first place."

"But it will be the last time we get to talk about it - I've lost my contract here and I've got a new one in Birmingham. I was wondering if you would come with me..." His voice tailed away and Carla shook her head at his desperation.

"Sorry, not interested, have a nice life - oh and I hope you find someone special who deserves you. Oh, look, there she is over there! " Carla waved over to Jennifer then grabbed Alex by the arm to stop him from running away. She then patted him hard on the shoulder, took a great big step back as she picked up her tray and walked away, to the cheers of her group at the table.

They decided to head back to Carla and Paul's for a few more drinks and to end the night on a high, instead of waiting for something else to go badly wrong at the ball.

Carla, as she walked out, saw Alex in the corner with the girl she had waved to - he looked depressed and, for a split second, Carla felt sorry for him. The feeling didn't last long as she laughed, leaving the room thinking about the strange recent turn of events...

Chapter Twenty-Four – Sweetly ever after.

A year later, Rachel was running between two shops, serving not only her own customers, but Carla's too. Carla was busy planning a wedding.

Drew had proposed seven months after they finally got together and Rachel had been in 'I'll do it' mode ever since. This willing attitude allowed Carla to plan everything exactly the way she wanted.

The cake was being custom-made, by a friend who owned the bakery a few streets from her own shop. The hairstyles were decided upon; the flowers chosen; outfits picked for the groom, best man and bridesmaid. The venue was to be her back garden.

The only thing Carla couldn't get right was her dress. She began to panic that she would have to settle for second best, which was the last thing she wanted to do on her special day.

Carla was in a veritable state of despair by the time a miracle turned up in the form of Rachel's mother who had been on holiday over in Thailand and heard about the upset from Rachel.

"Carla, it's my wedding present to you - think of it as your 'something new'," Rachel's mother said as she handed it to her. Carla could not contain her delight at how beautiful the dress was and how perfectly it fitted her. So that was it - everything was finally sorted and everyone could start to relax…

*

On the morning of the wedding, Rachel, the maid of honour, had taken over her duties in a complete panic. She could be seen running from room to room looking for problems that didn't even exist.

Carla, on the other hand, was as calm as could be, standing in front of her mother's double-mirrored wardrobes, stroking the soft fabric of her veil, smiling at the prospect of getting married.

"Mrs Carla Matthews, Mrs Carla Matthews…" she murmured to herself.

Then Rachel screamed at the top of her lungs.

"Oh, crap!" She ran to Carla's door, knocking it frantically.

"Are you decent?"

"Yes, come in." Carla was still calm, despite her best friend's apparently-imminent breakdown.

"Carla, who's walking you down the aisle?" Carla went over to Rachel, took her by the arms, smiled then guided her to the bed and sat her down.

"Honey, you asked me that ten minutes ago, and ten minutes before that, and it's still the same answer."

"Who's that, then?" Rachel was shaking with nerves.

"Paul is, so sit there and wait because I will need you to help me into this dress…"

As Carla was getting dressed, Paul was downstairs pacing the entire lower floor of the house, unable to sit being watched by the bridesmaid, Sarah, and flowergirl, Rebecca (the child from the sweet shop who fancied Paul). Finally, Carla was ready.

As she came down the stairs Sarah and Rebecca 'ooh'd' and 'ahhh'd' in astonishment.

Paul, who had been in the kitchen pacing at the time, ran out to see his sister, but when he reached the foot of the stairs, Carla had already made her way down and was talking to the girls.

"What you did - the whole coming down the stairs thing. I didn't get to see you," Paul said as he stood behind his sister. Carla turned around to show him the outfit and to tell him off for telling her off on her wedding day. But before she could even open her mouth, Paul's eyes filled with tears, to everybody's horror.

"Paul - what's wrong? I'll go back up to come down again if it really means that much to you!" Carla exclaimed, holding her brother's hands tight.

"No – it's OK – it's just you look so…"

"Beautiful!" the girls finished for him. Paul straightened up and said: "No!"

"Huh?" they all replied.

"No - she looks like shit!" They all gasped, except for Carla, who knew he only said this because they had finished his comment for him.

Carla laughed with Paul, while the others looked confused. Carla went back upstairs, but as she was half way back down, Rachel shrieked in a frightful way.

"Stop!"

"Oh, what now?" Carla stopped walking and leaned against the wall.

"I need my camera - someone should be filming this!" Rachel ran past Carla on the stairs, Paul ran into the lounge to get the video camera and Rebecca needed the toilet, so Sarah went with her to help her with her dress, leaving Carla leaning against the wall, calmly checking her newly manicured nails. Five minutes later, the four of them were back standing at the foot of the stairs as Carla once again attempted to walk down the stairs, for the benefit of two flashing cameras. Meanwhile Paul was telling them to stop looking at their cameras and look at the video.

Then it was off to the church, with the bridesmaids and flower girl in the bridesmaid's car. The car was in front of the bride's car, in which sat a very nervous but very excited Carla and an exceedingly quiet Paul, who was quietly letting tears fall over his face, but didn't want to let on.

Carla noticed and she couldn't help but feel that anyone who looked into her wedding car would think that the bride on one side looked happy and the young man on the other side – whom they would presume to be her husband - was crying like it was the biggest mistake of his life.

*

A significant crowd had now gathered outside the church waiting for the bride and groom to emerge. Several young children, not part of the wedding party, were watching over the stone wall, waiting to see the newlyweds come out of the church. They eventually walked into the grounds of the church, by invitation of one of the guests and given handfuls of confetti in order to join in.

Drew's mother was sobbing her heart out into her husband's jacket; his sister was standing flirting with the bride's driver, while everyone was becoming increasingly impatient, because the photographer had asked for more time in the church, so he could get as many pictures as possible.

Finally, the happy couple emerged to rapturous applause and cheers of joy, the noise of which attracted many of the neighbours and passers-by to stop and watch in curiosity.

Carla and Drew then delighted everyone with a lovely kiss on the top step of the church entrance, before getting into the car and heading to the reception...

They all headed back to Carla and now Drew's (and Paul's) home for the reception, where a beautiful banquet was already set out for them. Of course, for dessert, there could only have been cakes from the very best sweet shop in town.

The wedding cake itself was then wheeled out and Carla suddenly realised that Rachel had persuaded her to get too big a cake for the number of guests that were there. She turned to Drew.

"Well, at least you know what you're going be eating for dinner for the next four months." Drew looked confused before he looked at the cake and realised what she was talking about. They struggled to get to the cake for laughing. The speeches, predictably, were rather entertaining telling silly memories of both the bride and groom as they were growing up.

Paul did his usual taking the Mickey out of everything and everyone, before wishing the happy couple: "Lots of love, happiness, the joy of children and dentist bills for the amount of sweets they will be eating." Drew's father was a very largely-built man, whose speech was slightly pompous but well-meaning. He was the complete opposite to Drew and his speech was all a bit too much for everyone, as he lectured them all about the dos and don'ts in marriage and how to make a successful marriage. It amused Drew's mother no end - at one point, she laughed so much at her husband that she broke his train of thought. This interruption was all that was needed for Paul to stand up and signal to the band to start playing before he could start again.

This earned Paul a round of applause from the guests, but Drew's father misinterpreted it for him and sat back down in his seat at the top table beside the priest who had married his son and daughter-in-law. He then proceeded to bore the priest for the rest of the night, much to his relief the priest got a call on his mobile and made a swift exit, but not before congratulating the happy couple. Carla handed him an envelope with some money in it as a donation to his church, to thank him for his service and kind words, which he received graciously as he made his escape.

*

The rest of the reception went exceptionally well, until the bride and groom tried to leave. They were persuaded to have one more dance alone on the floor, before going to get changed for their honeymoon.

On the dance floor the pair fell into a deep conversation. .

"You do realise that you're forever more stuck with me?" Drew asked as they danced.

"Oh, no - you're kidding me? That's not what this circular band means, is it? Ah well, at least I won't suffer alone... but are you sure you can put up with me?"

"Oh, I might manage." They laughed as they had a look around.

"Well, let's just enjoy this moment, because as soon as we stop, we are going to be at everyone's beck and call."

"So - no fast quiet exit for us then?" Drew pretended to be shocked.

"What do you think? With my Rachel and your Sarah, you thought we could get away quietly? As long as we don't have to pose for any more pictures - my cheeks are aching." The music stopped abruptly, and Rachel took to the floor to confirm their worst fears.

"Right, you two - it's time for pictures."

"Aww! No more, please!" the married couple said in perfect harmony.

"If I thought it was going to be this much work, I wouldn't have bothered," Carla said quickly.

"Hey, you know your hubby, isn't to far away, here," Drew responded, which amused the guests.

"Oh - shut up, you know what I mean!"

*

Carla and Drew headed upstairs to get changed and get their bags before heading off to the airport. The guests, meanwhile, headed to the front of the house and waited with yet more confetti. Twenty minutes later, Mr and Mrs Matthews came down the stairs: Marti and Paul took their cases from the landing and loaded up the hire car that was taking them to the airport. Getting to the car, Carla turned to face the guests.

"Right, girls, are you ready?" she announced. She then launched her bouquet of flowers up into the clear night sky. When it came down, it landed right into Rachel's hands, to the shock and horror of Paul.

"Oh, really Carla - very funny, you did that on purpose." Rachel ran over to him.

"Shut up, you big lump." Rachel kissed him, which was met with a rapture of applause and giggles. Jumping into the car, Drew and Carla stood up out of the sunroof to wave everyone goodbye.

"Can I trust the pair of you to keep your hands to yourselves long enough to look after the shop?" Carla yelled to Paul.

"Driver, get them out of here!" Paul shouted to the driver as the others laughed. The car passed the crowd and headed towards the long driveway. As it moved slowly down the drive, the guests could see that, on the back of the car someone had draped a banner.

It simply said, in big, bold, red lettering: 'Love So Sweet.'

The End

www.ingramcontent.com/pod-product-compliance
Lightning Source LLC
Chambersburg PA
CBHW032141020726
47496CB00003B/667